10/15

P9-DUX-381

Original stories by three of the most exciting writers in women's fiction today!

For my Daughter

Margot Early, Jan Freed and Janice Kay Johnson explore the often wonderful, sometimes difficult relationships between mothers and daughters— and men and women.

These are stories you'll want to share with your own mother...and daughter.

ABOUT THE AUTHORS:

Margot Early's first Superromance novel,
The Third Christmas, was published in 1994 and was a
RITA Award finalist for Best First Book. Her husband's
parents owned a roller rink—similar to the one in this
story. When first married, Margot and her husband lived
there, and late at night when the rink was closed the two
enjoyed skating together. He's also a musician, and he
played "Soul Kitchen" on the guitar for her while she
was writing this story. Later this year watch for Margot's
miniseries, The Midwives, coming in September from
Superromance.

Jan Freed is proud to write in a genre that presents a
hopeful view of life without diminishing its hardships.
Her heroines are "strong, gutsy women who safeguard
traditional values against all odds—sort of John-Wayne-
in-panty-hose types." Her debut novel, *Too Many Bosses*,
won a *Romantic Times* Reviewer's Choice Award:
Best Superromance of 1995. Her third novel,
My Fair Gentleman, was nominated for the same award
for 1996, as well as the RITA Award. Look for her fifth
Superromance novel, *The Wallflower*, in June 1998.

The author of thirty-four published or upcoming books,
Janice Kay Johnson has written for adults, children
and young adults. When not writing or researching her
books, Janice quilts, grows antique roses, chauffeurs her
two daughters to soccer and play rehearsals, takes care of
her cats (too many to itemize!) and volunteers at a no-kill
cat shelter. In 1999 watch for her exciting new
Superromance trilogy.

MARGOT EARLY
JAN FREED
JANICE KAY JOHNSON

For my
Daughter

Harlequin Books

TORONTO • NEW YORK • LONDON
AMSTERDAM • PARIS • SYDNEY • HAMBURG
STOCKHOLM • ATHENS • TOKYO • MILAN
MADRID • WARSAW • BUDAPEST • AUCKLAND

ISBN 0-373-83357-1

FOR MY DAUGHTER
Copyright © 1998 by Harlequin Books S.A.

The publisher acknowledges the copyright holders of the individual works as follows:

SOUL KITCHEN
Copyright © 1998 by Margot Early.

THE MIRROR ADDS TEN POUNDS
Copyright © 1998 by Jan Freed.

MOTHER KNOWS BEST
Copyright © 1998 by Janice Kay Johnson.

CONTENTS

THE MIRROR ADDS TEN POUNDS
Jan Freed

I dedicate this story to Alta White and Stephanie Freed, my mother and my daughter. Mama, you made me believe I can achieve anything I set out to do, a gift I recognize as priceless now that I'm an adult. Stephanie, you've got it all— brains, beauty and heart. There's not a thing in the world you set out to do that you can't achieve. (Just ask your grandmother!) I love you both more than words can express.

CHAPTER ONE

LESS THAN A MONTH before The Wedding, in the middle of folding laundry, Lindsey Howard took a long hard look at the state of her underwear. In a horrified leap of logic, she realized Adam would soon look at it, too—most probably while on her person, instead of stacked on the couch.

Ten minutes later she hopped in her minivan and headed for the nearest mall.

At her first glimpse of the overflowing parking lot she almost turned around. Saturday in suburban West Houston was, as any veteran resident knew, the shopping day from hell. And her porcelain-laminate veneer awaited her at the dentist's office in only two hours.

But she persevered. She searched fifteen minutes for an empty space before karma sent a Mercedes backing out in front of her van rather than immediately behind it. She walked in thin sandals over a hotbed of asphalt toward the promise of inner tranquillity and cross-your-heart support. Because obsessing about the small stuff kept her mind off the cosmic implications of agreeing to a mere five-week engagement to Dr. Adam Sullivan, aspiring chief of cardiothoracic surgery at Holcombe Hospital.

The man who, arguably, had killed her first husband.

Lily's Lingerie
2:00 p.m., 26 days before The Wedding

DUCKING INTO the potpourri-scented dressing room, Lindsey hung five padded hangers on the wall hook and slumped in relief. Close call, there. A gaggle of girls bouncing into the crowded intimate-apparel store had included several of her daughter's friends.

What business thirteen-year-olds had in a place noted for sexy lingerie, Lindsey didn't want to imagine. But she could clearly picture Megan's reaction to snickering reports of her mom trying on the merchandise.

"Oh, hi!" a girlish voice chirped into the room. "I thought I saw you slip in here."

Lindsey stiffened, turned...and released a long breath. The blonde hovering inside the doorway was petite and young—but not someone she'd served cookies to in her kitchen.

"My name's Monica, by the way. I was going

to offer you help earlier but got sidetracked by those *kids.*" The sales assistant rolled her eyes, as if she wasn't only about eighteen herself. "When I looked back, you were flying toward the dressing rooms."

"Yes, well, guess I can still move pretty fast— for an old lady," Lindsey said, dropping her purse on the plush carpet.

"Old lady? Yeah, right."

What a pleasant young woman. "Well, maybe not *old.* But compared to the other customers in here, thirty-eight is definitely not young."

"You're *thirty-eight?* N-not that thirty-eight is old," Monica backpedaled valiantly, but too late. "I mean, you *look* a lot younger. My mother would never be able to shop here, even if she wanted to, and she's two years younger than you." The girl's distressed gaze flickered away, obviously searching for a distraction, and fastened on the satin, lace and snaps dangling from the wall.

Lindsey willed herself not to blush.

"Oh, good, I see you found our 'Just for Him' rack. Ver-ry sexy."

By now Lindsey felt about as sexy as Yoda. And since the only Force with her at the moment was a throbbing pressure behind her left eye, she'd have to pull a disappearing act through mortal means.

Glancing at her wristwatch, she made a show of surprise. "My gosh, where did the time go? If I don't leave now, I'll be late for my dental appointment."

From her expression Monica wasn't buying the excuse.

"No, really. See?" Lindsey bared her teeth and pressed a finger pad against the bicuspid chipped long ago by a line drive straight to her mouth. "Ah'm 'etting thith 'ixed."

Bestowing the kind of gentle smile reserved for toddlers telling a whopper, Monica tilted her head. "Let me guess. This is your first time in the store, right? Hey, don't be embarrassed." She flapped a soothing hand. "It's cool to want to look hot for your man."

This is what I get for bypassing JC Penney.

"So what's the occasion?" Monica persisted. "New boyfriend? New husband? Anniversary? Second honeymoon?"

Resigned to being trapped, Lindsey crouched down and rummaged in her purse. "New husband. No—second honeymoon. Well, both, actually. I mean, it'll be my second honeymoon, but not Adam's. We haven't been on a first honeymoon yet. Together, that is."

Drawing a calming breath, she located her aspirin bottle and shook out two pills into her palm. Her infrequent headaches had grown more intense and regular since Adam's proposal last week. "I'm a widow getting married next month," she finished with as much dignity as selecting "Just For Him" lingerie allowed.

"All ri-ight! Congratulations. I just got married myself last month."

So happy. So naive. So damn young. "That's nice," Lindsey lied, then popped the aspirin in her mouth. In a pinch she didn't need water.

"Yeah, it's pretty cool. I bought all my honeymoon stuff here. Oh, wait a minute! Did you know our crotchless panties are on sale?" Monica asked every customer within a thirty-foot radius.

Choking in midswallow, Lindsey couldn't answer.

"Buy two, get the third one free. Would you like me to bring you a pair?"

"No, thank you," Lindsey rasped out, suppressing the urge to add, "Shh!" Rising, she turned her back, reached for the first hanger and released two scraps of matching satin, a blatant hint to be left alone.

"That Wonderbra will make your boobs look huge. The bikini brief comes with matching garter belt and fishnet stockings. Would you like me to—''

"No!" Lindsey dropped the incriminating evidence and darted a nervous glance through the open door. *She* might not be interested, but the young man waiting for his girlfriend at the entrance of the dressing-room area was obviously intrigued.

"Look, Monica, I appreciate your help, but I don't need a thing right now." *Except a little privacy.* "Would you please close the door?"

"Oh. Sure." The girl's animated features fell. "Sorry 'bout that. I'll just get out of your way, then." She pulled the door halfway shut, then paused. "I'd...appreciate it if you'd tell the cashier I helped you."

Lindsey's irritation dissolved into understanding. Selling lingerie was a hard way to make a buck. "I won't forget," she promised gently, and was rewarded with a flash of gratitude in vulnerable blue eyes.

The door swung closed, sealing Lindsey in with memories of another time, another young bride at the mercy of customers' whims. Without a college education, her employment opportunities after high school had been limited. She'd sold as many as three separate product lines on commission all over the greater Houston area to help Pete and his brother, Larry, launch their construction company. Sink or swim. Spaghetti with meatballs…or without. She'd eaten a lot of vegetarian meals those first few years of marriage.

But by the time she'd quit after Megan was born, steak was a regular on their menu and Lindsey was a focused organizer, perceptive listener and articulate communicator. Valuable skills for a widow applying for a job in Holcombe Hospital's marketing department three years ago.

But polished enough for the wife of an ambitious surgeon now? an annoying inner voice asked.

Huffing, Lindsey pulled off her "I am woman, hear me snore!" T-shirt. She wouldn't hold Adam back from attaining his career goals, despite their different backgrounds. Hadn't their engagement restored the hospital board's complete confidence in his coronary surgical therapy? Not that being Pete's widow was the main reason he was marrying her…was it?

Damn that Larry for putting these doubts in her mind! There must be *something* else about her that had lured a thirty-nine-year-old trophy surgeon out of contented bachelorhood waters.

Quickly, before she lost courage, Lindsey stripped off her remaining clothes and faced every woman's worst nightmare: the sight of herself naked in a dressing-room mirror. At the last craven minute, she focused above her neck.

Okay, her eyes weren't terrible. Large and dark brown, they were blessed with a double fringe of lashes that made mascara overkill. Her olive skin and curly black hair came from her Italian dad, may-he-rest-in-peace; her heart-shaped face and dainty nose from her homogenized mother, may-she-give-nagging-a-rest.

That wide generous mouth, though, was a cruel throwback to some unidentified ancestor; possibly Grandma Edna's crazy great-aunt Norma, reputed to have joined a touring circus from Hungary to become its first female sword swallower. Reminding herself that mirrors add ten pounds to reality, one of the few Grandma Edna adages Lindsey chose to believe, she sucked in her stomach and lowered her gaze.

Flawed, flawed, flawed! She'd been right to insist on turning off the lights before turning down the covers to Adam. So far his demanding hospital schedule and Megan's few sleepovers had aided Lindsey's ploy. Infrequency had bred urgency and he sure hadn't quibbled about the dark. But once they were married she'd have to deal with lamps and that pesky dawn's early light.

Grimly she surveyed the damages of gravity

and childbirth. Although she weighed almost the same now as she had at age twenty, everything had...dropped. Not a lot, maybe. But compared with the surgically improved bait that was cast and jiggled in front of Adam, Lindsey was a top floater in a bucket of lively swimmers.

She closed her eyes and smoothed palms over her flesh in a detached clinical way. Her skin was soft, her waist narrow enough, she supposed. But her hips were way too padded for her liking, and her stomach...

Spreading sensitive fingers over her hated tummy swell, Lindsey recalled the span of larger dexterous surgeon's hands in the same location. She inched her fingertips lower, caught her breath, stopped short of the sudden focus of all her senses.

A sunburst of heat spread upward to warm her palms. She opened her eyes and gazed into dilated pupils. Awareness flickered, followed by shock, chased by chagrin.

She jerked up her hands as if scalded.

Good grief, this was a public dressing room! Why did the mere thought of Adam's touch make her feel things she'd never experienced with Pete—kind, funny, *dear* Pete—who'd adored every inch of her flawed body and soul? In truth Adam's potent charisma was as disconcerting as

it was thrilling. He'd used it to move from surgeon to friend to lover to fiancé, the last change
within three dizzying months.

Somehow he'd even extracted her promise to
sell her modest three-bedroom house and move
lock, stock and daughter into his larger West
University home. Not that she'd had the courage
to tell Megan yet.

Every time Lindsey had sought to slow down,
to question his love and their future together,
he'd blanked her mind with drugging kisses until—addicted—she'd feared his answer too much
to ask.

Knock-knock-knock.

Hand pressed to heart, Lindsey whirled toward
the door and prayed the handle wouldn't turn.
"Yes?" she squeaked.

"It's me. Monica. Could you open the door,
please? I have something to show you."

Lindsey scooped up the nearest clothing; the
discarded Wonderbra and matching briefs. "Just
a minute," she called jerkily, hopping on one
foot while stabbing the other through—dammit!—the wrong leg opening. Correcting her error, she hoisted up the briefs, then thrust her arms
through black straps, her breasts into satin cups.
Nicer than dingy cotton, but nothing remarkable.

Hooking the front clasp changed her mind, as

the bra swelled her flesh into wondrous chin-touching mounds. Lindsey couldn't resist glancing in the mirror. Whoa! They did, indeed, look huge. She angled this way and that, more impressed by this marvel of modern engineering than by the last five shuttle missions combined.

Knock-knock-knock. "Are you okay in there?"

She was feeling pretty darn good, actually. Moving to the door, Lindsey cracked it open and peeked through with one eye. An anxious blue orb stared back.

"I know you wanted your privacy, but I couldn't resist showing you this honeymoon negligee. It officially goes on sale tomorrow, but I talked the manager into giving you the thirty-percent discount today if you like it."

A thin strip of filmy white chiffon appeared through the crack. Intrigued, Lindsey opened the door wider.

"See the imported Belgium lace? The bodice roses and seed pearls are hand sewn. Isn't it totally awesome?"

Lindsey nodded. For once the youthful word wasn't an exaggeration. The negligee was a stunning combination of sensual sophistication and virginal innocence. In it, she might have a chance to arouse the same mindless desire in Adam as he produced effortlessly in her with a single intense glance.

"Would you like to try it on?" Monica asked hesitantly.

"I'd *love* to." Lindsey swung open the door and pressed her spine against the handle. "Thanks for talking to your manager for me."

The grinning sales assistant swept past, her arms cradling a cloud of snowy chiffon. She shook out the floor-length confection, hung it on an empty wall hook, then stepped back to admire the effect.

Mesmerized by the display, Lindsey had to instant-replay the sharp gasps behind her before they sank in. But the juvenile snickering that followed penetrated instantly, causing her stomach to slide to her toes. Her bare toes. The ones that matched the great expanse of naked skin saved from indecent exposure by mere scraps of black satin.

Slowly, as inevitably as the baby-sitter in a horror flick climbs the stairs toward certain doom, Lindsey turned her head.

The cluster of thirteen-year-old girls pressing hangers of padded bras to wishful breasts gaped bug-eyed at her chest. The boldest among them, a red-haired sprite fond of Grandma Edna's oatmeal-cookie recipe, swept her gaze down...up... and then smirked.

"Hello, Mrs. Howard," she said in a singsong voice. "Did Megan come to the mall with you?"

Lindsey blinked the glaze from her fixed stare. "Uh, no, Catherine. Megan stayed at home," she said vaguely, at last gathering the wits to pull the door shut.

"Would you tell her—" Catherine craned her neck to stay in sight "—that I'll call her later about my party decorations? She said she'd help."

Click. "Sure thing," Lindsey told the louvered slats.

Proud of her outward calm, she turned and faced Monica's sympathetic gaze.

"Is Megan your daughter?"

"Yyy-ep."

"Any chance her friend will only talk about decorations?"

"Nnn-ope."

"Oh. Well." Monica's expression brightened. "If she gives you any mouth, tell her she's grounded from using the phone. That shapes up most kids real fast."

"Thanks. I'll remember that." Good advice, Lindsey admitted.

Too bad Megan wasn't—and never had been—like "most kids."

Cool Clothes
12:30 p.m., 25 days before The Wedding

TRAILING HER DAUGHTER'S rigid spine into the small dressing room, Lindsey stopped just short of a ponytail slap as Megan whipped around.

"Mo-om, I can get dressed by myself," she announced with supreme disgust, her blond ponytail swaying to a stop, her slim arms draped with thirty minutes' worth of unrestricted browsing.

The resentful green gaze wrenched Lindsey's heart. Not so long ago Megan would have wanted "Mommy" to come into the dressing room—a beloved security blanket, outgrown but not yet discarded.

"Mo-ther."

"I'm going, I'm going." Backing her offensive presence out just shy of the saloon-style doors hitting her nose, Lindsey bit back a reprimand. Patience, she counseled herself. "I'll be right here if you need me, honey."

Silence met her statement. Puberty and The Wedding had conspired to encourage independence and more than a touch of rebellion.

Hitching up her shoulder bag, Lindsey joined two other mothers relegated to leaning against the wall opposite the daughters who'd once craved their attention. The brunette on her left offered a frazzled smile, the blonde on her right a commiserating shake of the head.

Lindsey added a "those darn girls" look, punctuated by a gusty sigh, and settled back to endure a pounding disco song she hadn't grown any fonder of since its release when she was a teen. "Everything old becomes new" was another Grandma Edna-ism proving to be true, Lindsey mused. Even "Spare the rod, spoil the child"—which she'd thought outdated and cruel during her daughter's preteen years—was beginning to sound more humane all the time.

So why had she canceled brunch with Adam to shop at a trendy teen clothing store she hated? Why was she rewarding her teenager's sass with a poorly disguised attempt to buy back respect?

Because she hated confrontation even more than she did disco music, her conscience admitted. And because for an instant—right after she'd suggested buying an outfit for Catherine's year-end party—the sullen young girl masquerading as Megan had smiled. Nothing short of a miracle, considering the scene after Catherine's dreaded phone call the night before.

"Mom?"

All three slouching women snapped to military attention.

Louvered double doors parted. A dark-haired replica of the frazzled brunette peeked out and scowled at her mother. "Okay, I've got it on, and I *told* you I'd look stupid. *Now* can I get the yellow one?"

Scurrying forward, Mom number one plunged into the war zone of her daughter's private space and murmured contesting compliments. Lindsey tuned out the increasingly heated battle and returned to her own silent skirmish.

There was no doubt she'd broken an unwritten rule for mothers of thirteen-year-old girls. The one that said moms should be loving—but sexless—and certainly not interested in *looking* sexy.

Good old Mrs. Howard's wholesome image had undergone a dramatic transformation in Lily's Lingerie, beginning with shocked young gasps. And who could blame the girls? That black satin ensemble she'd modeled would've made June Cleaver suck up her pearls.

"Mom?"

Lindsey and the blonde straightened. The latter hustled forward to enter the third dressing room, leaving Lindsey alone with the bass-guitar pulse of dance music for company. The wallflower pretending she didn't care.

Ridiculous, this sudden sting in her eyes and nose. She'd never been the weepy sort, even those horrible first months after Pete's death. Crying never changed reality. Lord knew, if it did, her mother would have transformed her dad into a "successful" businessman.

By focusing fiercely on a spot beneath Megan's dressing-room doors, Lindsey managed to blink back tears, even found her lips quirking in exasperated affection. Her daughter was such a slob.

Khaki shorts and a white T-shirt slumped wounded against the baseboard, casualties of a careless fling against the wall. At opposite ends of the floor, two off-the-rack shirts lay crumpled inside out, their coveted labels sprouting price tags Lindsey had studiously ignored.

Megan's trim ankles were currently shackled by shiny black material—a cross between bicycle shorts and bikini bottoms, Lindsey recalled with a shudder. She watched purple polished fingernails dig into fabric and tug upward. Heard the telltale rattle of hangers as another shirt was removed. Waited as glossy purple toenails shifted this way and that in front of an unseen mirror.

"Mom?"

Pitifully eager, Lindsey suppressed her urge to rush forward. Maybe all Megan wanted was the correct time. "Yes, honey?"

A Toni Braxton ballad started up. The "yellow one" argument died down. Mother-daughter debates and sultry croon merged into a background hum.

"Would you come in here and tell me what you think?"

The sudden golf ball in Lindsey's throat prevented her answer, but not her beaming smile. She pushed off the wall, shouldered through the double doors, then pulled up short.

Mama mia!

CHAPTER TWO

LINDSEY'S SMILE fluttered feebly.

"I *knew* you wouldn't like it!" Megan exclaimed.

Uh-oh, land mines ahead. Lindsey tiptoed forward. "It's not that I don't like it, exactly. It's...well..."

More like she loathed, abhorred and detested the low-rise short shorts and midriff-baring crop top suitable for a red-light district street corner.

She tried again. "Don't you think they're both a little—" *sleazy* "—small?" she finished tactfully.

"No. Why'd we even come here if you won't let me get what I want?"

Eyeing her daughter's purple-hued pout, Lindsey yearned for the days when denying a second grape Popsicle was her toughest parental decision. "I didn't say you couldn't get it, honey. But you haven't tried on everything yet. You might find something you like better."

"I won't. This is perfect."

"You don't think it's too—" *sleazy* "—casual? You're going to a party, after all."

"Mo-om. The DJ's setting up in the backyard. Catherine has this huge deck that's perfect for dancing. She said we'll probably sweat, so we shouldn't wear anything dressy."

"Okay. That makes sense. But...wouldn't you rather have a casual outfit that's, you know—" *not sleazy* "—something you can wear to school, as well as the party?"

"There're only two weeks of school left. And this is what I want to get." Period. End of discussion.

Whirling, Megan preened in front of the mirror, obviously enchanted with what Lycra did to small firm breasts and a lithe body toned by eight years of ballet lessons. The shriek of triumph from the room on their left didn't help Lindsey's case. Mom number one had surrendered and said yes to the "yellow one." On the right, the battle still raged. But from the sound of things, Mom number three was losing ground fast.

"Have you checked the care instructions?" Lindsey asked, a last desperate rally. Taking silence for a negative, she moved close behind her daughter and peeled back the yoke, then the waistband. Yes! "Megan, this says 'dry clean only.' A special-occasion dress is one thing, but casual shorts..."

"I won't get them dirty," Megan promised irrationally. "And if I do, I'll pay for dry cleaning out of my baby-sitting money. Please, Mom? You've picked out all my clothes for The Wedding, and I'll never wear any of them again." She met Lindsey's gaze in the mirror and twisted the knife. "Can't I get something that's just for me?"

Ouch. "Megan—"

"Please?" Eyes the same pine green as Pete's pleaded with little-girl appeal.

Weakening, Lindsey forced her own gaze lower.

Uh-uh. No way. "Sweetheart, a girl who wears tight and revealing clothes sends a clear message to boys. I can't send you to the party dressed like that knowing you aren't ready to handle the responses you might get."

"Oh, puh-leeze." Such scorn in those green eyes now. "What do you think's going to happen, anyway? Catherine's parents will be right inside the house."

"Unfortunately nothing has to happen. Gossip doesn't have to be true in order to spread and hurt you. There's no sense in your helping to create a reputation for being a...a..."

"Slut?"

Lindsey blinked, then sighed. "Well, yes, if we're being truthful. At your age it doesn't take much to start nasty rumors." She placed a conciliatory hand on her daughter's tense shoulder.

Megan wrenched free and spun around, every vestige of little girl replaced by a sneering stranger. "What about at *your* age, Mother? You don't think parading almost naked in front of my friends started any rumors? You don't think they figured out why you were trying on slutty lingerie?"

"Megan," Lindsey warned, aware of their neighbors' unnatural quiet.

"Am I embarrassing you? Well, good! How do you think I feel about you wearing that stuff for *him?* Sick, that's how. Sick, sick—"

"That's enough!"

Megan's chin came up, her ponytail lowered. "Daddy loved you, Mom. I thought you loved him." Accusation swam in her brimming glare. "How can you forget him so soon? How can you marry his murderer?"

Oh, baby.

So this was what was behind Megan's hostility toward the man she'd once adored. Trembling, Lindsey drew a ragged breath. At its peak, she swallowed a hysterical laugh. So much for avoiding confrontation.

In the adjacent dressing rooms, rustling sacks and urgent murmurs to "come on" announced imminent departure. Relieved, Lindsey signaled to wait for privacy. Her "baby" nodded, the dainty mouth Lindsey had checked before counting fingers and toes pursed in righteous disapproval. Then they were alone.

How to begin? "Your stereo was turned up so loud the other night I thought you couldn't hear your uncle Larry and me talking."

"Y'all were yelling."

Lindsey winced. "I guess we were, honey. I'm sorry you had to hear."

"Uncle Larry said Adam needed a guinea pig for his research. That he talked Daddy into unnecessary surgery when he was vulnerable and scared."

"That's not—"

"He said the only reason Adam made friends with us was for insurance until some, some... statue of liberation or something let him off the hook."

Statue of...? "Statute of limitation," Lindsey corrected, anger sluicing the apology from her voice. Damn Larry for causing not only her but Megan to question their worth in Adam's life!

Noting her daughter's heightened color, Lindsey struggled to moderate her tone. "Your father's death hit Uncle Larry hard, Megan. He lost his brother *and* his business partner, and needed someone to blame. Adam got picked.

"When Howard Construction began suffering financial losses, Larry asked me to sue for medical malpractice. I refused, but your uncle hounded me until the two-year statute of limitation ran out. After that he pretty much left me alone."

Threading wayward curls behind each ear, Lindsey sighed. "I thought he'd come to terms with his anger after all this time. But when I told him that Adam and I were engaged he—"

"Went ballistic?" Megan supplied.

"Yes." An apt description. "And I swept it under the rug. Like always."

Megan fingered her ever-present gold bracelet, Pete's gift for her ninth birthday. "You don't like confrontation," she murmured.

Lindsey's gaze jerked up. *Out of the mouths of babes.* "I hate it more than disco music," she admitted, smiling at this woman-child who was her greatest challenge—and joy. "But we have to confront another issue here, honey."

Suddenly nervous, she snatched up the nearest shirt from the floor and began turning it right side out. "You were still so young when your father was forced to quit work, you may not have realized how guilty he felt."

"Guilty? But that's stupid."

So simple to grasp—for females. "Not to a man used to supervising as many as six construction sites at a time. Working out of a home office seemed sissy. Plus, that was Larry's side of the business. Your father hated everything about it. But since his heart wasn't damaged severely enough to put him on the list for a transplant, he was stuck. He…wasn't a happy camper," Lindsey ended wryly.

"I remember how much he hated being cooped up."

"Hated" was putting it mildly, Lindsey thought, unhooking a hanger and slipping it inside the wrinkled shirt. Pete had felt emasculated by his weakened stamina. And nothing Lindsey had said or done seemed to alleviate his frustration or misery.

Only news of Adam's partial-left-ventriculectomy surgery had done that.

"So Uncle Larry was right?" Megan picked up the second shirt and draped it over a hanger. "Daddy didn't really need an operation?"

"He could have lived a very restricted life," Lindsey conceded. "But he *begged* Adam to do the surgery, Megan, even knowing the procedure was controversial. Even knowing he was choosing possible death over certain life with us. Since I had to sign the consent form, he begged me, too...'' And she'd begged right back, for him to please believe in her love, in her happiness with the man he was now.

But he hadn't. He'd opted, instead, for the chance to improve his quality of life—and had died two days after surgery of probable embolization, leaving Lindsey to deal with guilt and anger on top of her grief.

A tentative tapping on the door brought her back to the present. ''How're you guys doing in there?'' asked one of the two teenage girls overseeing the store.

Lindsey angled her head. ''Fine, thanks. We'll let you know if we need any help.''

''Okay, that's cool.''

Turning back to Megan, Lindsey leveled a stern look at her. ''Calling Adam a murderer is slanderous and irresponsible of Uncle Larry, and I won't tolerate you parroting his words. Is that clear?''

''Yes, ma'am.'' Pink cheeks heightened the green in Megan's eyes. ''But I'll *never* love Adam as much as Daddy,'' she vowed, her implied accusation clear.

Lindsey's mouth twisted, but she said only, "Come on out to the three-way mirror and see if you're still in love with that outfit."

Leading the way, she walked to the end of the dressing-room corridor and stepped aside.

Megan was unable to hide an instant of startled dismay at her three-dimensional image. "It *is* kinda tight."

The surge of emotion expanding Lindsey's chest demanded action. She closed the gap between them, turned her daughter around and dropped a kiss on the beautiful mouth with the awful purple lipstick.

"I love you more than life, Megan. And I loved your daddy the same way. Nothing and no one can ever replace either one of you in my heart, understand?" This wasn't the time to explain the human heart's infinite capacity for love and Adam's equal share of her affections.

Even before Megan's gaze moved beyond Lindsey's shoulder and widened, she knew. Her quickening pulse, a faint whiff of sandalwood, the nerves playing jumping jacks beneath her skin were all familiar clues. She looked in the three-way mirror, her heart kick boxing her ribs.

"Hello, Adam."

As USUAL her sloe-eyed gaze sent a jolt of adrenaline straight into Adam's bloodstream.

Mother and daughter turned from the mirror with matching surprise and guilt. Lindsey's eyes held an additional warmth he latched on to with pathetic hope. He wouldn't—*couldn't*—think about what he'd just heard, or he'd never get out of here with his pride intact.

"I can't believe you left your Sunday news-paper to track us down," Lindsey said. "How'd you know where to find us?"

"The salesgirl said it was empty in here except for a mother and daughter. The description fit." As far as it went. Which was way short of Me-gan's skimpy clothes.

Good Lord, when had that happened? He tried hard not to stare. But damn, when had *that* hap-pened? His future stepfather responsibilities sud-denly doubled in scope. He'd been so worried about Megan's resentment toward him he'd never considered other problems. Namely, teenage boys. Eddie Haskel clones, grasping Adam's hand at the front door and Megan's surprising new body in the car. If anybody dared touch that girl, they'd have to answer to—

"Adam?"

He blinked. Lindsey was looking at him strangely.

"Are you planning to punch someone out?"

"Huh? Oh." He unclenched his fists. Stuffing

both hands in his jeans pockets, he jabbed open a swinging door with his right elbow, jerked in the opposite direction, rammed his left funny bone. Hard. Pain resounded through his body in tuning-fork waves.

"Omigosh, are you all right?" Lindsey asked, suppressed amusement in her voice.

His handball game would suffer for days. Rubbing his elbow, he turned and met her merry brown eyes. "Go ahead and laugh."

She bit her lower lip.

"You know you want to."

"I want to laugh *with* you," she agreed.

He was a renowned surgeon, a member of the prominent Sullivan family, a combination that prompted respect and, in some cases, awe. Yet Lindsey was smiling as if he were a cute clumsy puppy—and damned if he didn't feel like rolling over for a tummy scratch!

Megan snorted. From her expression he might've just lifted his leg on the baseboard.

"So, did you have some shopping to do in the mall?" Lindsey asked, knowing full well he hated to shop.

"I was starving, and I thought you ladies might be hungry by now," he bluffed. "Want to take a break for lunch?"

Lindsey moved closer to Megan, reached up

and fiddled with her ponytail. "What do you think, honey? Are you hungry?"

If "honey" looked any more sour, Adam thought, she'd be a kosher dill.

"No."

Frowning, Lindsey slipped an arm around her daughter's waist and cocked her head. "By the way, Adam—"

"Ow!"

"—how did you know we'd be in Cool Clothes?" she said smoothly, ignoring the reaction to her pinch.

Adam controlled his smile and shrugged. "Megan told me this was her favorite store."

"I did not!" The girl transferred her indignant glare to him.

"Sure you did. Indirectly. The last time we played poker you got creative with the stakes, remember? A new shirt from Cool Clothes was part of the pot. At least, it was if *you* won." Sniffing loudly, he brushed an imaginary speck of lint from his Harley-Davidson T-shirt, the one she'd had to buy him, then leaned a shoulder against the wall.

The barest hint of a smile curved Megan's mouth. "You'd lost the last five hands. Who would've thought you'd draw a straight flush?" Lowering her gaze to the silk-screen print on his chest, she shook her head in a tsk-tsk fashion. "I thought I told you to wash that inside out in cold water."

"I do."

"It sure has faded a lot in two months."

"It's been washed an awful lot. This is my favorite shirt." Adam let that sink in, then raised the emotional ante. "I could use a replacement, kiddo. Anytime you're up for some five-card stud, let me know."

For a minute he thought she missed their weekly game of poker as much as he did. Thought she missed his front-row applause at her last ballet recital, the threesome they'd all been before he'd decided to make the ties of friendship something stronger. Her gaze grew suspiciously bright, then swerved away. Lindsey's turned downright misty, and her arm pulled Megan close for a hip-to-hip squeeze.

Watching them, Adam rode a swell of fierce tenderness. They'd be a family, a *real* family, where money and privilege wouldn't substitute for love. He would've mocked the sappy sentiment three years ago—before he'd recommended Pete's widow for a position in the hospital's marketing department. Lindsey had invited him home for a thank-you meal, and he'd been drawn back to the oasis of laughter and warmth again and again.

"Thanks for driving all this way," Lindsey said, her soft expression worth a trip across the Sahara. "We'd love to go to lunch, wouldn't we, Megan?"

The blond lashes swept down, came up on renewed resentment. Twisting, the girl directed her displeasure full force at Lindsey. "I'm not hungry. Besides, this was *supposed* to be our quality time together."

"Megan!"

"Well, that's what you said last night after Catherine called. Didn't you mean it?"

Flushing, Lindsey glanced at Adam. "That's no excuse for your rudeness. Apologize to Adam this—"

"No," he interrupted, straightening up from the wall. Megan's spoiled-brat routine was an act, a defense against selling out her father's memory. He'd deal with her guilt later. But Lindsey couldn't be allowed to waver before The Wedding.

"Megan's right," he admitted. "I can see that this is a 'girls only' kind of thing. I'm sorry I intruded. But what about—"

"It's no intrusion, really." Lindsey pulled

away from her daughter and crossed her arms. "*Is it,* honey?"

Adam's attention strayed to the pull of her red cotton T-shirt across plumped-up breasts. In twenty-six days they'd spend a glorious week alone in San Francisco. Preferably never leaving their bed.

"I guess not," Megan finally muttered.

With a last warning glance, Lindsey turned to Adam and hooked her unruly hair behind each ear. "We'll be finished in a few minutes, if you want to wait for us outside. But I'm not fit to go into a nice restaurant." The downward sweep of her hand encompassed running shorts and shapely tanned legs. "Would you mind too much if we ate at the food court?"

The dark curls behind her ears had already slipped free. They'd coil around his knuckles if he plunged his fingers deep. His gaze drifted lazily to the lush mouth he never tired of kissing.

She tucked the stray curls back in two self-conscious swipes. "Or we can go somewhere else…"

Reading the uncertainty in her eyes, he silently cursed his mother. Ann Sullivan had Lindsey's mom terrified of committing a wedding faux pas. In turn, Mrs. DeMitri constantly criticized her daughter's lack of concern for "appearances," both social and physical.

"The food court would be fine," he assured Lindsey. "But I've decided to go on home to my newspaper. No—" he raised his palm to stop her protest "—I shouldn't have shown up unannounced. You two take your time here."

"You're sure?"

"Positive. But, Lindsey?" Holding her gaze, he waited until she was there with him. "You look pretty damn 'fit' to me. I'd take you—" *here. Now.* "—anywhere and be proud."

Her eyes darkened to the color of French-roast coffee, her cheeks to sun-ripe peaches.

He wished like hell his loose khakis had been draped over the lamp shade this morning instead of snug Levis. "Since lunch is out for today, I'd like to take you to dinner tonight. Do you think you can make it?"

"Mo-om."

Lindsey blinked, then dragged her gaze to Megan's stony expression.

"You said we could rent a movie and order in pizza tonight."

"We'll go to Luigi's," Adam promised ruthlessly, reclaiming Lindsey's attention. "We haven't been there…in a long time."

Her lips parted, telling him she remembered

their intimate Italian dinner, remembered afterward...the first time they'd made love. She cast a tormented glance at Megan, turned a beseeching mother's gaze upon him.

Say yes, he commanded silently. *Say yes and I'll leave you in peace.*

"All right," Lindsey murmured.

His surge of triumph was fueled as much by panic as anticipation. If he couldn't hold her through love, then he would, by damn, hold her through lust. Lindsey made the debutantes and divorcées his mother had thrown in his path seem like beautiful stiff mannequins. Not a one of them had ever challenged his arrogance, tested his temper, made him laugh and feel alive like the woman he'd just manipulated. A woman so guileless he'd had to talk himself blue in the face before she'd agreed to live in his luxurious home after The Wedding.

A woman who still loved her dead husband more than she ever would him.

"Oh, good," said a voice behind Adam.

He turned to meet a cheeky grin and lively blue eyes. The red-haired teenager who'd directed him to the dressing rooms breezed into the corridor and stopped beside him.

"I got to thinking I'd better check out your story. A big guy like you—" her gaze swept his chest and shoulders appreciatively "—well, you could do a lot of damage if you were an ax murderer. But I guess everything's cool." She glanced at her female customers and back. "Is that your wife and daughter?"

"My father's dead," Megan announced before Adam could answer.

In the conspicuous silence, he pretended his heart wasn't hemorrhaging. Lindsey wouldn't meet his eyes.

"Bummer, man," the friendly girl finally said.

Remember The Wedding, Adam told himself, grateful now more than ever for his foresight. He'd pulled strings to ensure a sudden cancellation at Brazos Bend Plantation during its busiest June season. Once Lindsey said "I do," he'd have a lifetime to earn an additional three-word commitment.

Now if she just wasn't so damn stubborn about refusing his help with The Wedding costs…

Oblivious to the undercurrents, the salesgirl moved forward to circle Megan, whose pale stomach flushed as prettily as her face. "Wow, look at you! That is, like, so-o-o cool. Don't you just love the way it fits?"

Megan appeared startled, then smug. "Yeah, I do, but my mom thinks I look like a slut."

Lindsey's mouth slackened, then grew tight.

"What happened to thinking those clothes are 'kinda tight'?"

"I...changed my mind."

"Well, I didn't, and *I've* got the money. You can try on something else, or you can get dressed and we'll leave."

"But—"

"Your choice, Megan."

Megan turned desperately to her teen ally. "You sell a lot of these shorts and crop tops, don't you?"

"Well, yeah. We can barely keep 'em in stock."

"See, Mom? Everyone dresses like a slut these days. I'll look stupid if I don't."

Adam mentally cringed.

"Stupid? You'll look stupid if you don't dress like a slut? Are you *listening* to yourself?" Lindsey demanded. Clamping her mouth shut, she walked away two steps, then whirled to confront the blanching salesgirl. "Tell the truth, now. Don't you also have a lot of returns from girls who bought those clothes without their mothers—mothers who refused to let their daughters look promiscuous?"

"Well, yeah—yes, ma'am," the redhead answered warily. "At least, the part about returning clothes is true. I don't know about the other. I think girls are just trying to look good. Not look, you know, like they sleep around. But I guess you'd have to ask a guy's opinion to know what dudes really think.''

The silence pulsed as each female pondered the problem.

Sensing the shift in wind, Adam eased toward the dressing-room exit.

Blond, brunette and red-haired heads swiveled as one.

O-o-oh, hell, Adam thought.

CHAPTER THREE

Wedding Belles
3:00 p.m., 22 days before The Wedding

"O-O-OH, DEAR, tell me you *didn't* ask him that," Judith DeMitri wailed, pricking Lindsey's nerves worse than the row of straight pins cinching her satin wedding gown.

"She just told you she did, Judy, so quit that awful whinin'. You know how I hate it when you whine."

"You know how I hate being called Judy, Mama, but that never seems to stop you."

Perched on matching Queen Anne chairs across the large fitting room, Lindsey's mother and grandmother faced off. Again. Joey De-Mitri's life-insurance settlement five years ago had allowed his wife to buy a house, which Judith had promptly invited Grandma Edna to share.

"I don't see what in Sam Hill is so wrong with

Lindsey askin' Adam's opinion about Meggie's party clothes.''

"Megan, Mama. Her name's Megan. And I'll tell you what's wrong. Lindsey put him on the spot, that's what's wrong. No matter what Adam said, he was bound to upset one of them. The poor man probably wanted to run for cover.''

"Humpf. If that's all it takes to make the dog tuck tail, then he shouldn't be sniffin' around Lindsey's privates.''

"Mama!"

A gleeful cackle answered.

Arms held aloft, Lindsey obeyed the circular hand motion of the seamstress kneeling at her hemline and presented her left side for adjustment. When would her mother learn that acting scandalized was Grandma Edna's reward for saying outrageous things? Lindsey had caught on by age five. By the time she'd turned twelve, she could top her grandmother's most colorful country comeback and had ceased to be a target.

Angling a look now at the incorrigible tease, she hid an affectionate grin.

Edna Spencer had segued into a sales pitch for serving her famous "wienie-dog bites" at the wedding buffet—and was obviously enjoying her "citified" daughter's sputters.

By rights that wicked-witch chortle should

have accompanied a stooped body and wizened green face. Instead, she sat as straight as the ivory-handled cane supporting her stacked hands, her sculpted face a handsome decoupage of pearly rice paper. She'd protected her complexion from farm sunlight for seventy-eight years. But what ultraviolet rays had failed to do, a lifetime of laughter had accomplished.

Webbed crinkles feathered out from her periwinkle blue eyes and smirking mouth, the whole topped by a silver crown of coronet braids. Unraveled, those braids were a waist-length silver waterfall. Irresistible summer entertainment for a visiting tomboy granddaughter who refused to play with dolls.

Who *still* hated playing dress-up, Lindsey admitted, grimacing down at the petite seamstress tugging at her waist.

Trinh Nguyen glanced up and blinked. "I hurt you?"

"No, no. I'm fine." Lindsey had quickly gotten over the incongruity of a Vietnamese family buying a business called Wedding Belles. American families could take a lesson from the hardworking cohesive unit.

Trinh inserted a final pin, bent to tweak the dragging hemline, rummaged with a bit more force than necessary through a sewing kit. The equivalent of shouting in a culture that prized self-restraint and politeness.

Lindsey inched her Nike cross-trainers back from the satin puddled on their laces. "I'm sorry I forgot my heels again. I put them on my kitchen table last night specifically so I wouldn't forget. I had to walk right past them on my way to the garage." Her "silly me" laugh earned a glance that obviously agreed.

"Need shoes for hem," Trinh said, continuing her search through the kit.

"I know." *Guilt, guilt, guilt.* "But hey, at least they made it out of my closet this time. That's progress, don't you think?"

Not by Vietnamese standards, Trinh's silence clearly said.

"Next week I'll put my car keys on the shoe box so I won't forget. Really. I promise."

"You bring Thursday?"

"Yes, Thursday!" Lindsey nodded her irresponsible American head for emphasis.

"You bring Thursday, then we no worry." Rising on the alterations platform, Trinh moved behind Lindsey and fiddled with the long row of buttons down her back.

No worry. Right. Lindsey curbed an impulse to throw back her head and laugh insanely.

She should've eloped like she had with Pete,

despite Adam's coup of booking their ceremony at Brazos Bend Plantation. But Mrs. Sullivan's disappointment in her future daughter-in-law had seemed somewhat appeased by the prestigious wedding site. And Judith DeMitri's excitement over a chance to rub elbows with elite society had tipped the scales.

An assistant manager at Barnes & Noble, she'd ordered every book currently available on wedding etiquette and studied them at every opportunity. "We can't disgrace ourselves, Lindsey," was her constant refrain.

In a distant part of her consciousness Lindsey heard her mother and grandmother bickering. She lifted a shaky hand and swept back the curls sticking to her clammy forehead.

Sweat? She couldn't sweat! Not on her mother's heirloom satin wedding gown she was spending half a month's salary on to alter. Not when approximately three hundred guests would gather at the bottom of a red-carpeted grand staircase in twenty-two days to watch an unstained bride descend in stately dignity...

Or trip and ride her butt down the steps.

"O-o-oh," she moaned miserably, and wilted forward.

A wastebasket was suddenly thrust beneath her nose, her bowed forehead cupped by cool fingers.

Soothing. Supportive. Their faint scent of Jergens hand lotion a genetic imprint she would know anywhere. *Mother*.

"Take a deep breath, baby, there's a girl. That's right. Now another. Feel better?"

"A little."

"Aim for the basket," Grandma Edna called.

"I get water," Trinh said from behind.

The wooziness was passing now. Lindsey straightened and looked at the plumper, prettier and much less striking version of her grand-mother's face. She'd taken her mother's comfort for granted all her life. God willing, Megan would do the same with her.

"Thanks, Mom," Lindsey murmured, reach-ing out to squeeze her mother's hand. "I love you."

Startled pleasure replaced the discontent nor-mally shadowing Judith's eyes. "I love you, too, baby. You had me worried there for a second."

"How'd you know I felt sick?"

Judith laughed, revealing a glimpse of the girl she must've been, the beauty Joey DeMitri had fallen hard for the summer he'd baled hay for Grandpa Spencer. "You had that just-off-the-merry-go-round look. I've cleaned up too many of your 'o-o-ohs' not to recognize the signs. Was it something you ate, do you think?"

A sharp rap on a chair leg caught their attention. "That dog didn't knock you up, did he, Lindsey?"

"Mama!"

Grandma Edna settled her cane back into the plush mauve carpet. "Well, it makes sense, don't it? The girl's about to lose her breakfast, she's got ever'body in a tizzy rushin' into this fancy weddin'. Take a good long look at that *fee-ahn-say* of hers and tell me he hasn't slipped into her kennel whenever he gets the chance. He'd make my tail wag, too, if I was twenty years—"

"Mama, *really!*" Every trace of the sparkling girl was gone, replaced by a scowling blond matron.

"Really what, Judy? I'd say growin' a baby 'fore a man's leash is buckled tight is about as real as it gets. And it ain't always the right reason to get married, now is it?"

The two exchanged a long look, the younger woman's color rising as the elder's gaze softened.

Lindsey stiffened. Poor Mom, always wanting better than what she had. Poor Dad, never able to make his auto-body-repair shop do more than pay the bills. Lindsey had asked him once—before cancer had rendered him speechless—why he suffered her mother's constant complaints when divorce was a logical option. His dark eyes had filled with weary tenderness.

If we could choose who we fall in love with, there'd be nothing to look forward to in heaven, he'd told her.

"I'm not pregnant," Lindsey blurted, speaking to the dressmaker form draped in seed pearls and lace on her right. "That's not why we're getting married."

Grandma Edna was the first to respond. "That's good, honey. Real good. Why *are* you gettin' married?"

Lindsey's mouth might've been packed with cotton. She could no more answer her grandmother than she'd been able to chat with her dentist.

"Good grief, Mama, what a silly question!" Judith interceded, patting her lacquered bouffant Texas hair. "Besides being rich and handsome, Adam is crazy about Lindsey and Megan. Anyone with eyes can see that."

Turning away from her grandmother's all-too-probing gaze, Lindsey jerked at the heavy satin folds twisted around her legs.

A flurry of movement drew her grateful attention. Trinh, rushing to the rescue in more ways than one with the promised water. She stepped up onto the dais and wrapped Lindsey's fingers around a glass.

"Drink. You feel better."

"Thank you." She met her mother's eyes. "Would you mind getting three aspirin from my purse?"

"You want *three?*"

"Two, then." She'd take another one on the sly later. When her mother returned, she felt everyone watching as she downed the pills. The throbbing in her head increased. She handed back the glass with a bright false smile. "Thank you, Trinh. I feel much better."

Judith's worried frown remained. "Have you asked Larry yet to take your father's place at The Wedding?"

"No, Mother. I told you—I'm walking down the stairs alone."

"But he could hold you steady. And it's perfectly acceptable to ask him. All the books say so—"

"*Mo-ther.* Larry and I aren't feeling very charitable toward each other lately. I told you that. You'll have to hope I won't disgrace you by falling, because I'm walking alone."

"All right, all right, no need to bite my head off." Judith walked to her vacated chair and scooped up her knock-off Gucci handbag.

"Come on, Mama. If we leave now, I can drop you off at home and just make it to my hair appointment on time."

"But I wanted to see Lindsey in her veil."

"*Mama.* I told you we could only stay here an hour—"

"I'll drive Grandma Edna home if it'll help," Lindsey heard herself offer, a penance for snapping at her mother earlier.

"Oh, would you, baby? That would be wonderful! André hates it when I'm late."

"*Ahn-dray.*" A snort sounded from across the room. "Don't forget it's bingo night at the church, Judy. The one thing in this dang city I like to do, and you have to go and get dolled up," Grandma Edna grumbled. "That reminds me, Lindsey. You never did tell us what Adam had to say about Meggie's party clothes."

So she hadn't. Remembering his measured response now, Lindsey felt herself soften from the inside out. "He said that Megan would get lots of male attention the rest of her life no matter what she wore. But that she had to decide now what *kind* of attention she wanted. And he said she could wear clothes that focused a guy's concentration on her body, but personally, he thought her brain could win Miss Universe."

Megan had looked as surprised and pleased as

Lindsey had felt at the time. The fact that he'd ended up canceling their dinner date to handle a patient emergency had been keenly disappointing.

"Well?" her grandmother prodded. "Is that all he said?"

"Hmm? Oh, not quite." Lindsey arched a brow. "He said any guy who touched her wrong at the party would eat a fist sandwich for breakfast."

"Hot damn, I like that dog! No wonder you're in such an all-fired hurry to get married."

No wonder, Lindsey agreed. Then again, there'd never been any question why she was marrying him, but rather, why a man who could have his pick of society's darlings would "buckle his leash" to someone like her.

B. A. King, Men's Fine Apparel
12:35 p.m., 19 days before The Wedding

LINDSEY REMOVED her sunglasses and blinked in confusion. The elegant foyer wasn't like any men's-store entrance *she'd* ever seen. Of course Pete's idea of high fashion had been chinos and button-down-collar shirts from the Gap.

In the chaos of squeezing too many errands

into her lunch hour, had she gotten the address wrong?

Her heart sank. Adam had been working insane hours in order to take his vacation earlier than the hospital had anticipated. Their sporadic moments together were too precious for her to waste on— Ah, good!

She tucked away her sunglasses as a dark-suited man swept into the foyer. A tasteful brass badge identified him as Regional Manager.

"May I help you, madam?" he asked in a clipped British accent.

She stiffened under his swift head-to-toe inspection that obviously dismissed her as unimportant.

"Lost your way, have you?" he concluded before she could form a response. "If you need directions, there's a petrol station round the corner that sells maps."

He was every butler who'd directed riffraff from the front door to the servants' entrance, every maitre d' who'd seated nobodies near the noisy kitchen. And suddenly she wasn't a petite ho-hum brunette in a navy jumper and red flats, but a tall stunning blonde in a black sheath and high heels. "This *is* B. A. King, isn't it?"

"Why, yes, madam, it is."

"I believe Adam Sullivan is expecting me for

his tuxedo fitting? I'm Lindsey Howard—'' she arched a brow in her best Grace Kelly imitation ''—Dr. Sullivan's fiancée.''

The manager flushed to the roots of his distinguished gray hair. ''Of course, Ms. Howard. Dr Sullivan arrived ten minutes ago. If you'll follow me, please, I'll take you right to him.''

Lindsey hid her surge of satisfaction behind a regal nod. Hot damn, this princess-power thing wasn't half-bad!

As befitting the future Mrs. Doctor Sullivan, she started after the manager at a stately walk. Squeak…squeak…squeak. The leather vamp of her left shoe mocked her pretensions every other step.

Her guide paused and cocked his ear.

She stopped and froze.

He proceeded forward and so did she—this time hobbling Long John Silver-style in an effort to minimize the pressure on her left foot. A quick look around the store assured her no one was witnessing her loss of dignity. The place was empty except for a salesman shelving packaged shirts in a far corner.

A second more leisurely scan provided a feast for her senses. Incandescent lighting, antique armoires, the scent of fine leather and wool. Oil landscapes glowing richly on the hunter green walls. Classical music drifting soothingly from a hidden source.

The round racks of elegant clothes she passed might have been crowded tables in a posh restaurant. Any minute a sports jacket would elbow a neighboring coat and whisper, "The poor woman must have thought the sign read Burger King, not B. A. King."

Everything about the elite London-based store emphasized the extent of the chasm between Adam's worldliness and her own middle-class sensibilities.

Anxious questions crowded in to nag her, along with the first faint throb of another headache. What if, after they were married, she botched a fund-raising party critical to his continued research? What if she became a burdensome bore—or one of a hundred other nightmarish scenarios?

Squeak…squeak…squeak.

Realizing belatedly she'd resumed her normal walk, Lindsey dropped all pretense. Better to confront Adam with her squeaks now than later. Before he came to associate sealing their vows with being binded to a ball-and-chain wife.

"Here we are, Ms. Howard," the manager said, approaching and opening a paneled wood door. He indicated she should go in without him.

"Dr. Sullivan is in the back with Mr. Broadmore, our senior tailor. I'm sure you'll be pleased with his work. He's been with our American division for twenty years."

Entering a small waiting room furnished with a burgundy leather sofa and matching chair, she peered into the opposite hallway. Empty.

The echo of a thousand motherly admonitions to "mind your manners" brought Lindsey around to face her guide. "Thank you for escorting me here, Mr...?" She smiled at his surprised expression.

"Jones, madam."

"Really?" Her smile warmed into a friendly grin. "How about that? There are Joneses in my family on my mother's side, most of them in the Boston area. We don't mingle with that branch of the family much. We're not sophisticated enough for them, I think." She couldn't resist a teasing glance up through her lashes. "I don't suppose you have any relatives living in Boston, do you, Mr. Jones?"

His stare seemed more bemused than offended.

She laughed. "I guess not. Well, thank you again for your courtesy."

He cleared his throat. "You're quite welcome, Ms. Howard."

Lindsey started to turn.

"Might I bring you a spot of refreshment, perhaps?" he offered. Lindsey swung her head back around.

Whoa-ho! Chalk up another victory for the colonists. "That's very thoughtful, but no, thank you."

"You're certain? It's beastly hot outside."

Mr. Jones wasn't such a bad chap, after all. "I'm sure—but keep talking. I love to hear you Brits speak. Y'all make everything sound so...civilized."

"Do you think?" He straightened his boring navy tie with a pleased little motion, leaned forward conspiratorially. "I rather like the way you Texans drawl, myself. The home office says I've picked up quite a bit of your accent—"

"That's all very interesting," a deep voice interrupted, gunning Lindsey's heart into drag speed. "But unless you like the way Texans *brawl*, I'd suggest you stop flirting with my fiancée."

CHAPTER FOUR

LINDSEY WHIRLED around.

Arms folded across his wide bare chest, feet crossed at the ankles, Adam leaned negligently against the hallway doorjamb—tall, dark and pirate sexy in black tuxedo pants and a crushed black silk cummerbund.

"Of course, Dr. Sullivan. I meant no disrespect."

Sobering, Adam sighed. "Lighten up, Harry. It was a joke. Now close the door and leave us alone."

"Certainly, Dr. Sullivan. Right away." *Click.*

Adam rubbed the nape of his neck, tousling his black hair. "The joke wasn't *that* bad, was it?"

She stared at the underside of swelled biceps a shade paler than his bronzed face and couldn't breathe, much less muster a protest.

Lips canting, he lowered his arm and hooked a thumb in his cummerbund. "Gee, and here I thought I was pretty funny."

Funny was the last thing she would call him. Gorgeous, maybe. Virile, definitely. If darkness had prevented him from seeing her the few times they'd made love, it had also deprived her of seeing *him*. Shameless, she let her gaze roam hungrily over the man who would soon share her life and, praise the Lord, her bed.

Unhemmed black gabardine pants fit his wide stance closely, revealing more power lunches on the handball court than in a trendy restaurant. Those long muscular legs flowed into lean hips and a trim waist. His cummerbund cinched a prizefighter hard stomach. And that chest! A beckoning playground for her fingers amidst a whole amusement park of temptations.

After weeks of a quick shared lunch here and a hurried dinner date there, she was starving to touch him—to be touched *by* him. In only nineteen days the park gates would open... Damn!

They needed to talk before then.

"Adam?" She lifted her gaze and forgot her next words.

His burnished gold eyes watched her hotly. Intently. Above a surgical face mask those eyes had been nothing short of mesmerizing. "I'm the best," they'd reassured before her husband's operation. Right now they promised his skill wasn't confined to surgical techniques.

This was what she'd never felt with anyone else. This exquisite push-pull of emotional fear and physical desire. She'd tried so hard not to love him, had even succeeded for a while. Until his Dr. God act had crumbled and he'd fallen in love—with her little girl.

His dark-shadowed jaw clenched once. Twice. "I think you'd better go on back and pick out cummerbunds with Mr. Broadmore."

Some devil made her look slowly down his ab muscles, rippling piano keys under her gaze. His cummerbund received passing attention, his burgeoning arousal her lingering appraisal.

"I like the one you're wearing," she managed in a thick voice unlike her own.

A vicious curse. A powerful rush of movement.

Oh, the feel of those powerful arms crushing her to his pounding heart! She pressed closer, wrapping her arms around his waist, wanting to stay just like this for the next forty years or so. He was warm and strong and confident and *Adam.* And while he held her she had no room for loneliness or confusion. No fear of suffering her father's fate—or worse—being divorced and left to wither. To *die,* as she almost had after Pete's death.

A second abandonment would kill her as surely as a bullet in her brain.

"Lindsey, Lindsey," Adam growled in a half laugh against her ear. "You picked a helluva time and place to look at me like that. Do you want me to ravish you against the door?"

"Yes." The immediate pulse of his erection against her stomach prompted an answering tingle in her own swollen flesh. "But I'll settle for a kiss."

"Trust me, that's not a good idea." His voice sounded pained. His hands moved restlessly up and down her rib cage. "Albert is waiting."

"I'm a better kisser."

He choked out a laugh, deposited a swift peck on her forehead. "There. Are you happy now? Come on, let's go."

She stood on tiptoe and nibbled the underside of his square jaw. Mmm, warm salty sandpaper smelling faintly of aftershave. She trailed her tongue down his throat, felt him swallow hard.

"Lindsey, please... God, woman...I'm dying here."

She threw back her head and glared. "Then for pity's sake, Adam, kiss me farewell. And do it *properly*, this time."

His eyes flared, white-gold match tips in the face of a man pushed to his limits. Gripping her waist, he steered her firmly, thrillingly backward at a steady walk.

Her spine met hard wood, her chest, stomach and thighs unyielding muscle. She blinked up at his descending dark head and exulted, *Yes! Show me I wasn't imagining the magic. Remind me it isn't one-sided.*

And then his mouth was moving against hers, annihilating conscious thought in a blast of heat. It mushroomed from his stroking tongue, melting bones and sinew. Destroying her ability to stand had he stepped back.

Instead, he crowded forward, his palms slipping down to cup her rear, lifting her effortlessly off the floor. She clutched his bunched shoulders, spread her pliant dangling legs. Broke off the kiss and gasped at the press of his hard length at the center of her need.

It was decadently good, deliciously erotic. The friction of fabric against fabric closed her heavy eyelids. The building heat, steamy and wanton, wrung a moan from deep in her throat.

A small detached part of her listened, appalled, to the sound.

The rest of her leaned forward for another openmouthed kiss.

Adam obliged with flattering enthusiasm, filling her with his swirling tongue, his musky sandalwood scent. Realizing she could touch him at last, she massaged the crisp dark hair covering his skull. Explored the hard slabs of his chest. Kneaded his muscular shoulders, back and buttocks—

He shifted suddenly, braced his feet to hold her with one hand. His free hand gathered up her jumper fabric as her mollified ego urged him on.

Yes, yes! This is magic. You wanting me as much as I want you.

That distant part of herself heard a distressed, "Oh, my."

The rest of her concentrated on the warm fingers sliding up her thigh.

"Remember yourselves, please!"

Adam and Lindsey froze. Their eyes popped open. She wondered if she looked as dazed as he did. Wrenching her mouth away, she stared over his shoulder at a diminutive bald man standing near the hallway, a half-dozen cummerbunds draped over one forearm. His scandalized gaze centered pruriently on her exposed thigh.

She wriggled like a hooked worm. "Adam!"

He stepped back hastily.

Her feet hit the floor with a thud. She jerked down the skirt of her jumper, heard Adam swear beneath his breath and echoed it wholeheartedly in her mind.

According to Adam, the Sullivan men had shopped here for generations, along with most Texan men of professional, political or social power. And, as most women eventually did, Lindsey had learned the truth of another Grandma Edna-ism: men flapped their tongues worse than laundry on a clothesline in March.

Her fiancé turned around as if he owned the store, his frigid stare challenging the tailor's audacity to judge Dr. God. "Was I keeping you from a more important appointment, Albert? Because I can certainly take my business elsewhere if you're…impatient with delays."

The tailor's face drained from pink to white with alarming speed. "N-no, Dr. Sullivan. I didn't mean to sound impatient. Take your time and join me in the back room when you're ready to come—that is, when you're finished. I mean—" his gaze darted resentfully to Lindsey and back "—I'll be happy to fit your tuxedo at your convenience."

Backing up, he hit the wall, reddened, then turned and fled down the hall. Adam chuckled, the indulgent male with his reputation restored— no, enhanced.

But Lindsey knew that, despite the "liberated" freedom of her gender, she'd just locked in her image as a gold-digging trollop.

Dillards, "After Five" department
11:10 a.m., 15 days before The Wedding

HER ARMS LADEN with grandmother-of-the-bride
selections, Judith DeMitri frowned at the closed
dressing-room door. She'd specifically asked her
mother to leave it ajar. "Open up, Mama, it's
me."

"Me who?" demanded a wavering but feisty
voice.

Grinding her molars, Judith counted to five.
She'd promised herself she wouldn't lose her
temper today. "Would you *please* open the door?
My hands are full."

A strained heave and grumble, a prolonged rattling of the brass knob, a *pop* as the button lock
disengaged—and the door cracked open. "Well,
hell, Judy, why didn't you say it was you?" Her
mother swung the door inward, backed away, re-
settled her rear on a small chair and her cane on
the plush carpet. "A body can't be too careful in
the city. Remember my egg money."

As if you'll ever let me forget.

Twenty-two years ago on a rare visit to Houston, her mother had stopped at a grocery store on
her way to make a bank deposit. While stowing
ingredients for Lindsey's favorite oatmeal cookies in the trunk of her Oldsmobile, Edna had been

approached by a man with a knife demanding her purse. The fifty-six-year-old woman had given it to him, all right—directly between the eyes with considerable force.

Fifteen rolls of assorted change packed a serious punch.

Judith finished hanging her armload of dresses and closed the door. "How long are you going to hold that one incident against an entire city, Mama? Houston is perfectly safe if a person uses common sense and doesn't take chances."

"Are we watching the same news at night?"

Judith plowed on gamely. "Think of the shopping, the restaurants, the entertainment here that you can't enjoy in the country. Think of the culture."

"Speakin' of bacteria, did you send off that soil sample to the agriculture-extension service like I asked?"

Oh, darn. Her mother wouldn't get the experimental hybrid tomato plants she grew for the service until they analyzed the Ziploc bag of dirt in Judith's purse.

Her mother pounded her cane once. "Dang it, Judy, I asked you a week ago! I'm already late gettin' my tomatoes in."

Four years in a row Judith had argued in vain against her mother's backyard garden. "For the last time, Mama, I wish you'd relax inside the house while I'm at work. Read one of the books I brought home for you. Watch TV. You don't need to break your back out in that hot sun growing your own vegetables anymore. That's the nice thing about having grocery stores nearby.''

"Tell it to someone who hasn't been mugged."

Mentally counting to five again, Judith sifted through the hangers and jerked out a pale pink silk dress. "What about this one, Mama? How do you think the color would look next to my yellow suit in the receiving line?"

"Like washed-out tomatoes next to sick lettuce—the kind they sell in grocery stores." She met Judith's eyes challengingly, then expelled an aggrieved breath. "Oh, all right. I suppose I could try it on, since you won't let me wear my Sunday dress."

"Talk about washed-out color." Rushing forward, Judith helped her struggling mother rise. "That thing is fifteen years old if it's a day, and it never *was* in style. What would Ann Sullivan think if you showed up at The Wedding looking like you just fell off a turnip truck?"

"Well, hell, Judy, I don't know. Maybe that I used to live on a farm?"

Scowling at the shrewd twinkle in her

mother's eyes, Judith helped slip off the faded blue cotton shirt, the loose elastic-waist knit pants. She offered a steadying hand, which her mother accepted and then stepped oh, so slowly out of the pant legs.

The fact that Edna the Independent allowed such assistance gave Judith pause. In a quick sweeping glance she saw just how shrunken, how thin, how very *old* her mother's once strong body had become.

The sight slapped her into awareness. Of the inevitable loss ahead that she'd denied to herself for years. Of her own fragile mortality, equally denied for the same reason.

Joey's death had left an emptiness she hadn't realized he'd filled until he was gone. Lindsey loved her, yes—but the emotion was tainted by mistakes Judith had made. With horrible clarity, she sensed the yawning void her mother's death would leave.

Who else on earth would love her so unconditionally?

"It's enough to scare the spit out of you, ain't it?" her mother said wryly.

Realizing she'd been caught staring, Judith turned and fumbled with the dress zipper. "What is?"

"Other people gettin' old. Realizin' *you're* no

spring chicken, either. Inside, you're still eighteen. Last week you was only thirty. How can this have happened when you wasn't lookin', when you ain't ready?''

Wide-eyed, Judith looked over her shoulder.

Her mother bestowed an ageless smile that warmed and reassured. "Fifty-six ain't old. Hell, at that age, I knocked a mugger flat on his back. And don't put *me* in a pine box yet, either. I'm havin' too much fun aggravatin' you to give up the ghost anytime soon.''

The pressure in Judith's chest grew painful. "You'd better not.''

"C'mon, now, none of that. Let's get me in that dress and cover up this sorry bag of bones. I wouldn't want to upset Annie and her la-di-da friends by lookin' like a field scarecrow.''

Judith welcomed her twinge of annoyance. "*Ann*, Mama. Her name's Ann—'' she turned and floated an umbrella of pink silk over her mother's upraised arms "—and you'd better not call her anything else.''

"Not even Her Highness?'' The muffled cackle grew raspingly clear as a silver coronet of braids popped through the scooped neck.

A traitorous voice inside Judith secretly agreed. Ann Sullivan had always been cool, but when she'd called the day before wanting a final head count for the rehearsal dinner, she'd been downright frigid. The possible explanations for her borderline rudeness had kept Judith up all night worrying.

"Don't even call her *Ann* until she invites you to use her first name. The same goes for Tom and Daniel—Adam's father and grandfather. They're a lot more formal than people back home."

"They sound as uppity as the Jones clan in Boston."

"They're just high class, is all. You'll understand when you meet them at the rehearsal dinner. Hold still." Judith adjusted the neckline, tugged down the hem, steered her mother around and zipped up the back.

"There now, what do you think?"

CHAPTER FIVE

JUDITH STUDIED her mother's full-length reflection in growing pleasure.

Shimmering pastel silk narrowed from padded shoulders to just below the knees, a flattering camouflage for painful thinness. Rhinestone buttons flashed elegantly at the cuffed long sleeves. Her mother's old-fashioned hairstyle suddenly seemed regal, her pronounced bone structure classic.

Edna met her daughter's gaze. "This Daniel...how old did you say he was?"

Judith frowned at the saucy glint in periwinkle blue eyes. "Don't even think about it, Mama. Just sit quietly at the table and follow my lead. I'll probably never have another chance to eat at Capri again, and I don't want to be a nervous wreck worrying about you drinking someone else's water or using the wrong fork. *Or* propositioning Adam's grandfather." Worms of anxiety writhed in her stomach.

"Humph! I'll try not to blow my nose in my napkin."

"I'm serious, now. We can't disgrace ourselves, for Lindsey's sake."

"Lindsey likes me just the way I am. Hand me my cane."

Judith scooped up the mahogany stick, flinching as her mother jerked it out of her hands. "Are you angry?"

"No, I'm not angry. I'm *mad*. If I embarrass you so much, why don't you just take me back to the farm where I can grow bright red tomatoes and deep green lettuce and eat 'em with any damn fork I want to? George Henderson is a decent enough tenant farmer, but he'd be glad to have my advice—don't think for a minute he wouldn't."

That again. "I'm sorry I made you leave the farm, Mama. I know you loved it. But you forget. I used to live there. I know what kind of accidents can happen in the country."

"Like gettin' mugged?"

Judith narrowed her eyes. "Like breaking an arm falling off the barn-loft ladder. Like nearly losing an eye helping Daddy string barbed wire."

By the time Judith was eighteen she'd had scars and calluses to make a city girl shudder. Her one consuming desire had been to escape a lifetime of adding to them. "Leasing out the farm and bringing you here was for your own good, Mama. It wasn't safe anymore for you to live in that godforsaken place alone."

Her mother's mouth pruned. "I did just fine on my own for eight years without seeing hide nor hair of you on Spencer land. God didn't forsake that place, Judy." *You did,* her accusing silence added. "If I hadn't had Him—and Lindsey's visits, bless her heart—I don't know what I would've done after Garth passed on."

Guilt burrowed its stinging barb deep in Judith's conscience. Whirling, she pawed through the hanging clothes and yanked out a blue knit. "Of course you wouldn't thank me for insisting you move. Lindsey deserves all your praise. After all, she's a saint. Never complaining, always smiling, nursing her father night and day, visiting you at the farm—" she hung the suit smartly on a separate hook and smoothed the skirt "—standing by Pete after his heart attacks. Now she's got one of the most eligible bachelors in Houston twisted around her little finger. And why not? She's nothing like *me*. I'm just a nagging shrew—"

"Judith Lynn!"

The rare use of her proper full name stopped Judith's ranting as effectively as it had during her youth. She released the knit fisted in her hand and turned.

Leaning heavily on her cane, the impish light snuffed from her eyes, Edna Spencer looked every one of her seventy-eight years. "I hope that's not jealousy I hear in your voice, 'cause that would pain me somethin' fierce."

Judith endured a wave of hot shame. Dear God, she was *worse* than a shrew.

"You know them special hybrid tomatoes of mine that taste so much better'n the store-bought kind?"

Tomatoes? What in the world?

"They're finicky as hell to grow, always needin' more water, or sunshine, or calcium in the soil, or cooler nights. Then as soon as they get what they need, it's too much, or too hot, or somethin' you can't figure out for the life of you." Her mother's look asked, *Are you with me, here?*

She was, and it hurt.

Taking a halting step forward, Edna stroked a gnarled knuckle over Judith's cheek. "I didn't say the trouble wasn't worth the reward, daughter. It's just that our Lindsey is more like okra. It'll take root in just about any kinda soil and pretty much grow strong no matter what nature throws at it. But give it some pamperin'…"

Catching her mother's hand as it drifted down, Judith noted the wet residue of her own tears in surprise. "Like Adam will pamper her?"

The light slowly returned to her mother's eyes, bathing Judith in the glow of unconditional love. "Just think how she'll thrive *then*, Judy."

"Oh, Mama, I don't begrudge her a wonderful new life. She's my baby. I don't know what makes me talk so mean and spiteful sometimes."

"I don't know, either...baby." Mother and daughter exchanged a brief tender smile. "But I do know spite has a way of cuttin' short a person's life. Like I said, you're young yet. You got plenty 'a good years left to live—especially if you're willin' to see the good in 'em."

Wedding Belles
9:30 a.m., 9 days before The Wedding

LINDSEY STOOD in front of the three-way mirror and angled this way and that, trying to see her image through the eyes of her future in-laws.

Would they find the dress as timelessly beautiful as she did? Or would they think, *She* would *flaunt her body. There's not a discreet bone in it.*

Mr. Broadmore, Adam's gossipy little-hen tailor, had flapped his mouth just as she'd predicted.

News of her wanton behavior had filtered to Ann Sullivan, who'd telephoned with a discreet account of the rumors and given Lindsey an opportunity to deny everything. She had to give the woman points for fairness.

Too bad—in fairness—she'd had to confirm the tales. Absolutely the most wretched and humiliating moment to date in a lifetime that included some doozies.

Trinh scurried forward to billow out the skirt to her satisfaction. She met Lindsey's eyes in the mirror and stilled. "You no like?"

Spinning around, Lindsey caught the frowning woman's smaller hands in her own and squeezed. "I love it, Trinh! And so will everyone else. You're a genius with alterations. Thank you so much."

The seamstress had transformed her mother's gown from that of an eighteen-year-old bride's into one suited for a mature woman. If the Sullivans couldn't appreciate the dress, or her undebutante maturity, then the hell with them.

Big talk, now. But wait'll you're standing at the top of that grand staircase. Stifling a groan, Lindsey turned for one final inspection in the mirror.

The dress was constructed entirely of heavy ivory satin, as lustrous as a South Seas pearl. A shawl collar hugged her upper arms, dipped low to form a sweetheart point. She stared critically at her healthy hint of cleavage and bare shoulders. Too much skin? No, not with her long satin gloves.

They fit wet-suit close, as did everything between the bodice and the dropped waistline. A damn good reason to resist the Rocky Road ice-cream binge she'd felt coming on for days.

From midhip the satin flared into yards and yards of floor-length skirt. Raising her arms and pirouetting, she watched the graceful shimmer and swirl of fabric above her ivory satin heels.

"You big happy, yes?" Trinh asked.

Lindsey stopped.

Was she happy? Loaded question. She felt like her first alarm clock, a simple hand-wound piece of junk bought to satisfy a child's whim. The spring mechanism used to spend weeks frozen in a tight coil, then unloose its clanging shriek without any forewarning.

"The dress is beautiful," she hedged. "Can I take it home now, or is there something left to do?"

"You happy, I happy. Take home and make pretty picture."

Ah, yes. The bridal portrait. Another waste of her limited time, patience and money for the sake of Sullivan tradition. "I'll do that," Lindsey managed.

Trinh's dark eyes grew peaceful and serene. "You no worry. Look like princess."

No worry. Right.

Lindsey smiled at her unlikely fairy godmother, then moved behind the changing screen to undress. She would push aside the thoughts that robbed her of sleep at night. Like the promise she'd made to move into Adam's palatial West University home before the fall school term started. And the fact she'd failed to inform Megan of that minor little change in plans.

There were other more immediate problems to face. Her appointment this afternoon with the florist who demanded full prepayment. The meeting tomorrow with the caterer who kept pushing a "nice liver pâté" over the low-fat dips she'd requested. The "Rehearsal Dinner" chapter she'd promised her mother she would read and review with Grandma Edna.

"Trinh?" Lindsey called. "Could I please have—"

A small tray was thrust behind the screen, balancing a glass of water and four aspirin.

"Thank you, Trinh. You're a lifesaver." Smiling ruefully, Lindsey accepted the offering and told herself to take every day one hour at a time.

Then maybe—just maybe—she'd get through the next nine days with her sanity intact.

Lindsey's dressing room
5:05 p.m., 4 days before The Wedding

SEATED IN THE SMALL dressing area between her bathroom and bedroom, Lindsey clipped shut the large barrette and eased her hand away. Would her topknot hold? The damn thing had tilted or fallen three times already.

So far so good. Amazing.

She released her breath just as the first curl escaped. Then another. "No-o-o," she wailed, staring at her image in the vanity mirror.

The photographer was already setting up in the backyard. She had to be out of her robe and into her wedding dress when the light captured the trellis exactly right. No matter that the bride looked and felt more like something to shovel *on* the roses than pose in front of them.

The bedroom door cracked opened. Her mother's head poked through. "Do you need any help, baby?"

"I need André. My hair's impossible."

It was all the invitation her mother needed. Judith bustled into the room, her eyes widening as she assessed the damage.

"I *told* you it was horrible," Lindsey said.

"Now, now, it's not horrible. It just needs a little brushing, is all."

"Mother, I've brushed, sprayed, pinned and unpinned for twenty minutes now. A bad-hair day is a bad-hair day." In the mirror her mother's face suddenly appeared over her shoulder.

"You need more blush," Judith said bluntly.

"If I put on any more, I'll look like I'm running a fever."

"I don't think so, but if you feel comfortable like that..."

Snatching up a makeup brush, Lindsey swirled it in pink powder and stabbed both cheekbones. There. Bozo with a 104-degree temperature. That oughtta make her mother happy.

"Hmm. What lipstick are you going to wear?"

The coil inside Lindsey tightened. "I'm wearing it."

"Oh."

Here it comes.

"But you look so pretty in that lipstick I gave you for your birthday. The color makes your teeth seem whiter."

Lindsey yanked open the vanity-table drawer and pawed loudly through her jumbled makeup. Where was that awful thing? Ah, here, in the plastic bag of free samples she never used. She uncapped the tube, leaned forward and applied bloodred Copa Cabana to lips better downplayed than emphasized.

Perfect. A tribute to Stephen King's novel *It*. Clowns in the sewer had nothing on her. Surely her mother would admit as much. She bared her teeth in a ghoulish smile.

"See, didn't I tell you they'd look whiter? Hmm. Your lashes could use another coat of mascara."

Unbelievable.

"And a little powder on your nose will take the shine right off—"

"Mo-ther."

Judith blinked. "What? I want you to look your best. It's an honor to have your portrait hanging among generations of Sullivan brides. Your great-great-great grandchildren will some-day look at your portrait and remember you like this."

Lindsey sank her face into cupped palms. "Oh, God. I'll be the first Sullivan bride to send kids screaming from the gallery," she mumbled. "They'll have nightmares about me breathing heavily under their beds, popping out of the closet, staring from every street gutter they ride past on their bikes."

"Oh, honestly, don't be ridiculous!" Judith

unclasped the barrette sliding toward Lindsey's ear and dragged a brush through her hopeless curls.

Head bowed, Lindsey closed her eyes. *I can't do this.* The thought raced round and round her brain, a panicked wild thing seeking escape.

The back kitchen door slammed, rattling perfume bottles on the vanity table.

"Mom!"

Her distressed tone brought Lindsey's head up. She swiveled on her stool.

"In here, Megan," Judith called.

Seconds later 105 pounds of teenage angst burst into the bedroom, marched close and thrust out an opened envelope. She'd obviously cleared the mailbox on her way in.

"What's this?" she asked, her body taut, wariness in every line of her stance.

Lindsey's heart lurched. "What's what?"

"This stuff about Keeton Academy. Why are you getting registration information?"

The bottom fell out of Lindsey's stomach. She'd sent for the school brochure and registration forms three days ago, but hadn't expected a response so soon. And certainly not addressed to her *and* Megan.

"Omigod." Megan paled.

"Lindsey, that's wonderful!" her mother exclaimed. "I never understood why you'd want Adam to move in here when he has that big gorgeous house so close to the hospital."

"We're moving into Adam's house?" Disbelief gusted through Megan's stormy green eyes.

Oh, God, I can't do this.

Judith smiled at her granddaughter. "Keeton is one of the most prestigious private schools in the city. You'll love it."

"I'll *hate* it, Nana! All my friends are going to Preston High. We've been waiting for *years* to get out of middle school."

Lindsey roused herself enough to murmur, "You don't have to go to Keeton."

"I don't?"

Imbecile. Idiot. "If you'd rather go to public school, you can."

If she lived to be a hundred, Lindsey would never forget the betrayed incredulity in her daughter's look.

"When were you going to tell me, Mom?"

The coil in Lindsey's gut was a sharp pain now.

"Well?"

"I'm sure she was going to tell you soon," Judith interceded, placing a supportive hand on Lindsey's shoulder.

"Soon." Megan huffed her contempt. "Like, when the moving van pulled up to the house?"

Lindsey huddled into herself. She had no excuse, no valid defense.

Her daughter's chin firmed and lifted. A very bad sign. "I won't go. You can't make me."

"Oh, honestly, Megan," Judith muttered.

"No way am I going to some snotty private 'academy,' Nana, or a public school where everybody's known everybody since kindergarten. I'll drop out first."

"You don't mean that."

"I do, too. Sherry Douglas's older sister dropped out and has her own apartment now and everything."

"Ask Sherry's sister how much she likes paying her own rent and utilities, buying her own food and clothes. I'll bet she'd trade places with you in a minute. Why are you talking such nonsense?" Judith squeezed Lindsey's shoulder. "Tell her I'm right, baby."

I can't do this, I can't do this.

Tap-tap-tap. "Um, excuse me, Mrs. Howard. I called down the hallway twice, but I guess nobody heard me."

Mr. Thompson, the one-hundred-bucks-an-hour photographer Adam's mother had recommended, hovered at the bedroom doorway. Embarrassment and irritation played tug-of-war on his thin face.

"I'd like to start shooting outdoors in about five minutes. We only have a fifteen-minute window of opportunity to work with. Could you get into your dress, please?"

Dress? Lindsey blinked down at her white terry robe, twisted slowly to study her reflection in the vanity mirror.

"She'll be ready, Mr. Thompson," Judith assured the man when Lindsey didn't respond.

"Okay." He sounded doubtful. "I'll be waiting in the backyard."

"Thank you, Mr. Thompson."

"Fifteen minutes isn't very long."

"We'll hurry." His footsteps shuffled off. "Prima donna," Judith muttered under her breath. With a final pat on Lindsey's shoulder, she moved to the closet.

The grate of the sliding doors sounded faraway. Lindsey stared blankly into her mirrored eyes.

"Megan, hon, help me get your mother into this dress."

"But we were talking, Nana."

"You heard Mr. Thompson. We'll have to finish this discussion later. Your mother's bridal portrait is very important."

"And I'm not."

"Honestly, did I say that?"

"You didn't have to. *Everything* these days is more important than me!"

The gnawing pressure in Lindsey's stomach spread up into her chest.

"The stupid flowers in the bouquet. The stupid food for the reception. The stupid thank-you notes for the stupid presents taking over our dining-room table. Why don't I just go live with Catherine after The Wedding and make everyone happy?"

"Lower your voice, Megan. Such dramatics."

"You'd be dramatic, too, if your whole life was ruined."

Judith sighed. "Talk some sense into your daughter, Lindsey. Her life is going to be wonderful."

I can't do this, I can't do this.

"Don't worry, Mom," Megan said. "I won't bother you anymore. Catherine has two extra bedrooms, and her parents like me a lot. I can live with them and go to Preston High, and you and Adam can live alone in his big gorgeous house. That's what y'all want, anyway. Admit it."

"Honestly, Megan. You're being ridicu—" Judith broke off on a gasp. "Adam!"

Lindsey sensed Megan whirl around.

"We weren't expecting you. How nice," Judith said, strained cheer in her voice.

"I got out of the O.R. early. Nobody answered my knock at the front door. Lindsey, are you okay?"

I can't think, I can't breathe, I can't do this.

"She's moving a little slowly, Adam. Would you mind telling Mr. Thompson in the backyard we'll be another five minutes?"

"Lindsey," Adam repeated. "Are you okay?"

He'd noticed in fifteen seconds what her mother and daughter hadn't in ten minutes. Somehow that made everything much much worse. The past weeks of doubt and tension roiled within her, demanding release. Lindsey swiveled around to face her fiancé.

Still dressed in his green scrubs, his brown-gold eyes warm with concern, he was handsome, respected, brilliant, wealthy... The list went on and on while her own was pathetically short. When the physical chemistry wore off, she would inevitably bore or embarrass him. She'd avoided the truth long enough.

"I can't do this," she whispered, holding herself together with superhuman effort.

"Of course you can." Her mother said. "I'll have you buttoned up in no time—"

"You aren't listening, Mother. *I can't do this!*" she shrieked, her control splintering. Wild-eyed, she twisted her robe sash, exposing her raw insecurity to three startled stares.

"All right, baby. I'll talk to the photographer," her mother said carefully. "Maybe he can reschedule for tommorrow."

Lindsey saw Adam go rigid and knew that he, at least, had heard what she hadn't said.

"No, Mother. There isn't going to be any bridal portrait because there isn't going to be any bride. For once I'm glad you bought all those wedding-etiquette books. We've got guests to notify, presents to return. Wouldn't want to disgrace ourselves using the wrong protocol, would we?"

Oh, it hurt to hurt her mother, pain on top of pain. Instead of apologizing, she turned to a new victim. "Don't worry, Megan. I won't bother you about new schools anymore. We're staying right here. You can go to Preston High in the fall."

Far from triumphant, Megan looked shocked. "Mom, I didn't mean... I wasn't trying to..."

"Stop the stupid wedding? Gee, you could've fooled me. You've done nothing but complain or be rude to me and Adam since I told you we were engaged."

"But I didn't think you'd call it off. Not really. I was just, you know…"

"Complaining and being rude?"

Megan's bottom lip quivered. "Yeah, I guess so."

"Did it ever occur to you to think about *my* feelings? I have them, too, you know. Oh, puh-leeze, don't tell me—tears? You're crying? Good grief, I thought you'd be happy. You are damn hard to please, you know that?"

"I'm sorry," Megan said thickly, her wet lashes spiked, her green eyes remorseful.

For the life of her, Lindsey couldn't stop, couldn't turn off the hateful jangling alarm. She could only let her pain run its course. "Hey, that's okay. You were right. Adam and I should never have gotten engaged. *Thank you,* Megan. You saved us from making a big mistake. Inter-marriages between clowns and aristocrats are doomed to fail. I can admit that now."

Megan's stricken gaze skittered away, searched Judith's stunned face briefly, veered toward the doorway and clung. A child's plea for comfort in a world turned unfamiliar and scary.

Adam responded instantly, striding into the room, opening his arms as he approached. In a movement combining strength and tenderness, he pulled Megan close for an enveloping bear hug—

their first embrace in months. They stood locked in the grip of strong emotion, eyes closed, features taut in a near grimace.

Watching, Lindsey felt the first hot tear spill free and puddle in the seam of her trembling lips.

Adam kissed the top of Megan's head, pulled away, smoothed back strands of long blond hair sticking to her wet cheeks. "Your mother is exhausted. She's been under a lot of stress. She didn't mean to hurt anyone. You know that, don't you?"

Megan nodded, her tears falling in earnest now.

Almost as freely as Lindsey's.

"And for your information, kiddo, I don't want to live in my big gorgeous house with her alone. I need you there to protect me," he teased, coaxing a small watery smile from her reminiscent of earlier days. Swiping two big thumbs beneath her eyes, he grew dead serious. "I can't replace your father, Megan. I wouldn't attempt to try. But I love you and your mother very much. I'd like us to be the family I never had."

Lindsey stiffened.

"If you can't think of me as family, then let me be your friend. We were pretty good friends once, weren't we?"

Sniffing loudly, her tears starting afresh, Megan nodded.

"Okay, you think about it." He lifted the hem of his loose green shirt, dabbed her splotchy face, then turned her toward the door. "Now, scoot. We'll talk more later."

Lindsey barely noticed her daughter run out. She hadn't liked being talked about as if she wasn't in the room. But what he'd said... Oh, could she have been such a blind fool, all this time? Or had he only included her in his declaration of love to smooth things over?

She divided her concentration between replaying Adam's words to Megan and hearing his instructions to her mother.

"Tell the photographer I'll call him tomorrow to reschedule, and I'll make it well worth his trouble. Then take Megan out for a hamburger, would you please, Judith?"

Judith plucked three tissues from a box on the vanity table, handed two to Lindsey and blotted her eyes with the other.

Finished, she sent her future son-in-law an adoring smile.

"Good idea. I can pick up a Kid's Meal while we're out. Mother lacks one toy in McDonald's latest promotion. She'll drive me nuts until she has them all." At the door she paused. "Thanks for talking some sense into my daughter. Anyone can see you two are a match made in heaven.''

Adam's answer faded into the background as Lindsey remembered another deep voice. *If we could choose who we fall in love with, there'd be nothing to look forward to in heaven.* Her father's bleak words echoed tauntingly from the past.

No more deflecting confrontation, Lindsey decided then and there. No more pretending she was a princess. She was who she was, love her— or not.

''All right, Lindsey, we're alone. Would you like to tell me now what 'intermarriage between clowns and aristocrats' is all about?''

Lindsey blew her nose, threw her tissues into the trash and rose on unsteady legs.

CHAPTER SIX

ADAM WATCHED Lindsey square her shoulders and thought, *This is it. I've lost her.*

"It's about expectations, Adam. And partners who don't live up to them."

So. She'd decided. She couldn't settle for less than what she'd had with Pete. A helpless sense of failure unlike any Adam had known, even that of losing a patient, erased the lingering joy of his reunion with Megan.

He rarely assumed the Sullivan mask of aloofness anymore. Thank God it was like riding a bike. "I understand."

Her lashes fluttered and dropped, came up on unfathomable pools of brown. "Good. That's good. Because I've seen what disillusionment can do to a marriage. We're much better off living with a little embarrassment now than committing to a lifetime of…"

"Disappointment?"

Her bright red lips trembled, then compressed. "I see you do understand. I'm sorry it had to come to this. I'll make sure your shot at chief of surgery isn't jeopardized.''

What the...?

"We can still eat together in the cafeteria occasionally, things like that, and show everyone it was an amicable break—''

"Whoa-whoa-whoa, back up." He lowered his brows and set both hands at his waist. "You'll *what?*''

Lindsey's shuttered gaze moved to her neatly made bed as if the blue comforter had spoken, instead of him. "I'll make sure the hospital board knows our breakup had nothing to do with Pete's death. But I hope you'll continue to spend time with Megan. I saw her face when you said..." Her whip-sting glance flicked him once, then returned to the bed. "Well, Megan believed what you said.''

In that unguarded instant of eye contact, he'd seen hurt and considerable anger. Incredible.

Possibly wonderful.

"I don't give a flying flip about what the board thinks, Lindsey. If they'd thought I was remotely responsible for Pete's death, I'd have been kicked off the staff long ago. And I meant what I said to Megan.''

Her gaze leaped to his and stayed.

"Every single word," he confirmed.

"Then, why... I mean, you agreed so fast to call off The Wedding, I thought... I don't know what I thought. Or think."

The frantic flutter at the base of her throat shot his hopes up along with his pulse.

"Adam, do you love me or— Wait!" Her upraised palm stopped him three feet away. "Don't come any closer. I can't think clearly when you touch me."

Better and better.

She clutched the lapels of her terry robe together and frowned. "I'm not *going* to let you touch me until we talk. Do you realize every time I bring up life after The Wedding we wind up kissing?"

"We do?"

"Don't give me that innocent look. We need to talk about our differences. Great sex is not enough— Stop right there!"

Damn. He teetered just short of his goal.

Her nose was red, her makeup streaked, her curly hair a mess. She looked adorable. Extremely kissable. And so close. God, he loved the way she smelled. A warm lush scent that reminded him of her backyard roses in midday sun. Only more stirring, because *she* was mixed in there, too.

Adam would almost swear she wore nothing

under that terry robe but sweet female skin. He fisted his hands to keep from reaching out—

"Listen to me, Adam. I never saw my mother and father kiss or hug. Not in all my years growing up. But he would look at her so...yearningly. Whatever had drawn her to him in the first place had obviously died, and I hurt for him, you know?"

Yeah, he knew. He could've happily stared at Lindsey until cataracts clouded his vision.

"It took me years to forgive Mother for being ashamed of him, for not loving him as much as I did. But now I realize she was as unhappy as he was. Fair or not, she blamed him for holding her back from a life-style she wanted. Oh, Adam..." Her eyes pleaded for understanding.

His heartbeat faltered. He braced himself for the worst.

"I can't bear the thought of disappointing you like Dad disappointed my mother."

He blinked. "*You* don't want to disappoint *me*."

She nodded woefully.

His grin started out slow and crested on a surge of pure elation.

Paling, she whirled around and darted for the bathroom.

Damn. "Lindsey!" He passed her in three quick strides, cut in and turned.

She barreled into his chest, rebounded and spun toward her vanity table.

"Lindsey, you don't underst— Phew!" He spit out a powder puff, dodged a small jar of something, took a direct hit on the chin from a tube of lipstick.

"I pour out my heart—" she hurled a hairbrush "—I'm dying inside—" she threw four spiny plastic rollers in rapid succession "—and you start *smiling?*" She scooped up a box of tissues.

Lunging, he clamped her wrist on the windup and hooked her waist with his free arm. "Remember that day in Cool Clothes when you said you loved Megan and Pete more than life? I knew exactly what you meant, Lindsey, because that's how I feel about you."

Her back was arched, her flushed face tilted up, her expression wary—but intrigued. She looked away, then slowly back. "What did I mean?"

He almost smiled. Hell, she deserved specifics. He'd been a coward and a fool not to trust her with them before. "When I look at you, Lindsey Howard, my heart floats clear up to the ceiling. I forget fund-raising dinners and hospital politics.

I forget the fear and hope on patients' faces. I forget my cold-sweat nightmares about failing them and their families.

"I see your face and I'm...happy. I'm happy," he repeated wonderingly, humbled by the simple truth. "Just because you're near. Just because you're *you*. No other woman in the world has made me feel like that."

Her eyes had gone fawn soft, enchanted—and enchanting. She released a long sigh.

He did smile then. "Sappy, huh? You've turned Dr. Adam Sullivan into plain ol' sappy Adam. A man who can survive without you, but not *live*." He lowered his voice into a caress. "Don't make me live without you, Lindsey."

"I do all that to you?" she breathed, almost convinced, just a whisper away...

"Sweetheart, that's only the half of what you do to me."

Snugging her in tight, Adam pressed his advantage close. And harder than he could ever remember.

The box of tissues dropped from her limp fingers.

He draped her hand over his shoulder and dipped his head for a taste of her soft red mouth.

Adrift in spangled heat, Lindsey smiled against his lips. He loved her! Beyond lust or friendship.

The truth of it had shone in his tawny eyes, re-sounded in his tender voice. He loved her! Enough to risk sounding "sappy" and romantic. She made a happy purring noise deep in her throat.

He lifted his head an inch, his gaze urgent and intense. "I don't care how we marry, just so long as we do. Hell, we can call The Wedding off and go to City Hall if you want. I know you're still in love with Pete, but I swear I'll make you happy. I'll take you to Italy—you always wanted to see Venice and Rome. We'll hire the best ballet instructor in the city for Megan. She's got too much talent not to explore her potential...."

Dreamy and dazed, Lindsey could only cling mutely to his broad shoulders. Was this supremely confident man really whispering love bribes as if he needed them to win her heart?

"...your grandmother could have a gardener, someone to do the heavy work and leave the fun stuff for her. I know she's as stubborn as you are about accepting help, but dammit, what's the good of having money if I can't spend it to make you hap—"

Her open mouth stopped his foolish rambling.

She put all the emotion in her joyful heart—and a considerable amount of lust, as well—into a long stimulating conversation with his eloquent tongue. When she came up for air, they were both breathing faster.

Smiling tenderly, she cradled his jaw in her palm. "I'll always love Pete. You're right about that. But I'm *in love* with you, Adam. I have been for over a year. Totally and completely. With all my heart and soul."

Amazingly he looked as uncertain as she'd felt earlier.

"You want more sappy words, or would you like me to show you how I feel?" She lowered her lids to sultry half-mast. "I suppose I could do both..."

He turned his head sharply, his jaw rasping her palm, his lips soothing the tender skin with a fervent kiss. Above the mask of her fingers his eyes glittered like gold dust. Holding her gaze, he deliberately flicked the center of her palm with his tongue.

"I'm a man of action," he said, his breath icy-hot against her damp skin. "But whatever turns you on."

She stared into his mesmerizing eyes. "*Everything* about you turns me on."

With a guttural curse, he ripped his mouth from her hand and dove for her waiting lips.

They connected roughly, passionately, fighting

for dominance of the kiss, stoking the fire into leaping flames.

Lindsey gave no quarter. It had been so long, and she hadn't been sure he loved her then. Her new knowledge made everything different. More arousing. More meaningful. She needed to express her overwhelming emotion. She needed to bond in the ultimate act of commitment. She needed, needed, needed...

His hands suddenly clasped her bottom, holding her still for the grind of his hips. When her pleasure neared pain, when her frustration mounted to the point of mindless abandonment, she jerked loose the bow of her robe sash and spread the terry cloth wide.

Ah, yes. His cotton scrubs were negligible barriers to her naked skin. Much much better. But still not enough. Locked in the kiss, she strained closer against him from breasts to thighs.

Lindsey could feel his heart pounding in heavy thuds, feel the pulse in that part of him she wanted inside her. She'd never been so aware of her body in relationship to another's. Even her hair seemed to have developed nerve endings. When he thrust his fingers through her hair, a jolt of delight speared straight to her toes.

He closed her eyes with his hard-soft lips,

kissed a trail to her ear and swirled his tongue inside.

Shivery thrills streaked under her skin. Nothing existed but Adam.

"Lindsey, Lindsey," he crooned, a gruff male hosanna in her ear. One big hand found her left breast and paid it reverent homage. "I'm going to take you to that bed and make love to you like I've wanted to from the first. In the light, with no doubts between us." His mouth swooped down to capture her nipple.

Lindsey gasped. The hot moist tugs at her breast reached deep inside her, releasing a liquid rush of welcome for his possession. She swayed on her feet, woozy with lust, drugged with sensation. His mouth shifted to her right breast, and her legs buckled.

Adam caught her beneath the knees, swept her up powerfully against his chest. The room spun and they faced the bed. His strength excited her. Made her feel feminine and protected, in a me-Tarzan-you-Jane way. She twined her arms around his broad shoulders and enjoyed the ride.

Down, down she went, her back sinking into the comforter, her arms lying limp over her head, her robe a terry-bear rug beneath her decadent sprawl.

"Don't move," he ordered, pulling away quickly to lock the bedroom door.

Their eyes met across the room and held fast as he approached the bed. By the time he stopped, her heartbeat had tripled—at least a third of it due to anxiety. The same evening light filtering through the miniblinds to caress his face exposed her fully to him for the first time. She watched him look slowly down the length of her body and willed herself to remain still. What was he thinking? Oh, God, was he disappointed?

Cracking, she reached blindly for the edges of her robe.

He was on the bed in an instant, his stiff arms bracketing her hips and pinning down the terry cloth. "My electric bill is about to go up," he said thickly. "I may never turn off the bedroom lights again."

His hungry admiration was impossible to misread. The petals of her fragile ego unfurled.

With hands and lips and tongue he proceeded to show her his appreciation, murmuring erotic words of praise against her hollows, arousing her to a fever pitch until she tossed her head from side to side.

"Please," she managed at last in a strangled voice, plucking fretfully at his clothes.

Relenting, he hauled her upright, freed her

arms from the robe sleeves, then peeled off his scrubs in jerky haste.

When he blanketed her with hard muscle and hair-roughened skin, she gasped the pleasure was so great. When he slid into her slowly, inch by exquisitely hot inch, she moaned. When he moved with strong sure strokes to the rhythm of her wildly beating heart, she whispered "I love you" in counterpoint over and over. And when he pushed them both over the edge into exhilarating heart-stopping free fall, she cried out his name and clung tightly, trusting him to keep her safe.

When their breathing grew quiet and he kissed a tear from the corner of her eye, then cuddled her close as if she was his most precious possession, she sent up prayer of thanks. And tacked on a wish for her father's happiness.

Like him, she hadn't chosen to fall in love. Yet far from looking forward to contentment in the next life, she'd found heaven in Adam's strong loving arms.

CHAPTER SEVEN

Brazos Bend Plantation, ladies' dressing room 3:00 p.m., one hour before The Wedding

"HERE GOES NOTHING," Lindsey told her mirrored reflection.

She cautiously removed her hands from the small head cap anchoring her chapel train. It looked straight. She hadn't messed up André's handiwork pinning the thing on. He'd outdone himself creating her sleek chignon, softened by artfully selected curls around her hairline.

Rising, she turned from the vanity mirror stretching wall-to-wall above a rose marble countertop. "Ta-da!" she crowed.

"Walk a few steps," Megan advised.

Lindsey did, then faced her daughter. "Well?"

"The truth?"

Me and my new policy of up-front honesty. "Lay it on me."

"You look kinda stiff. Like you have a basket

of fruit on your head or something. Loosen your neck.''

Lindsey tilted her head left, right, back. So far, so good. Fairly confident her veil would stay put, she walked the length of the large dressing room, turned model style and headed back to Megan.

''Well?'' Lindsey demanded, astonished when tears welled and trembled in Megan's eyes.

''You look beautiful, Mom. Really. Just like a princess. Adam is lucky to get you.''

''He's lucky to get us both, Megan.'' The moment stretched. *Please don't start with the move thing now.*

Megan's chin came down. ''Yeah, you're right. He *is* lucky.'' A mischievous gleam lit her eyes. ''Poker every night. By the time I get my license I'll have enough saved to buy a car.''

Lindsey laughed, the joy piercing her heart a sweet pain. ''I wouldn't count on it. Who bought whom a Harley-Davidson T-shirt, hmm?''

Megan made a face. ''That was a fluke.''

Lindsey reached out and patted her daughter's shoulder. ''Whatever you say, dear. And speaking of princesses, you remind me of Cinderella.''

''Oh, Mom.'' Despite her tone, Megan looked pleased.

''My baby is a beautiful young woman.'' Pressing a palm against her heart, Lindsey blinked rapidly in a not-so-kidding show of emotion. "I think I'm going to c-c-cry."

Grinning, Megan leaned in to bump shoulders. "You are such a bozo."

True. And Adam loved her, anyway! Had any bride ever been so lucky? Lindsey couldn't stop smiling. "Give your mother some credit. You're gorgeous. Would I lie to you? Don't answer that." Lifting their joined hands, she forced her blushing daughter into a music-box twirl.

In her sashed powder blue dress with belled floor-length skirt, Megan was breathtakingly lovely. Her upswept blond hair made her seem older than thirteen. André would get four years of prom business out of this effort, Lindsey predicted.

The door opened just as Megan completed a full circle.

Resplendent in pink silk, Grandma Edna walked in haltingly and propped both hands on her cane.

Judith swept in behind and stopped short, her hand fluttering over her yellow cocktail-suit breast pocket. "Oh, my." She smiled mistily. "Just look at them, Mama! Have you ever seen anything so beautiful? They could be princesses at the ball." She snapped open a small clutch purse and pulled out a tissue. ''I think I'm going to cry.''

As her mother dabbed her eyes, Lindsey met Megan's gaze. They both broke into giggles.

''Looks like they hit the spiked-punch bowl already,'' Grandma Edna observed dryly.

If you could get drunk on happiness, she was wasted, Lindsey admitted. Today she had champagne running through her veins. Everything and everyone was beautiful, especially these women she loved.

''Oh, my,'' she mimicked. ''Just look at them, Megan! Have you ever seen anything so beautiful?''

Picking up her cue, Megan assumed a weepy smile, lifted her skirt and air-dabbed her fake tears. ''They look like…like…''

''Washed out tomatoes and sick lettuce?'' Grandma Edna suggested.

Lindsey turned a baffled gaze from her smirking grandmother to her mother.

''Don't ask.''

Tap-tap-tap. ''Excuse me, Mrs. Howard, but I finished up early with the groom.'' Mr. Thompson, strapped in bulky camera equipment, stood hesitantly in the open doorway. ''I could get that generational shot you wanted out of the way now. It'll free up more time for the wedding-party photos after the ceremony.''

What a difference four days made. ''Wonderful! Come in, come in,'' Lindsey urged. ''Where do you want us?''

He pushed the door wider, swung around to pick up a tripod from the hall, then clattered inside, sweeping the room with a professional gaze. ''Around that wing chair, I think. Give me a few minutes to set up here first. Are you ladies ready to be recorded for posterity?''

There was a beat of silence. Then all four females headed for the vanity mirror. A long upholstered bench, one of three in front of the marble counter, accommodated them all within reach of a cluster of cosmetics.

Four hands pilfered from the array and set to work.

''Does this lipstick look okay, Nana?''

''Hmm. Why don't you try my Copa Cabana? It'll make your teeth seem whiter.''

''Oh, Judy, you and your red lipstick. To hear you go on, you'd think you'd discovered fluoride.''

''Well, excuse me for living, but I know what I know. Here, Megan, put a little of this on.''

''But only old people wear red lipstick, Nana. I mean, not *old* people, but...you know...''

"Anyone over eighteen," Lindsey clarified, leaning forward to powder her nose. "Heaven forbid Megan should embarrass herself wearing red lipstick when she can look like something dug out of a grave." She met her daughter's eyes in the mirror. "I saw that black lipstick you slipped into the grocery cart."

Megan grinned unabashedly. "Pretty cool, huh?"

"Corpses usually are."

"Hey, Meggie! Can I borrow it sometime?"

"Honestly, Mama. Why would you want to wear black lipstick?"

"For that dang-fool mailman. He's always yellin' in my ear like I'm dead, anyway. If I sit real still on the front porch with my eyes closed, it oughtta scare the pants off 'im."

Four feminine laughs ranging from cackles to giggles intertwined and faded pleasantly.

"That yellow is really pretty with your hair, Mother," Lindsey said.

"Do you really think so? I loved this suit when I bought it. But now I think I should have gone with a darker color. I look so...fat."

"No way, Nana! I hope I look like you when I'm ol—your age. Besides, the mirror adds ten pounds, you know."

Mascara wand in hand, Lindsey paused.

"That's right, I forgot. I feel much better. Thank you. Mama, are you sure you don't want a little more blush...."

The chatter continued unnoticed as Lindsey absorbed the impact of Megan's breezy comment. A seventy-eight-year-old woman's irrepressible personality had been captured and stored in her great-granddaughter's memory. Megan would undoubtedly pass the legacy on to her children, along with Lindsey's outlook and teachings. The responsibility was awesome and frightening. But empowering, as well.

The nurturing and shaping of young lives was one of the best things about being a woman. So it had been for countless generations of mothers. So it would be for countless more.

Lindsey's gaze moved lovingly from the spirited humor in Grandma Edna's eyes to the hope for approval in her mother's to the fierce independence in Megan's, traits they all shared in varying proportions. The *rightness* of it all enriched her contentment.

"You conductin' music over there or somethin', Lindsey?"

Laughing, she capped her mascara. "No, just daydreaming."

"With that handsome devil waitin' downstairs, can't say as I blame you." Grandma Edna's sparkling eyes said she knew Lindsey's heartbeat had just sped up, knew and rejoiced in her love for Adam.

"Okay, ladies, I'm ready for you now," the photographer called.

Amid much bustling, grousing, laughing and shifting, he positioned Grandma Edna in the mauve wing chair; Lindsey on one arm; Judith standing at the opposite arm, her body angled toward the camera; and Megan on the floor, her hand resting on Grandma Edna's knee.

"Beautiful!" Mr. Thompson said, backing up and moving around to peer into the camera's viewfinder. "Perfect! You're going to treasure this one for years."

Lindsey knew he was right. But the image she would treasure most had already been captured earlier: the sight of four generations of women primping in front of a mirror.

"Okay, on the count of three, say cheeseburger."

Lindsey's genuine smile grew progressively stiffer through a series of different camera settings, film speed and light changes. At last he pronounced them finished.

"About damn time," Grandma Edna grumbled. "All those cheeseburgers made me hungry. Think we've got time to grab a Kid's Meal?"

Judith looked at her watch. "Oh, good heavens! Mama, we need to get downstairs and take our seats! Megan, you're supposed to be standing next to Reverend Wheeless in *five minutes!* Lindsey, get your bouquet!"

"Mother, relax. Take a deep breath—that's it. Everything is perfect, thanks to your advice and help."

"Oh, that makes me so happy, baby."

Lindsey lifted a glorious cluster of magnolia blossoms, baby's breath and peach roses from a florist's box. "Hey, now, don't ruin your makeup. Go on, I'm right behind you."

She followed the procession of females out into the hallway. Thirty feet ahead, the grand staircase loomed.

Her instant panic attack put her mother's to shame.

"Don't faint on us now, girl," Grandma Edna said, laying a gnarled hand on Lindsey's shoulder. "Got your somethin' old?"

Nodding, Lindsey fingered the antique cameo pendant nestled at the point of her sweetheart neckline.

"Somethin' new?"

She touched one of the pearl-and-diamond earrings Adam had given her last night at the rehearsal dinner, along with an eloquent toast to his bride.

"Hey, now, don't ruin *your* makeup, either. A man doesn't want to see his bride cry on her way to get hitched."

With a valiant effort Lindsey forestalled a disaster.

"Good girl. Got somethin' borrowed? Oh, yeah, Judy's dress. How 'bout somethin' blue?"

Lindsey patted her thigh and winked. "Garter belt."

"Ha! That'll make the lucky dog sit up and beg. Now you come down those stairs with your head held high and a smile on your face, hear?"

"Yes, ma'am." Lindsey leaned down and pressed her cheek to the soft papery one. "I love you," she whispered, and heard the same whispered back.

Suddenly there was no time left except for a quick hug from her mother and daughter before they all hustled toward the set of back stairs. At the doorway Megan turned with an impish grin.

"Break a leg, Mom," she called, and ducked out of sight.

"Funny," Lindsey mumbled, heading on trembling legs for the grand staircase. A swell of organ music announced the arrival of the immediate family. Her cue would come any minute.

Four steps out of sight she stopped, her hand over the heart that hammered in anticipation. She closed her eyes.

Thank you, God, for the blessings I am about to receive.

The music came to a halt. The tension of three hundred people holding their breaths and lifting their gazes stretched all the way up to tighten Lindsey's chest. Then the majestic opening chords of "The Wedding March" trumpeted the announcement: Here comes the bride!

It was time.

Lindsey moved to the top of the red-carpeted stairs and heard a collective gasp, but she saw only one uplifted face. Bronzed and sinfully handsome. His eyes burning possessively, full of obvious pride in his future wife. She snapped her groom's picture with her internal camera to store for the remainder of her life.

Then she smiled, because to do less would dishonor the moment, and he smiled back, making the moment perfect.

Head held high, she took that first step down on the strength of his love. Then another. And another. She might actually do this without disgracing herself. But if she tripped...well, she wouldn't worry.

After all, Adam was there to catch her.

Dear Reader,

When faced with the happy task of developing a romance also featuring a mother/daughter relationship, I struggled with nailing down the main characters. The hero was easy: a virile, successful surgeon who forgoes choosing a trophy wife in favor of true love. What's not to like? Ah, but the heroine was another story. The problem was, which of her stories should I choose?

Should I focus on a new mother's love for her infant? Nah, that was the honeymoon stage. How about those preteen years, when a daughter still believes her mother knows something about anything? Gee, where was the challenge in that? Okay, then, what about a mother and her (shudder) teenage daughter? Plenty of challenge there. But maybe a little too much angst?

Well, heavens. Mothers had mothers, too—*and* grandmothers. Increased life expectancies and the relationship between children and aging parents is a hot topic to baby boomers. What to do, what to do?

In the true Jan Freed fashion of making things more complicated than they need to be, I wrote a multigenerational story. And I'm so glad I did. The fact is, relationships constantly evolve, and each stage of a mother's and daughter's life offers an opportunity to deepen their complex bond. I hope after reading about Megan, Lindsey, Judith and Edna, you'll be reminded to nurture and treasure your own bonds.

Life is short. Tell your mothers and daughters how much they mean to you.

Warmly,

Jan Freed

P.S. I love hearing from readers. You can write me at:
P.O. Box 5009-572, Sugar Land, Texas 77487

MOTHER KNOWS BEST

Janice Kay Johnson

CHAPTER ONE

WASHTEL'S POTLUCK picnic was in full jovial swing by the time Rosalind arrived. Long tables covered in white paper had been set up in the middle of the mown grass between the playground and the covered barbecue area. Already laden with food, the tables were vanishing beneath Crock-Pots bubbling with Boston beans and plates of fruit and bowls of chips as each arriving employee brought another contribution. To one side, a clown performed for a cluster of mesmerized children. Laughter drifted from huddles of adults. In the roofed area, white-aproned men Rosalind knew from work flipped hamburgers over coals.

Poised to set her own casserole dish on the table, Rosalind stared aghast at another offering already temptingly displayed. "Oh, no! I never thought to ask Mom what she was bringing."

A casual friend of Rosalind's from work, Joan Dermott, took Rosalind's addition to the potluck meal from her nerveless hands. "Don't worry.

Your mother's chicken Divan is the greatest. You know it's always devoured. I'll bet yours is as good.''

No less disturbed, Rosalind watched the older woman plop her casserole right next to its mate.

"I use her recipe." She was absurdly ashamed to admit it. "Mine's identical."

"Well, then, it *is* as good," Joan said comfortingly. "Come on. Let's grab paper plates and start a line before the food gets cold."

Rosalind let herself be dragged away, knowing she was disturbed out of reason by a silly coincidence. So what if two chicken Divans sat side by side? There were probably four potato salads on that table. Ten fruit salads. Five or six crocks of baked beans.

But each would have its own flavor, a small voice in her head pointed out. Each would be individual. Subtly distinct. Hers wasn't. Her dish was her mother's. Hers was a clone.

She slapped potato salad on her paper plate. "For Pete's sake!" Rosalind muttered to herself. "You're making a trans-Atlantic phone call out of…of one word whispered into a tin can!"

"Did you say something?" Pete DeVries, a service rep, asked from beside her. She hadn't even noticed he was behind her in line. The unseasonably warm May sunshine had beads of sweat popping out on the dome of his balding head. The day had turned out perfect for the company picnic, being held early this year because someone had forgotten to reserve the park in July, the traditional month.

"Just talking to myself." Rosalind forced a smile. "This all looks wonderful, doesn't it?"

If he answered, she didn't hear. She'd reached the two wretched casseroles. Her mother's was on this side of the table, hers butting it so that the line snaking up the other side could dish up helpings more easily. A voice boomed, "Well, if this isn't Marge's chicken! Darned good stuff. Try it. Here." A man she knew only by sight spooned some of *her* casserole onto a woman's plate.

"It smells delicious," his companion agreed, moving on.

"Oh, Margaret brought her chicken Divan!" cried a female voice.

Rosalind gritted her teeth and took a second helping of baked beans. The texture and even the color of each dish was subtly different. She wanted to sample both.

She and Joan had no sooner settled at one end of a picnic table on the small bluff above Perry Creek when her mother sat across from her, dainty helpings of half-a-dozen separate dishes

distributed over her plate, none touching. Rosalind's looked much the same. She glanced with
distaste at Joan's overflowing plate, where wa-
termelon and strawberries oozed into potato
salad, and baked beans buried beef stroganoff.
Her mother had taught her daughters to be fas-
tidious.

And to be copycats?

Don't be silly, she scolded herself. Smiling,
she said, "Hi, Mom. How are the great kitchen
plans going?"

She was glad her mother had finally decided
to do something for herself. Mrs. Kirk had spent
too many years working hard just to raise her two
girls and pay for their college educations. She
only wished her mother had indulged in her real
dream, a trip to somewhere exotic. It was true,
though, that the 1920s-era bungalow hadn't been
updated beyond a coat of paint in Rosalind's lifetime. The kitchen was way overdue for some
work.

Joan chimed in with questions about Margaret
Kirk's plans, and they chatted about cabinet features and tiles and garbage compactors as they
ate.

"I can hardly wait for the built-in micro-
wave—" Mom interrupted herself midsentence.
"Did you make the second chicken Divan?" she

asked, lifting elegant brows. At Rosalind's nod, Mrs. Kirk smiled. "I thought so. I knew Penny was bringing that nice Mexican rice dish."

Also Mom's recipe. Rosalind had made it herself just last week. It ought to be no surprise that Rosalind's sister, who also worked for WashTel, would have used a familiar recipe.

"Well, we'll get plenty of compliments on the chicken," Mom said with a pleased nod. "Like mother, like daughter."

Rosalind's answering smile felt as genuine as the effusive friendliness of a telemarketer. She wasn't like her mother! Penny was, but not her. She was the creative one, the rebel, the dreamer. Everybody had always commented, smiled indulgently. Why, she didn't even *look* like her mother and sister, both petite slender blondes. Her own dark hair and five-foot-seven height had come from her father, according to Mom.

But the coincidence of that damned casserole niggled at her for the rest of the day. She left the picnic early, not quite in the mood for the gossip and games, or for the beer that began to appear from coolers. Nothing on television appealed to her, either, and her mind kept wandering from the book she finally chose.

Why did that darned casserole bother her so much?

Because her thirtieth birthday loomed, she finally decided. Lately she'd been going through a process of self-examination, which was perfectly normal. The trouble was, she couldn't help realizing that she was nowhere near where she'd intended to be in life by this milestone. Not that she was worried, exactly; it wasn't as if thirty was middle-aged. She had plenty of time.

Nonetheless, she continued to brood as she went through her bedtime routine. She put an exact half inch of toothpaste on her brush, then began on her upper right molars, keeping an automatic eye on the clock. Thirty seconds, and she switched to her lower right molars.

It wasn't as if being like her mother was so terrible, she thought. If only Penny hadn't already fallen in line so docilely. For Pete's sake, she'd even let Mom pick out her husband! Being like Mom might not be so bad, but Rosalind refused to be just like her sister.

Thirty seconds more, and she switched to the upper left side of her mouth. She brushed faster, remembering the scene at dinner one night when Mom had said, "Penny, honey, have you met John McKenzie? He's in sales. I hear he's at loose ends right now, and I feel sure you two would be perfect together. He has a wonderful smile, and he's bright and ambitious. Do you know someone who'd introduce you?''

Penny had nodded meekly. A week later, she and John had been dating. Six months later, pledging their troth at the altar.

Rosalind had tried. ''Are you sure you love him?'' she'd asked privately. ''You aren't marrying him just because *Mom* thinks he's perfect?''

Penny had laughed the notion off.

But Rosalind still had her suspicions.

She frowned at herself in the mirror, then glanced at the clock. Oh, no! She was brushing her front teeth, with absolutely no idea whether she'd done a thorough job on the rest of her mouth. She always watched the clock! Thirty seconds on each section, Mom had taught them.

Her hand stilled. At twenty-nine years nine months old, she felt guilty because she hadn't brushed her teeth exactly to her mother's specifications?

It was only habit, she tried telling herself. But she couldn't help looking past herself in the mirror and noticing the towels, perfectly spaced on the rack and folded in thirds. Just like Mom's.

Her linen closet was also organized like her mother's. Her reluctant mental tour of the apartment moved on to the kitchen. The cupboard contents there could be interchangeable with her mother's, too, down to the packets of soup and sauce mixes, alphabetized in their own little white wire box.

Rosalind stared at herself in the mirror, appalled. But it wasn't so bad to be organized, was it?

Maybe not, but that didn't explain why, eight years after graduating from college, she still worked at the telephone company in the job her mother had gotten for her. Why she'd never followed her dreams.

She rinsed out her toothbrush. Her mother had even helped her choose her living-room couch!

Oh, God, she thought. *I'm not a rebel. If I was ever creative, I'm not anymore. I'm a clone! I've turned into my mother, next generation.*

If she didn't make some changes—now—next thing she knew she'd be turning forty, married to some man her mother had approved, worrying about the mortgage on the house Mom thought was a great buy, teaching her own children that security and practicality were more important than dreams.

But they weren't, and the time had come for her to prove it.

WITH DEEP SATISFACTION Rosalind looked around the empty interior of the building. Open beams gave it character, in her opinion, and she loved the loft that ran the full depth of the narrow storefront. It had just room for floor-to-ceiling bookcases along the wall, and waist-high ones along the railing. She'd put mysteries and science-fiction up there; dedicated readers wouldn't mind the stairs.

She made one final turn, imagining the bay window filled with a magical display, a cosy children's space in back, case after case of books, comfy chairs, posters, music, customers eager to dip into her wares...

Okay, the rent was higher than she'd budgeted for, but the location was perfect, sandwiched (to use a pun) between a bakery/deli and an art gallery. Two antique stores occupied other spaces on this block, and slanted slots along the street offered plenty of parking.

She had done her research—too thoroughly. While in college, Rosalind had worked in a bookstore, determined to learn the business. For the past six years, she'd subscribed to *Publishers Weekly,* the trade journal of publishing and bookselling, poring over articles about clever marketing, great window displays, card and magazine sidelines. She'd repeatedly investigated costs, rents, overhead. Every time she had concluded that a bookstore could be a paying proposition here in Perry Creek. Every time she'd chickened out before she took any real step toward a future her mother had dismissed as "risky," the one time Rosalind had tentatively voiced her dream. But now...

"I'll take it," she decided.

The real-estate agent smiled. "You won't be sorry. Let's go back to the office and get started on the paperwork. As I mentioned, the lease is for a minimum of one year, and first and last month's rent is required. The owner must approve any radical remodeling, but I don't think anything you have in mind will be a problem."

She tuned him out, terror mixing with her elation. This was a huge step—no, not a step, a gamble. A leap from an airplane with a parachute packed by an amateur. Her mother would be horrified when Rosalind told her what she'd done.

But, oh, what fun she was going to have! And she hadn't really, really had fun in a long time.

Her life would change, Rosalind thought dizzily. She'd make new friends: writers, intellectuals, artists. She could throw away her wardrobe of suits and prim dresses. Perhaps a caftan in peacock blue and imperial purple would help create the right ambiance. Or she could wear jeans and Mexican embroidered cotton shirts. Sip espresso and listen to a poet reading from his work, then ring up purchases as dozens of fans lined up to buy his latest book.

The changes would spill over to her apartment. Pale cool colors reflected her mother's personality, not her own. She'd go for...oh, primary colors, or grand dark ones taken from a Turkish rug. She'd slip over to the art galleries and antique stores on her lunch break, pick up little bits of this and that, which together would reflect *her*.

Somehow she'd come to be back at the real-estate office. Still in a pleasant fog, she signed the lease and a truly enormous check, which was just the beginning. There was so much to do—publishers and book distributors to contact, accounts to establish, a contractor to be hired, a CPA to set up the books...

Oh, it would be worth every penny and every backbreaking minute of work! Even having to tell her mother that she'd quit her job and was committing her savings and her future to such a risky venture was a small price to pay for finally beginning a real adventure.

Since she thought it *was* worth losing her money and possibly alienating her mother, she must be doing the right thing. Goodbye, Rosalind-the-clone, she rejoiced. Hello, Rosalind-the-rebel.

CHAPTER TWO

"I DREAD HAVING my kitchen torn apart." Rosalind's mother shuddered, then took a delicate bite of her pasta salad. "But I tell myself it'll be worth some inconvenience to have cupboards with real storage and to get rid of that Formica countertop." She nodded toward the swinging door that led to the kitchen.

She and Rosalind often met for lunch on Saturday or Sunday; this week Mrs. Kirk had suggested they eat at her house. She continued, "You don't think I'm being extravagant to redo the kitchen, do you?"

"Don't be silly, Mom. You should have done it years ago." Rosalind smiled despite the lump in her stomach. She'd told herself their weekly luncheon was the perfect time to tell Mom her plans. So why hadn't the right moment to drop her bombshell come? And she'd thought it would be easier, here in the familiar comfort of her mother's house. Home.

Coward, she accused herself.

"You know perfectly well I couldn't afford to remodel the kitchen years ago." Her mother's grimace emphasized a few lines on a face that was still charming despite her fifty-four years. As attractive as Margaret Kirk was, Rosalind had always wondered why she'd never remarried. Mom sipped her coffee. "Probably I can't afford it now, either, but with both you girls through college and safely launched on careers, I thought, well, now or never! So I'm interviewing contractors this week." She waved her fork. "Oh, I must show you the tiles I'm considering. Don't let me forget. They're in the kitchen."

"I'd love to see them." Rosalind bit her lip. "Mom, speaking of careers, I have news, too."

"Really?" Her mother nibbled on another bite while raising her carefully plucked brows in inquiry.

A deep breath failed to fill Rosalind with courage. No way of easing into the unpalatable truth came to her, either. *Just do it,* she told herself.

"I've quit my job. I'm going to open a bookstore here in town."

"You've *what?*" Mrs. Kirk's fork clattered to the floor. Neither she nor Rosalind bent to pick it up.

"I've quit my job," Rosalind repeated. "I've

rented a building on First and I'm opening a bookstore.''

"But…'' Her mother's mouth opened and closed. Her throat worked as she dealt with the unimaginable. "But you have such a good job!''

"Mom, I'm an administrative assistant. A glorified secretary. I don't like my job! It's not what I ever wanted to do. It was supposed to be temporary.'' She groped for a way to make her mother understand. "I'm almost thirty. It won't *be* temporary if I don't make a change soon. Running a bookstore has always been my dream.''

Her mother's expression was frozen between shock and horror. "But you'll strip your savings. And you know how hopeless starting a small business is!''

"Not hopeless. Some make it.'' Rosalind leaned forward, half pleading—although why, she didn't know. An act of rebellion wouldn't count if the person you were rebelling against cheered you on. Except, of course, that she wasn't rebelling, she reminded herself hastily; she was taking control of her life. She said persuasively, "Perry Creek is perfect, Mom! The antique stores and art galleries are thriving, and you know how crowded all those little lunch spots for tourists are every day. It used to be just summer, but with the ski area, now people are stopping in

Perry Creek even in the winter. If an art gallery can make it, a bookstore can. I really believe that.''

Mom, of course, pointed out the pitfalls. A chain bookstore might open nearby; if snow didn't fall this winter, no skiers would pass through Perry Creek; if Rosalind didn't correctly guess what people wanted to read, they probably wouldn't darken her door a second time.

She responded to each objection, but her mother's disapproval didn't waver.

''All right,'' Mrs. Kirk said at last. ''You're going to try to start a small business. Fine. But wouldn't it make sense to keep working while you get it on its feet? You won't be able to open for months...''

''I'm shooting for August first.'' Rosalind held up her hand. ''I know that's quick, but I want to get some of the summer trade. I've already contacted distributors and publishers and set up accounts. I don't have *time* to keep working.''

Hurt in her eyes, Mrs. Kirk said, ''What I don't understand is why you didn't discuss this with me before you made irreparable decisions.''

''So you could have talked me out of it?'' Rosalind smiled tentatively. ''Come on, Mom. I may be crazy, but I'm not stupid.''

Her mother did *not* return her smile. ''Honey,

I understand that you're feeling as if something is missing from your life. It probably doesn't help to see Penny so happy with John and so enjoying motherhood. But...well, your turn will come." A hint of tartness crept into her tone. "Although it might come sooner if you'd date more often. There *are* nice men around. You're just not looking."

She should have been insulted that her mother assumed her venture was a substitute for a man. Yes, she *had* wondered lately, just a little wistfully, whether she would ever meet the man of her dreams. But career and marriage were two different things. Besides, she'd concluded that she *wasn't* going to meet her knight in shining armor at WashTel. Perhaps he'd be a poet. He would write odes to her. "Mom..."

"This...this scheme of yours is such a gamble! You'll lose everything if you fail! If you meet a wonderful man, you won't be able to start a family right away, unless you plan to go back to work six weeks after you have the baby. And even then half your salary would go to pay child care. And you have enough now for a nice down payment on a house, don't you? Do you have any idea what I would have given to have any real savings when your father died? Please, please, don't throw every bit of security away."

Rosalind gave up. Quietly she said, "I already have, Mom. A week from Friday will be my last day at WashTel. I'm sorry if that disappoints you."

Her mother bristled. "*I'm* not the point. You are. Your future is."

"Yes. And this is my choice for it." Rosalind pushed away her plate, her appetite gone. She had an odd sense of displacement; this was her home, she'd grown up here, but suddenly she was a stranger in the dining room where she'd set the table a thousand times, cleared the dirty dishes, fought with her sister, learned good manners and made pretend trains with the maple chairs inherited from her grandparents. Defying her mother had turned out to be more costly than she'd imagined. Would their relationship ever be as close again?

She stayed to help clean up and look over the tiles her mother was considering, but their conversation was stilted. A barrier—Rosalind's foolishness—had risen between them.

But her pride was intact, and she refused to beg for a blessing her mother wouldn't give. She eventually said a stiff goodbye and strolled out to her car as if nothing was wrong. In case her mother was watching, she started it up immediately and drove away. She went three blocks before she pulled over to the curb, set the emergency brake and began to cry.

PENNY STOPPED by Rosalind's desk the next morning at work to repeat all Mom's arguments and add a few new ones. "You know, Mom's terribly upset," she said as the clincher.

Rosalind was presumably supposed to apologize, tell her boss that she'd made a mistake and wanted to stay on after all, and cancel her lease. She said only, inadequately, "I'm sorry. I can't make every decision in my life based on whether Mom would approve." *Unlike you,* she had the tact not to add.

Penny swept off in a huff, anyway.

Mom called the next evening. As though having conversation with a stranger at a cocktail party, Mrs. Kirk asked with polite interest about Rosalind's plans and progress. Rosalind answered just as courteously. Then they talked about the antics of Penny's three-year-old. Mrs. Kirk's voice warmed immediately. Rosalind hung up feeling scared and alone. She wasn't going to be able to count on any help from her family.

Her certainty and her loneliness stayed with her over the next couple days. Neither her mother nor sister called; she saw neither woman during breaks at work. She was forced to realize how much her family meant to her. She had friends, naturally, but Mom and Penny were her closest ones. She knew they wouldn't cut her off, but...well, maybe they'd stayed close because their goals and lives were so similar. Maybe now that hers had changed, she had nothing in common with them. With difficulty she summoned up an image of those new friends she'd be making: the poets and writers, the artists, the gallery owners. They'd sip wine and espresso and listen to harp music—which she hated, but never mind—and talk about insights and the human condition, instead of the latest gossip whispered at WashTel. She would be just fine, Rosalind told herself firmly. The mold she'd been scrunching herself into didn't fit; of course there were aches and pains now that she was stretching. But they would go away.

Still, the sound of her mother's voice on the phone Thursday evening brought a rush of complicated feelings to knot in Rosalind's chest.

"Are you free for dinner tomorrow night?" Mrs. Kirk asked. "The contractor I've hired will be stopping by at five-thirty, and I thought you might like to meet him. Unless you've already hired someone to do the inside of your store?"

"No, I've interviewed a couple, but either they

wanted too much money, or...oh, I don't know, I just wasn't impressed.'' She was interested despite herself. If she let her mother pick a contractor, was that a step backward? On the other hand, wasn't it perverse to refuse to talk to the man just because her mother suggested it?

"I have a proposition for you, as well, dear." Mrs. Kirk's tone was warm, caring, concerned. Everything it hadn't been during their last couple of conversations. "I've been worrying about your finances, of course, and an idea came to me. Why don't you let your apartment go and move home for a while? Until the store is on its feet." Only the tiniest pause suggested what she was undoubtedly thinking: *if it ever gets on its feet.* "Even if you help with expenses, you could save a great deal of money."

Move home? Rosalind's first reaction was horror. She was starting a new life, striking out on her own, and her mother wanted her to move back into her old bedroom? She pictured it, the white lacy curtains and bedskirt of her childhood mixing awkwardly with the posters of rock stars and the half-burned candles of her teenage years. Rosalind shuddered.

"You can't possibly want me," she said weakly. "Aren't you enjoying your independence?"

"Nonsense," her mother returned, brisk as always. "Obviously you treasure yours, but it needn't be for long if the store takes off right away. And if not..." She didn't need to finish the sentence.

Rosalind reluctantly thought about the checks she'd been writing lately, about how everything seemed to be costing more than she'd anticipated, how she'd miss the sick leave and vacation and health insurance that had been free from WashTel. If she could save the $700 a month rent, plus the cost of utilities...

"I...well, I'll think about it," she conceded. "And dinner sounds lovely, thanks."

"Oh, good. I'm sure you'll be as impressed with Craig Morrow as I am." Mom's tone held something indefinably disturbing. Satisfaction, out of proportion to Rosalind's simple agreement to come over to dinner?

Rosalind hung up feeling bothered, but she succeeded in dismissing her uneasiness. She didn't *have* to hire the man. She wouldn't let her mother railroad her. How awful to be suspicious of her own mother, for Pete's sake! Why not just accept that she was being helpful, now that she'd gotten over the shock of Rosalind's decision?

And Mom was shrewd and practical. If she'd chosen this contractor for her kitchen, he was

probably the very best. *So have an open mind,*
Rosalind scolded herself. After all, he might be
perfect for her, as well. Even if her mother *had*
chosen him.

CHAPTER THREE

ROSALIND HEARD VOICES the moment she let herself in the front door of her childhood home. First her mother's, then a slow deep response that bespoke patience and confidence and competence. Reassured, Rosalind let an image form in her mind. He'd be an older man with worlds of experience, not only in building and remodeling, but also in dealing with the vagaries of the people who hired him. He'd know how to keep the work on schedule without irritating everybody. He'd *listen* when Rosalind explained what she wanted, unlike the one contractor who had smirked and told her why, if she had any sense, she'd want something different.

"Hi, Mom!" she called.

"Oh, hello, dear, we're out here," her mother returned gaily. "I'm so glad you're early."

Rosalind sailed into the kitchen, expectations firmly in place, a smile on her lips.

Mrs. Kirk stepped aside; for an instant Rosalind saw only the broad chambray-clad back and dark—not gray—head of the man who stood contemplating the dining alcove. At the sound of her footstep, he turned, in slow motion it seemed, giving her expectations plenty of time to crash and shatter on the worn linoleum.

He was most certainly *not* older. The broad back matched wide shoulders, muscled forearms below rolled-up shirtsleeves, a strong tanned neck above an unbuttoned collar. That chambray shirt was tucked into worn blue jeans pale with plaster dust. His hips were lean, his legs long.

Reluctantly she looked up to his face, a narrow intelligent face, the mouth clever and sexy, the eyes brown beneath dark brows that drew together during her long stunned scrutiny.

Oh, dear. He was gorgeous. Thirty-five, if that. *Not* seasoned by decades of experience. Not fatherly. Not at all comfortable.

What was her mother thinking of?

"I...hello," Rosalind said inadequately.

He nodded, unsmiling.

"Rosalind, dear, this is Craig Morrow. Craig, my youngest daughter, whom I've been telling you about."

"Pleased to meet you." He sounded not sure he meant it, but his voice was still slow, deep, patient. It wasn't, after all, *his* fault that he looked like Mr. July from a calendar of hunks in hard hats.

"Did I mention that Rosalind is starting a construction project of her own?" Margaret Kirk asked as if blithely unaware of the undercurrents.

"Yes. You did."

Which, Rosalind thought ruefully, Mom knew perfectly well.

"Is residential remodeling your specialty?" Rosalind asked.

His thoughtful gaze never left her. "No. My last job was the addition to the veterinary clinic. You name it, I do it."

"Are you a reader?" she asked on impulse.

Annoyance narrowed his eyes for a heartbeat. "I've been known to open a book."

Rosalind was embarrassed to realize that he'd assumed she was patronizing him. She hadn't intended to; just because he wasn't pale and intellectual-looking, because his hair was too short for a dark lock to fall romantically over his brow, didn't mean *War and Peace* wasn't his favorite novel. But how could she apologize or tell him she hadn't meant what he thought she meant without saying something that would probably offend him even more?

Mom rescued her by bustling forward. "Craig, can I talk you into staying for dinner? Rosalind and I are going to be informal tonight, just spaghetti and French bread and a salad, and we'd love to have you stay. I still have some questions."

Again his dark eyes narrowed for an instant, but not with irritation this time. Rosalind wasn't quite sure what he was thinking.

"Sounds good," he said easily. "I'm pretty grungy, though."

"Oh, heavens!" Mom waved an airy hand. "We'll just eat out here. Anyway, the whole house will be coated with plaster dust soon enough."

"I'll seal the doors with plastic..." he began.

"Which only slows it down, from what friends tell me." Mom chuckled. "I don't mind a bit. This will be so exciting."

She continued to chatter as she and Rosalind carried food to the table. He stood to one side looking awkward, answering questions in monosyllables. Not much of a talker, Rosalind diagnosed, but he did seem to listen. Each time Mom thought of a new problem, Craig Morrow mulled it over for a minute, then came up with a practical simple solution. Despite her initial wariness, Rosalind was impressed.

He didn't do much talking over dinner, either. She told him all about her plans for the bookstore. His few questions elicited all kinds of personal information from her, too; by the time the last salad green and slice of French bread were gone, Rosalind was somewhat shocked to realize she'd told this complete stranger how old she was, her major in college and what teacher she'd had for world history in twelfth grade.

He'd had Mrs. Jacobsen, too. "She's retired now, you know. Husband died last year. She hired me to turn the basement of her house into an apartment to sublet."

"You grew up here?" Rosalind asked in astonishment. "I don't remember you." She knew everyone. And he wasn't the kind of man you forgot, even if he had been sixteen the last time you saw him.

He'd been four years ahead of her, they determined, so they hadn't been in high school at the same time. Then she went off to college, and he went to work for the contractor who'd hired him summers.

Over blackberry cobbler, Rosalind asked if he'd be interested in giving a bid on her bookstore renovation.

A quirk of his mouth indented a groove in one lean cheek. "Sounds good. Your mom's is the only major job on my plate right now."

"And *I* can certainly be flexible," Mom contributed, smiling benevolently from her daughter to her newly hired contractor. "For Rosalind's sake."

They made an appointment for the next afternoon at five o'clock. Rosalind would have to go straight there in her prim work clothes, but it didn't matter what she looked like, did it?

Mrs. Kirk didn't say a word about him after he left, which surprised Rosalind a little. Probably she figured she'd done her bit. Either Craig Morrow's bid would be too high or it would not. No matter how she praised him, if Rosalind couldn't afford him, she wouldn't hire him. No matter how perfect he might be in other respects.

Ms. Rosalind Kirk was late, but Craig was a patient man. He didn't mind waiting for her, either today or in the future. He'd lied to her; he had more jobs right now than he knew what to do with, but this was one he wanted even if he lost money on it.

At the first sight of her he'd had a clutch of...well, hell, physical desire, sure—it was sharpening his anticipation now—but he'd felt more. He'd have sworn there for a second that he smelled cinnamon rolls baking, but then when she came closer it was more like a bouquet of the violets his mother used to grow.

Smelling things... He had to shake his head over that. All he knew was, she made him want something. Her. Only not in a way he'd wanted a woman in his life before. Across the breakfast table from him, carrying his baby... Okay, it was dumb; he didn't know her. Fortunately she'd handed him a way to fix that on a plate.

Now he surveyed the storefront she'd rented and nodded with approval. Even at five-ten, the street bustled. The wooden sidewalk echoed hollowly as browsers passed.

The bay windows were good. He'd be willing to bet she, not the landlord, was responsible for the sparkling clean glass. That was the kind of thing an eager new tenant did. He pictured her kneeling inside, washing each small pane and dreaming.

Craig turned when he heard a car pull into the slot right behind him. Cheeks flushed, dark hair slipping out of a topknot, Rosalind hopped out, slammed the car door and hurried toward him, righting herself when she tripped over the step up to the sidewalk.

"I'm sorry," she said breathlessly. "I'm late. I hope you haven't been here forever."

"Ten minutes. I've been looking the place over."

"What do you think?" She waited, eyes wide and hopeful.

He gave a firm nod. "Good location. Nice building, neighbors are suitable. You even have parking. Couldn't ask for more."

Her breath escaped in a rush and she glowed. Damn, she was pretty! Just like he remembered. He even caught a whiff of something irresistible. Sugar cookies, fresh from the oven.

Her words tumbled over each other. "That's what I thought. I love the front windows! And there's lots of storage space in back, and the balcony is wonderful, and... Oh." She collected herself. "I'm babbling. It's just that I'm so excited. Here, let's go in."

He stood back while she unlocked the front door, painted brown.

"Isn't this an awful color?" She didn't wait for an answer. "I've already picked out the loveliest rich green for the door and trim."

Leaving her by the front windows, Craig prowled through the empty interior, noting the condition of the drywall, the balcony supports, taking measurements. At last he returned to her side. "Okay, tell me what you have in mind."

She talked and he listened, nodding occasionally, happy to have an excuse to linger over every feature on her round gentle face. He was careful,

though, to pay attention to what she said; he
knew without being told how serious she was
about her new business.

"You've priced ready-made shelving?" he
asked.

She wrinkled her nose. "It costs the world.
Unless I went with metal. Or I could go really
rustic, but I don't like that. I want the place to
seem...established. As though it's been here forever. You know what I mean? Books don't look
right otherwise."

In his mind's eye he saw a bookstore: this one.
Dark glossy wood, fine moldings, leather uphol-
stered club chairs, stacks and stacks of books.
"Yes," he agreed. "I know what you mean."

"Only...I don't know if I can afford what I
want," she said unhappily.

His big mouth just opened itself. "I've done
cabinetmaking. I'll see what I can come up with.
I can keep costs down." By swallowing the loss.

Yes, but he'd finally pinned down that elusive
scent. Vanilla. Did she bake frequently? Or did
women use vanilla-scented shampoo or perfume?
He saw her stroking lotion onto silken skin, her
small hand moving in leisurely circles, working
the cream in, and damn, he wanted it to be his
hand.

They talked more about her plans; he contributed a few ideas and was amply rewarded by her shining eyes and brilliant smile, by the increasingly trustful way she confided her dreams for the store.

"I can hardly believe it might all really happen," she said at last, looking around with a bemused expression. "I've planned for so long..."

He nodded. "I was pretty sure I could make it with my own contracting business a couple years before I worked up the guts to actually try."

She sighed. "I've been thinking about this ever since I got out of college! I suddenly realized I'd be retiring from WashTel before I knew it if I didn't do something."

"Could you have afforded it right out of college?"

"Well, no," she admitted.

"Then don't be so hard on yourself."

Her grateful smile made him want to kiss her. *Big mistake,* he told himself, pretending to study the small notebook where he'd written dimensions. *Don't rush her.*

"As far as this job goes, I'll have to work up a bid," he said. "Right now, I'm thinking in the neighborhood of..." He named a price that had to fall under the ones she'd already been given. No one in his right mind would do the work for so little.

He guessed he wasn't in his right mind.

"Really?" Rosalind's eyes widened. "If you can come close to that—" she drew a visible breath "—then you're hired."

Craig held out a hand; after the tiniest of hesitations, Rosalind laid hers in his. It felt as fragile as those dreams she'd confided. A surge of wanting and triumph shook him. He tightened his grip, fighting the temptation to draw her toward him.

Instead, he smiled, slow and sure. "We'll make it work," he promised.

CHAPTER FOUR

"OH, YOU DID HIRE HIM!" Mom crowed. "I'm so glad! I knew you'd agree he was perfect for you."

Perfect for *you?* Suspicion ran its nasty little fingers up Rosalind's spine. "Exactly what do you mean by 'for me'?" she asked carefully, tucking her feet under her on the couch in her living room. The couch Mom had adored, and Rosalind had been lukewarm about, but had bought, anyway. The couch that at the end of the month—only a week away—would have to go into storage, along with most of Rosalind's possessions.

"You have to admit he's a lovely man," Mom rattled on. "The nice part is, he obviously has brains, too. And so far, he's even punctual! Hardly anyone in construction is, you know."

Rosalind removed the telephone receiver from her ear and stared at it for a moment. Punctual? Her mother's voice, made tinny by distance, was still chattering.

Rosalind shook her head in disbelief, then put the phone back to her ear. "Punctual?" she echoed. "Of course, I'm glad he is, since I'm on such a tight schedule with the shop, but—"

"Believe me—" Mom sounded firm "—it's an important quality in a husband, too."

There it was, that word, resounding against Rosalind's eardrum as though the telephone wires quivered with the force of it.

Her teeth ground together. "You think I should *marry* the man?"

The tiniest hesitation suggested that Mom had read her tone correctly. "Now, honey," she coaxed, "you can't deny you were attracted."

Wrong. Rosalind could deny it—if she lied. That she could do without compunction. "I wasn't. He's not my type."

"Don't be silly," Mom said serenely. "Of course he is. You just don't realize it yet."

A film of red slid over Rosalind's vision. "Mom, butt out!" she snapped. "I wouldn't marry Craig Morrow if he was the last man on earth! I want a…a poet. An artist. Not some sweaty Neanderthal with calluses on his hands! Which shows how well you know me!"

"Or," her mother corrected gently, "how little you know yourself."

A strangled growl rose in Rosalind's throat. "I

cannot believe…! Oh, forget it!'' She slammed down the phone.

Oh, God, she thought in despair. How could she move home again? Especially now that she knew the truth: Mom was trying to set her up with Craig Morrow, who would presumably be lurking in Mom's kitchen day and night!

Rosalind groaned and buried her face in her hands. What an idiot she'd been! She'd hired the man herself! When he wasn't in Mom's kitchen, he'd be at Rosalind's refuge, the bookstore. She'd never escape him.

I don't have to move home, she thought wildly. But she'd already given her notice to the landlord. And refigured her budget, easily spending on paper the money that wouldn't have to go to rent.

No, all she could do was pray that Craig Morrow was oblivious to Mom's scheme. And not the tiniest bit interested in her, Rosalind. *He* would see that they had nothing in common, she thought, reassured. Her angry breathing slowed as reason came to her rescue. Craig Morrow wasn't a puppet, any more than she was.

Thanks to his indifference, Rosalind wouldn't have to do a thing except enjoy Mom's disappointment. And she *would* enjoy it.

CRAIG STOOD WATCHING while Rosalind studied his bid. He'd chosen to hand-deliver it, both so he could see her again and counter any problems—lower the final tally further if need be, anything to keep her from hiring a competitor.

He was already going in the toilet on this one, so he'd at least anticipated some enthusiasm on her part. What he got was wariness.

She eyed him over the edge of the paper. "This looks very good. Almost, ah, too good."

Oh, hell. He'd figured she'd accept the gift horse without peering at the teeth. He should have guessed she was the type to want to know why those teeth were too damn white and shiny.

"Well, I'll tell you," he said, thinking fast. "I'm offering to do this at cost, sort of a loss leader, because I'm hoping you'll recommend me to other business folks. I want to do less residential remodeling and more jobs like this. Perry Creek is changing. I figure this—" he nodded at the bare building around them "—is my open door to the boom."

She scrutinized his face, fixed in eager ingratiating lines, and bought it. Hook, line and sinker. "But I feel almost guilty..." she said hesitantly.

"I've got your mother's job to tide me over at the same time," he reminded her, careful not to mention the half-dozen other jobs he was juggling.

"Well...if you're sure?"

"Oh, yeah." His certainty hadn't wavered. Today he'd have sworn he smelled lilacs. He wanted to bury his face in her silky dark hair and find out if that was where the tantalizing scent came from. "I'm sure."

"Then—" she smiled "—when can you start?"

Triumph rose in him, hot and powerful. He was careful not to let it show.

They talked about priorities on the job for a few minutes; she wanted the stockroom in back and the front window done first; that way she could start ordering and could put a display in the window to awaken interest in the community.

"I'll have a party for the grand opening," she confided. "Wine and cheese and maybe a string quartet. You know. Something classy."

Something boring, in his opinion. Right up there with poetry readings. "I don't know if Perry Creek is a string-quartet kind of town," he said tactfully. "If you could get Bruce Springsteen or Vince Gill to do an acoustic set or...oh, heck, some big-name author. And have kegs of beer. Now that's Perry Creek-style."

"*I* give this town more credit than you do," Rosalind said loftily.

He had a feeling he'd blown it. Hell, maybe she was right; maybe Perry Creek did boast a few fans of tinkling cascades of musical notes that went on and on and on and never seemed to get anywhere.

Abandoning the potentially dangerous subject, he said, "Listen, I don't know about you, but I'm getting hungry. Like to try that new place, uh, what's it called? Gianni's?"

The narrow-eyed look she gave him was beyond wary. "You're asking me out to dinner?"

A little annoyed—what in hell was wrong with a man inviting a woman to dinner?—he said, "Yeah, that's how it sounded to me."

"As in a date?" Now she sounded outraged, her pansy-soft eyes glittering.

Wounded feelings grated in his throat. "Is there something wrong with that? You're pretty. I thought we'd talk, see if we like each other." *See how soon you'd marry me, have my babies.* "If you're not interested, that's okay." A flat-out lie. He sought for something truthful to add. "I didn't mean to offend you."

She blinked. "No! I mean, you didn't offend me."

Could have fooled him.

"I just was hoping…" Her cheeks flushed rosy pink. "That is, I'd rather keep it professional. Not muddy the waters. You know?"

Okay. He could work fast. Have this place ready to open in record time. "Afterward…?"

Not lilacs. Maybe those big white lilies that smelled so sweet at night, when you stepped out into the yard to hear the crickets chirp and see the stars overhead. They damn near glowed in the dark, as white and mystical as a full moon. Sweet like lilacs, but the one was in spring, the other the heat of summer, more sultry.

"I don't think so."

Her answer, flat and final, jarred him out of the images that had risen, as seductive as the scent of those lilies. Of *her* in the dark, arms raised above her head as she shimmied out of some floaty nightgown, showing him the slender body that glowed, too, her breasts as white but for the duskiness at the tips…

"Fine," he said, mad as hell. He could have sworn she felt some of the same chemistry he did. The way she quivered a little when he was real close. The way her eyes shied away sometimes, when his sparked with more intent than he'd meant to show. "We'll keep it professional."

"Fine," she said, just as shortly. "Here's a key. The sooner you can get started the better."

"I'll have a crew here tomorrow morning." The sunroom addition on the Fenway house could wait; or maybe he could subcontract out some work he'd intended to have his own crew do. The drywall needed taping on the Toth job; he'd call Bill's Drywall and see if they could pick it up.

He was a goddamned idiot, Craig thought, risking his professional reputation for a woman who just wasn't interested. Or was lying because she didn't want to be. He wasn't sure which.

But he was a stubborn man. She didn't realize how well they'd have to get to know each other before this job was done. And he'd be sure to supervise work at her mother's house real closely, too, once Rosalind had moved back into the spare bedroom. He'd be everywhere she turned. Sooner or later she'd recognize his virtues.

He shoved down the fleeting depression that had him wondering whether she'd consider *any* of his qualities virtues. Her kind of man probably loved listening to string quartets and sipping wine.

No, he wouldn't face the possibility that he might not have a prayer with her.

MOVING DAY gave Rosalind a few pangs of...not regret, exactly. Panic? She wasn't burning her bridges, she kept reassuring herself. Her stuff would be in storage. If she got mad enough at Mom, she could move out again. If worse came to worst, she had friends who'd let her stay with them for a little while. Besides, this *was* just temporary. If she could really open by August first, the bookstore might make a profit right away. Why not, with a great location and the right planning?

Penny and her husband and several of Rosalind's friends helped carry her furniture and the boxes of pans and dishes and books and miscellany out to the truck she'd rented, then unload them all into the storage space. Penny and Mom stayed to help her give the apartment a last scrub, and then she followed Mom's car home.

She parked in the driveway, a sense of unreality sweeping over her. Carrying her suitcases up to her old bedroom made her feel ten years younger, as if she were home from college for the summer, not an adult taking temporary refuge. She put away her clothes in the closet and dresser, giving a practiced jerk to open the third drawer, which always stuck.

It was like being struck by déjà vu, she decided three days later, only the sensation wasn't momentary; she was trapped in it. She'd been transported back in time. She had automatically taken over the same chores she'd done before leaving home, stored her cosmetics on the same shelf in the bathroom medicine cabinet, settled in the same corner of the couch in the living room when she read or watched TV.

Thank God for the bookstore! Without the hope it gave her, she might have gone insane.

She might go insane, anyway, between her mother and Craig Morrow.

He had started work at her store the next day just as he'd promised. The back room was painted and shelves were going up before quitting time at five. He'd helped her try various layouts with lengths of string in place of shelving units, until they settled on final dimensions. And then he'd followed her home to check on the progress of the two men gutting her mother's kitchen. He hadn't done that quickly, with a brisk approving nod. Oh, no, he'd lingered, inspecting every detail, chatting with Mom.

Even when Rosalind had retreated to her room and curled up on the bed—she really had to get rid of those posters—or sat in the straight-backed chair in front of the student desk, where she felt as if she ought to be opening her geography textbook, she'd heard his voice, a low rumble rising up the stairwell. Even when it had quieted, she'd known to the moment when he'd left. She was spending so darn much time with the man, her senses were tuned to him in a way that infuriated her.

Okay, so he was sexy. So she looked, when he wouldn't notice. What woman wouldn't? But he *wasn't* her type, and she hated this constant awareness of his presence, this prickling up her spine when he approached, this glow she felt at his rare smiles, this eager waiting for his approving nod or opinion.

Maybe Mom was right about one thing. Maybe it had been too long since she'd gone on a date. She'd gotten discouraged these past few years. Her friends had set her up with single men. Either the friends weren't very picky, or else they didn't know Rosalind any better than her mother did. The mismatches were appalling.

Of course, she had also dated some men from work. She shuddered, remembering Sam Michaelson, the sales rep with the gleaming white teeth—surely capped—who was given to repeating his favorite stories about his favorite subject, himself. College-football triumphs figured largely in his monologues.

Still, she shouldn't have given up altogether. Other women met wonderful men and fell in love. One was out there for her, too. She must crave that…that romantic connection, the meshing of souls, the meshing of *bodies,* more than she'd realized. Otherwise she wouldn't be getting so hot and bothered about Craig Morrow, building contractor, now would she?

A date. That was the answer. She needed to spend time with some other men.

And she knew just where to start. The owner of the antique store two doors down had come by several times already, first to welcome her, then to check on the progress, he said. He'd suggested lunch one day when she'd been busy. She was pretty sure she could nudge him into offering dinner.

And she'd make darn sure he picked her up at her mother's house, preferably when Craig was there, *lingering.*

Now *that* would send a message, to her mother *and* him.

CHAPTER FIVE

CRAIG TILTED back his head and studied Margaret Kirk's kitchen ceiling, which one of his men had ripped out and was reframing. "Looking good," he finally conceded.

These old houses could be a bitch. On the one hand, they were solidly built, no question; on the other hand, time had caused settling and warping, and materials hadn't been standard to start with. Many hadn't been built by professionals. In one of his last jobs, the large front window had been two inches out of plumb.

Normally the ceiling wouldn't matter. But in the kitchen, the cupboards had to be built square and hung straight. The prep work was taking days.

Craig was feeling pretty good, though; so far, he'd juggled all the jobs successfully. Nothing was behind schedule, nobody was ticked off. And today he'd brought in the first bookcase for Rosalind's approval. He'd used alder, about the cheapest wood, but with precut moldings and a cherry stain had achieved a piece of furniture he thought looked damned good.

She'd thought so, too. She'd breathed a silent "Oh!" then chortled with pleasure. For one second he'd thought she was going to hug him. In the close quarters he could see the velvet texture of her skin and the fan of her lashes. "Oh," she'd said, aloud that time, "it's beautiful. Perfect. Do you mean that price? Can you really build enough bookcases fast enough for me to open the first week of August?"

Only if he lived, breathed and slept with sandpaper in one hand and a rag dipped in stain in the other.

"Sure," he'd said with a shrug. *Yeah, Superman*, he'd mocked himself. He felt like a kid performing gymnastics on the playground to impress the pretty girl in the ruffled pink dress.

The part he'd felt good about was that it had seemed to work.

Her smile and eyes had gone soft, sweet. "Oh, bless you." She'd made an abortive move toward him again, placing her hand on his upper arm.

God. That was all it had taken. Suddenly he hadn't been able to look at anything but her mouth, curved, lips parted. His body had tightened. His breathing had quickened. But he wasn't alone. He'd have put money on it. Some deep shift had occurred in her, too. Her lower lip had trembled, just a little. Her breasts had risen and fallen as though she'd shuddered for breath. Her eyes had darkened. He'd leaned toward her, intent clear, and she'd shivered but didn't move.

At which moment that sleazy jerk from the antique store had walked in.

Opportunity lost, but not for long. Hell, no. He felt it in his bones. She'd been yielding, softening. She'd *wanted* him to kiss her. A man couldn't make a mistake about that kind of thing. Whatever had been the sticking point early on, Rosalind had obviously changed her mind.

Tonight Margaret Kirk had asked him to stay for dinner. Maybe afterward Rosalind would go sit on the front porch swing with him. The night was fine, the roses in bloom. He saw it more clearly than the ceiling ready for new wallboard. Rocking gently, in tune with each other, his arm along the back of the swing. Night sounds, the fragrance of roses drifting faintly to them. Him turning to face Rosalind, her lashes shyly sweeping down to hide her eyes, but her chin tipping up. He'd bend down, their lips would touch—

"Oh, you're still here, Craig?" His reverie was not so rudely interrupted when Rosalind herself pushed aside the plastic sheet covering the kitchen door and looked inquiringly at him.

"Yeah. Your mom asked me to stay to dinner."

"Oh?" Her eyebrows rose. "How nice. It'll give you a good chance to talk about the changes Mom's considering."

You? Changes?

In the distance the doorbell rang. Rosalind turned her head, and for the first time he saw that she now wore a dress, a tiny black number that clung to rounded hips and breasts in a way that sent a surge of heat through him.

"Oh, that must be Jordan." She smiled vaguely, as though she were already putting him, Craig, out of her mind. "We're having dinner tonight. You know Jordan, don't you?"

Jordan? The sleazy antique dealer? She was having *dinner* with him?

This couldn't be happening.

He followed her, his good mood evaporated. Now he felt as baffled, as disbelieving, as betrayed as a dumb dog dumped by its beloved owner.

It wasn't happening, he tried telling himself. She wasn't dating the antique dealer. It was some kind of business discussion. A Rotary Club meeting. Something friendly, not romantic.

Then why was she wearing that short tight dress?

He was right behind her when she opened the front door.

"Jordan!" she cried in apparent pleasure. "Come on in. You know Craig Morrow, of course."

The two men nodded stiffly to each other. The antique dealer was handsome in a pretty-boy way, auburn hair curling at his nape, his pants too tight, the sleeves of his jacket self-consciously rolled up. His usual, too-ready smile was guileless, confiding. Craig had seen things for sale in the window of Jordan West's antique shop that he knew damn well were reproductions. With the country look big right now, "primitive" cupboards were all the rage. The ones West set out front on nice days sold only to be replaced by twins. Craig didn't like anyone who cheated customers. He couldn't believe Rosalind was taken in by this slimeball.

But she was giggling at some remark he'd made and gazing big-eyed at him as though he was some movie star come to sweep her off her feet. Craig could hardly contain his growl.

Then, "Mom!" she called, "I'm leaving. I'll see you when I see you."

What did *that* mean? Ten in the evening or three in the morning?

"I wish you'd told me..." Margaret Kirk

came down the staircase, lines between her pen-
ciled brows. She spotted West. "Oh. Why,
hello." She tried to sound cordial, Craig could
tell she did, but he was glad to note that she
didn't seem any more pleased about Rosalind's
date than he was.

Rosalind did introductions. The smarmy bastard gazed deeply into her mother's eyes and
smiled with practiced charm. Margaret was supposed to swoon. She didn't. Instead, her nostrils
flared as though she'd smelled something rotten.

"Good evening, Mr. West," she said coolly,
dismissively. "Rosalind, have a pleasant time."

Pleasant, hell. Craig hoped that within fifteen
minutes or so, she'd be bitterly sorry she'd gone.
After half an hour, maybe she'd call and ask to
be rescued.

She was gone, the sound of her laugh drifting
through the heavy closed door. Like the wisp of
a scent, he thought sourly.

He pulled himself together and turned to face
Rosalind's mother. Her gaze, bright and interested, was fixed on him, not on the door her
daughter had just closed. Craig was afraid his
disgruntlement must still show, but instead of
raising those aristocratic brows in surprise, Margaret Kirk smiled.

"I see you don't care for Mr. West."

Damn right he didn't. "No," he said simply. "I don't."

"I thought Rosalind had better sense than that."

He'd thought so, too.

"But I suppose it's my fault," her mother mused. "She always has been rather...well, rebellious."

Yeah, he could see that she might be. Which didn't explain what she was rebelling against.

"I suggested that she really shouldn't give up on men," Margaret explained, even though it was none of his business. "Of course, trust Rosalind to deliberately choose one I was certain not to like." She smiled. "I do think it's a good sign she was hanging on him like that. That kind of behavior isn't at all like her, you see. I'm sure she was trying to make a point. Although—" she tilted her head meaningfully at him "—possibly not for my benefit."

Craig stared at her. Was she suggesting...? Damn. Rosalind *had* thrown him an inordinate number of smiling glances. Testing his reaction, maybe? And she'd sure as hell made a point of tracking him down in the kitchen. To make sure he saw that she was going out with someone else?

He liked the idea that she was trying to make

him jealous. He just didn't see why she'd bother. He'd already told her he liked her, hadn't hc? All she'd had to do was tell him she'd changed her mind and would like to have dinner with him. How hard was that? Would he ever understand a woman's mind?

And come to think of it, why was Rosalind's mother looking like a purring Siamese cat sitting next to an empty fishbowl? Surely, even when their daughters were grown, mothers didn't like to see them date men as sleazy as Jordan West.

No, she hadn't liked that, Craig was forced to conclude. She'd looked perturbed as hell. It was *afterward,* when she'd seen his reaction, that her mood had lightened drastically.

"Well," Margaret said now, "I ordered from that nice Chinese place. I hope you like Chinese. It ought to be here any minute."

"We could have gone out—"

"Their food is excellent," she said briskly, "and this is so much cozier, don't you think? Besides, I had a few ideas I thought we could talk about."

Rosalind had said something about her mother wanting to make changes. Craig almost groaned. Why couldn't women just make up their minds? Why did they have to keep thinking, rearranging, fussing? But, hey. She was paying him.

Unlike her daughter, he thought sardonically. Heaven help his bottom line if Rosalind started changing her mind, too.

"Sure," he said with a shrug.

Excusing himself to wash his hands, he returned to his earlier train of thought. No, Margaret Kirk was not happy about Jordan West. What had pleased her was that he, Craig, didn't like Rosalind going out with West any more than she did. Which meant...

He frowned at himself in the mirror.

It meant that Margaret wanted him to like Rosalind. And Rosalind to like him. Good God, had she hired him because she thought he'd be suitable for her daughter, as if he were beef on the hoof?

Worse yet, was it possible that Rosalind *knew* her mother had cut him out of the herd with an eye to butchering him specifically for Rosalind's dinner table, so to speak?

Was she determined not to like him because her mother was determined she should?

It made appalling sense. He might have reacted the same himself, if his father had tried to pull that kind of crap.

So. Did he sound Rosalind out on the subject, see if she'd admit she knew about and resented her mother's machinations? Would she admit it?

He dried his hands on the miniature towel laid out by the sink—at least, he hoped that ridiculous lacy scrap of terry cloth was a towel and meant to be used.

Make Rosalind admit it? Or deal with the problem himself?

A man of action, Craig rather liked the idea of taking steps to win himself the woman of his dreams.

All he had to do, he figured, was make himself appear less desirable. E. coli on the hoof, instead of prime beef. In other words, tick Margaret off royally.

Craig grinned. How hard would it be to annoy a woman whose kitchen you were remodeling?

CHAPTER SIX

CRAIG MULLED the problem over that night—
when he wasn't picturing the scumbag with his
hands all over Rosalind. Sleep was in short sup-
ply.

It wouldn't be hard to make Margaret Kirk
mad as hell, Craig reflected, but what if he was
wrong about Rosalind's reason for rejecting him?
He'd have alienated a good client—one who happened to be the mother of the woman he was
pretty sure he'd fallen in love with.

About morning he came to a conclusion. Ask.
Put on the spot, why wouldn't Rosalind tell him
the truth?

The next day, at the bookstore, he did. Pretty
tactfully, he thought. He didn't even phrase it as
a question.

"I, uh, have the impression your mother would
like to see us pair up."

A thousand and one emotions ghosted across
Rosalind's gentle face. At last she eyed him.
"You noticed, huh?"

Craig went for blunt. "I didn't like the idea of you dating West. She could tell, and it pleased her."

"You didn't like..." Rosalind swallowed the rest of her sentence. Her cheeks pinkened. "Who I date is really none of your business."

He avoided that one. This was a fine time to show the manly vulnerability women supposedly craved. "It doesn't feel real good to have you turn me down, then watch you hanging on someone else." Especially a sleaze like Jordan West, Craig chose not to add.

"I wasn't hanging..." She apparently remembered that, yes, she definitely had been. Maybe embarrassment explained her burst of honesty. "If it makes you feel any better, I won't be going out with him again. As far as turning you down, it really wasn't you... Oh, dear. That sounds odd. But you have to understand, I don't dare give my mother ideas."

Yes!

Still, he wanted to hear it in plain English. "What you're saying is, if your mother hadn't pushed me at you, you would have gone out to dinner with me."

"Um—" she took a deep breath "—yes. I suppose so."

"You don't find me unattractive."

Pink cheeks signaled her answer. "Well... no."

"Ah." Should he point out the idiocy of letting her mother make her decisions for her in one way if not the other?

Nah. He had a better plan.

"THEY DON'T *FIT?*" Margaret Kirk repeated, teeth snapping shut between each word.

"Mistakes happen," Craig said easily, bracing himself for the fireworks.

They both contemplated the bank of cabinets, sitting askew on the bare plywood floor. The warm maple was beautifully crafted with paneled doors and gleaming brass hardware.

"You took the measurements yourself."

"Yeah." He shook his head in apparent puzzlement. "I don't know whether I wrote that width down wrong or what." He let his face brighten. "Now, if you can live with another real narrow cupboard there, instead of the drawers you had in mind, we could go ahead. I can rework these myself."

"What I can live with is the configurations we agreed on." Ice glittered in every word. "Exactly how long will it take you to redo my cupboards? Assuming," she added pointedly, "you drop everything else."

"Well—" he mulled it over, trying to look oafish "—if I put your daughter's bookstore on hold…"

"You claimed you could handle both jobs!" Now she sounded like a fishwife, as his mother would have put it. He didn't know what a fishwife was, but the label worked.

His gift for timing being what it was, Rosalind walked into the gutted room to hear her mom's shrill exclamation.

He hadn't seen her in a couple of days, so despite the tension, he let himself appreciate the sight of her in snug jeans and a tank top edged with lace at her cleavage. Little curls escaped the knot on top of her head. She liked to appear businesslike, but it was an uphill road when her hair wouldn't cooperate and her curves so nicely filled everything she wore.

"Is something wrong?" she asked, eyes widening.

Biting off every word, Margaret told her the story, accompanied by tight gestures at the offending cabinets. In fact, Craig had ordered them so that the error could be fixed fairly easily. He hadn't told Margaret Kirk that.

Maybe dragging his feet would have been enough to irritate Rosalind's mother. But he'd been afraid she'd excuse any delays because of the work he was doing for Rosalind. No, to make her good and mad, he had to foul up. Those same delays would be a lot more exasperating when she'd seen her beautiful new cupboards in the kitchen, then had them snatched away again. Because he, Craig Morrow, perfectionist, had made a mistake.

His pursuit of Rosalind was costing him not only a great deal of money, but his reputation. Panic flickered again, but he squelched it. She was worth any sacrifice.

"Thanks to Mr. Morrow's carelessness," Margaret was saying, her angry gaze shooting his way, "I will now be without a kitchen for weeks more. At the moment I'm very sorry I recommended him to you."

"Anyone can make a mistake!" Rosalind fired back. "You should see what beautiful bookcases he's made for my store! Goodness, Mom, what's a minor holdup?"

"Minor?" she repeated on an ominously rising note. "Two weeks? Three weeks? Do you have any idea how desperately I'd like to come home from work and put dinner on in my own kitchen? If I see another fast-food hamburger, I'll... I'll..."

Stuff it down his throat, her expression suggested. Guilt assailed him. It was eased by having Rosalind rush to his defense yet again.

"Now, Mom, I think you're overreacting. Look how beautiful the cabinets are going to be! And aren't you the one who told me that something always goes wrong during a major remodeling? What do you want to bet it'll be smooth sailing from here on out."

Craig didn't want her mother mollified too quickly. "I've got those new measurements right here," he assured her, patting his pocket. No paper crinkled, and he frowned. "Well, maybe not here… Now, where did I put those?" he muttered, pretending to search his pockets.

"I don't give a…a *darn* where they are," Margaret snapped. "Just so you get it right this time! One more mistake like this and you're fired!"

Hiding his satisfaction, Craig watched her stomp out of the kitchen. The swinging door didn't slam, but it whooshed shut so hard he felt a blast of air.

"I'm sorry I had to make such a dumb mistake," he said. "Your mom has been so nice."

"Don't worry." Rosalind laid a hand on his forearm, which tightened in instant reaction to her touch. "She's usually pretty understanding about stuff like this." Pause. "Not that I ever did anything *quite* like this.'' A giggle escaped her. "How did you? I mean, you're a *foot* off.''

Maybe he'd gone overboard. Would an inch have been more believable?

"God knows," he said ruefully. "Do you really think she'll get over this?''

"Of course she will!''

The balm of Rosalind's smile was clearly meant to soothe his damaged ego. The true effect was not soothing: he wanted to pull her into his arms and kiss that sweet mouth until she melted.

He shoved his hands in the pockets of his jeans in hope of disguising just how soothed he was. "I hope you're right. Well." He moved his shoulders awkwardly. "I guess I'd better get out of here. Your mom would probably rather not see me again tonight. Besides, it's dinnertime. You two are probably planning to go out.''

Worry crinkled her smooth brow. "What do you do for dinner?''

"Oh...usually fast food. I'm not much of a cook.'' He was glad to be able to tell the truth. Lying to her wasn't sitting well with him. A pretty straightforward guy, he'd normally consider the idea of tricking a woman into dating him pretty distasteful.

Rosalind's chin came up and she said with determination, "I'd like to take you out tonight.

You've had a bad enough day. You shouldn't eat a cheeseburger and fries all by yourself. We could do something nice. Maybe...well—'' she blushed "—you're the one who mentioned that new Italian place. Gianni's. Shall we try it?''

Hot damn. Things hardly ever worked out this perfectly.

"If I can come back for you after I go home and shower," he said, letting himself look pleased but not elated. Not that she'd have any reason to suspect what he'd done; what idiot would jeopardize his livelihood to convince a woman to go out to dinner with him?

With it put like that, he felt like a fool. A happy fool.

"I'll change, too." She smiled. "I'll talk to Mom. Who knows? Maybe she'll even join us. If that's okay?''

What could he say? She meant well. "Of course it is.''

"Then I'll see you in a bit," Rosalind said.

He raced home, showered, put on his going-out slacks and jacket, then tore back to the Kirks' house. Fingers crossed behind his back for luck, Craig knocked on the door.

Rosalind opened it a crack and slipped out with a swift glance behind her. Wrinkling her nose, she said, "Mom's still sulking. Sorry.''

He tried real hard to appear regretful. "I'll do a rush job fixing my foul-up."

"Don't worry," she said, squeezing his arm.

His blood heated. Tonight Rosalind wore a snug little dress in a silky blue-green fabric that clung to every curve and left bare slender legs that seemed to go on forever. Maybe because of the high heels that made her teeter and grab his arm again.

"Shall we go?" he suggested, clearing his throat after hearing how husky his voice sounded.

The drive to Gianni's, dinner—it was all just like he'd dreamed it would be. They talked with an eagerness he didn't remember feeling before. About high school, college, parents, work, football, music. About everything, and nothing in particular. He wanted to know what she'd experienced, thought, felt; *how* she thought.

The amazing part was that she seemed to feel the same. Eyes shining, her dress exposing an enticing view of her cleavage as she leaned forward, she hung on his every word, asked the right questions, laughed at the right places.

On the drive home he wasn't sure he could stand the anticipation. They'd stayed so late night had fallen, which was after ten o'clock at this time of year here in the Northwest. Occasional light from streetlamps fell through the windows of his car, making her legs shimmer and the creamy flesh of her throat and shoulders glow.

Over dinner he hadn't noticed that special fragrance that was her, but now the car was filled with it. Like a caramel apple when you first bit into it, tart and sweet at the same time. The image was damned erotic: creamy caramel exterior, crisp juicy apple inside. His whole body tightened.

In the driveway of her mother's house, he set the brake and turned off the ignition. The porchlight was on, but nothing over the garage, so in the sudden silence he could barely make out the pale oval of her face.

"Thanks for suggesting this," he said. "I had a good time."

"Me, too." Her voice was just above a whisper. "Thank you for taking me. I meant to pay for it."

"I wouldn't have felt right." Moving slowly so as not to alarm her, Craig laid his arm along the back of her seat. His hand itched to move those last inches and wrap around the back of her neck, feel the tiny hairs tickle his palm, slide up into her curls.

"I guess," she said as softly. "I was dumb to say no in the first place."

Not dumb. Not her. He felt the need to defend

Rosalind even from her own criticism. "I don't blame you for not liking the idea of your mother pushing us together. Makes you think of *Fiddler on the Roof* or something like that, doesn't it?"

"Yes!" New eagerness entered her voice; she turned her entire body toward him. "I love *Fiddler on the Roof!* It's one of my favorite musicals! Remember, our high school did a production. Penny took me—I think maybe I was still in the middle school. It was wonderful."

"I, uh, played Tevye," he admitted. He hated to think what the guys on construction sites would think if they knew he'd once upon a time had the acting bug, going so far as to put on makeup and prance about the stage.

"Oh…" Rosalind breathed. "Really? You were so good! Oh, I can't believe it! Sing something. Please?"

He was mighty tempted to go for Tevye's demand to know whether his wife, Golda, loved him after twenty-something years of marriage. Discretion being the better part of valor, he tilted back his head and launched into, "If I were a rich man…"

By the time he got to asking the Lord what it would hurt to give him a "small" fortune, Rosalind was clapping.

"I *love* that song! I'm so glad you remember it!"

"I hope the neighbors didn't hear."

She giggled. "Or my mother."

He groaned. "I already dread having to face her again. If she heard me out here, bellowing away..."

"She loves *Fiddler on the Roof,* too," Rosalind said earnestly. "Really."

He had to kiss her then. Just like that, his hand closed the distance; his fingers buried themselves in her hair. He bent and captured her mouth with his.

Her lips trembled; a tiny moan vibrated in her throat. His teeth felt the tender fullness of her lips, his tongue dipped inside to taste the sweetness. She was every treat he'd had in his life all wrapped up in one: cinnamon cookies, the rides at Disneyland when he was kid, the crowd in the high-school auditorium clapping and whistling for *him,* the keys to his first car handed over by his dad. Joy and hunger and a sense of rightness rumbled in his chest.

Rosalind stilled it with her small hand splayed over his heart.

He lifted his head. "Will you have dinner with me tomorrow night?" he asked roughly.

"Oh, yes," she whispered. "I would love that."

And I love you, Craig thought, but didn't say.

CHAPTER SEVEN

HOW DREADFUL to think that maybe Mom *had* known her better than she knew herself! On that unpalatable thought, Rosalind tossed and turned all night.

Of course, it didn't matter now, she reminded herself. In her mother's book, Craig was no longer the perfect man, so Mom wasn't likely to gloat now. In fact, she'd been flat-out mad when Rosalind had announced her intention of having dinner with Craig.

She'd turned off the television set with a snap that should have broken the remote-control case. "He's just been incredibly careless, made a major mistake on my kitchen, inconveniencing you, as well as me, and *now* you decide you like him?"

"I think you're being unfair…"

Mom's mouth had tightened and she'd said bitterly, "*I* think you accepted his invitation just to send a message. You only like men I don't. Fine. Message received. Go."

"Mom…"

The television had come on with a blast, showing the scene of a crowd demonstrating in Moscow's Red Square. Rosalind's mother hadn't answered. Craig's knock on the front door had come at an opportune moment. Rosalind had slipped out.

And had a wonderful time. An incredible time. Remembering, she hugged her pillow and uttered a small squeal, as if she were a teenager again.

He *listened*. Men never listened. And he had interests she shared. And a wonderful voice. Would he sing love songs to her? And, oh, how he could kiss! She'd almost melted into a puddle on the floor mat of his car.

The best part was, they were having dinner again tonight. They could talk and talk, and he'd kiss her again…

A tiny sigh escaped her. She'd never fall asleep at this rate!

Yes, but who cared? She could think about Craig all night. His big competent hands, the rough/gentle texture of his fingertips, the way the lines in his cheeks deepened when he smiled. She had a million mental snapshots to choose from: Craig at her store, frowning in concentration, the muscles in his thighs bunching as he dropped to his knees to inspect a heating vent; her first sight of him, dusted with plaster, stolid but intense; the shadowed planes of his face over a candlelit table.

Either she had a really big crush on the man, or she was falling in love.

With the man her mother had chosen for her.

No, with the contractor her mother was currently very, very angry at.

Two different things entirely.

She must have slept eventually, because she awakened with a tingle of excitement and a reason for springing out of bed. She didn't see Craig all day; he must have been on another job, maybe working on her mother's cabinets, assuming he would reconfigure them himself. She met with several publishers' reps, did some ordering, finally chose software to track inventory and replaced the display in the bay window. Formerly books about local history along with some unusual antiques from Jordan's store had—she hoped—caught the eyes of passersby. Now she poured a bed of sand—from sacks she'd picked up at the building-supply store—and set out books on Northwest travel destinations amongst creamy white sand dollars and dried starfish, picked up on childhood trips to the Washington coast.

It worked, she decided, standing outside on the

boardwalk. She wouldn't add a beach ball or any other paraphernalia. The artless scene whispered more commandingly for attention than a gaudier display could possibly have shouted.

"Nice," Craig said from behind her.

The sound of his voice was enough to make the shimmer of anticipation she'd felt all day froth like a bottle of champagne given a good shake.

"You're early."

"I thought about you all day," he said simply.

"Me, too." Rosalind blushed. "I mean..."

"I know what you mean." He smiled, his eyes darkening, and bent his head.

She rose on tiptoe to meet his warm mouth, tasting of passion despite his gentleness.

"We'd better go to dinner," he said huskily, "or else I may lose interest in eating."

She already had. But this was a little early in the relationship to do anything as drastic as undressing in front of him and slipping between the sheets of his bed, feeling his hair-roughened leg insinuate itself between hers, his big hand engulf her breast, his mouth...

Oh, dear. Her body didn't seem to think it was too early. Fortunately Craig was gently urging her to lock up, ushering her into his car, talking about something he'd heard on the radio that day.

The intense flush of sexual need became a faint ache. She could ignore it, enjoy talking to him, getting to know him. Find out whether last night was a fluke.

It wasn't. Tonight was just as good. More talk: he preferred dogs, Rosalind cats, but both thought they'd like to have one or two of each; two children would be just right, as well, they agreed. Unlike most men, he didn't especially hanker for a son to carry on his masculine genes and his name. Sons or daughters, either would be fine, he said with a shrug. Rosalind felt the same. In fact, it seemed miraculous how often they did agree. They argued amiably about the small stuff: music, books, whether dogs or cats were smarter. But where the big stuff was concerned, they were in harmony.

His kisses were even better tonight, more intense, more urgent. He wanted her, she realized with a thrill—really, really wanted her, and wouldn't be content to wait for long. Normally that would have scared her. She might have feared that after one night he'd be gone, but Rosalind knew without any doubt that Craig had a great deal more in mind. Partly her certainty came from some of the things they'd talked about. The careful way he'd brought up the subject of children, for example. Partly, it came from a deep-rooted belief that she *knew* him. Not everything about him, not yet. But the man himself, the core of values and strength and vulnerability that made Craig Morrow... Oh, yes, she knew him.

Once more, he was the one to end their embrace, to gently straighten her silk blouse, smooth her hair back from her face, ease her away from him. She ought to have been embarrassed to have so little self-restraint, but tonight her body sang with pleasure, and her mood was too rosy to allow room for anything so silly.

As he escorted her to her—well, to her mother's—front door, she walked sedately, but inside she skipped. *He loves me!* she thought joyfully. Would he ask her to move in with him soon? Rosalind sneaked a peek at him. Or was he romantic enough to ask her to marry him without an experiment in shared living first? She pictured him kneeling, sliding a shimmering diamond ring on her finger, murmuring words of passion...

"Good night," he said huskily, turning her for a quick last kiss. But his lips lingered and his hands slid up so that his thumbs pressed the undersides of her breasts. She rose on tiptoe to deepen the kiss. Craig didn't seem to mind.

"Good night," she whispered at last.

"I'll see you at the store tomorrow," he said, that thrumming note of intimacy still in his voice. "Maybe we can have dinner again?"

"I'd love to." Rosalind never had believed in coy games. She would have been crushed if he *hadn't* wanted to see her tomorrow night!

She let herself in, secretly hoping her mother would be long since asleep. The living room was dark but for one lamp. The light pooled on Rosalind's mother, sitting with feet curled under her on one end of the couch, a book open on her lap.

"Oh, hi," Margaret Kirk said serenely. "Did you have a nice time?"

Rosalind lifted her chin a notch. "As a matter of fact, I did."

"I'm glad." Her mother patted the couch beside her. "Why don't you sit down and tell me about your evening."

Suspicious, Rosalind said, "Were you waiting up for me?"

Mrs. Kirk's eyebrows rose. "Heavens, no! I know it's after my usual bedtime, but my book is a good one."

"Oh." Rosalind perched at the other end of the couch. "What are you reading?"

"A man tells about his travels in Tibet." Her mother held it up, although she wasn't diverted. "Where did you go for dinner?"

"That new Thai place."

Mom liked experimenting with other cuisines. Tonight she was uninterested. "I'm sure the food was good. Are you enjoying Craig's company?"

Casual conversation, a parental inquisition or a lead-in to more hurt feelings?

"I wouldn't have gone out with him two nights in a row if I didn't."

Her mother inclined her head graciously. "I'm glad. You deserve to have fun."

She did? With the man who was responsible for Mom having to eat french fries for weeks extra? Rosalind gazed at her mother with mild astonishment.

How to put it? "You're not, um, annoyed anymore?" she asked carefully. "I mean, because I'm dating Craig?"

"No, no!" Margaret Kirk gave a sunny smile. "You were absolutely right. I did overreact. Anybody can make a mistake. He's been wonderful all along, and he's done a truly lovely job on your shop. Did I tell you I took a peek in the window this afternoon? The bookcases are beautiful. Just what I was imagining. Gracious! I really do need to apologize to him. He must think I'm a cranky old lady."

"You're hardly old," Rosalind protested automatically, her thoughts whirling. Mom had forgiven Craig. She was delighted that Rosalind was dating him.

"Old enough to know better." Her mother patted her hand. "Well, I must go to bed. I just wanted to tell you I know I was wrong. I'm glad you saw more clearly than I did. Now if he were just in his fifties, I might give you a run for your money!"

The saying, given the context, repulsed Rosalind. Was that how her mother saw Craig? A prize? The biggest, gaudiest stuffed animal hanging above the carnival game?

Exactly. The one she wanted for her daughter. She hadn't been able to throw the rings herself; parents couldn't arrange matches these days. But she had certainly done her best to guide Rosalind's hands, give that extra little push.

And it looked as if the ring had landed neatly over the single gold-painted peg, winning the coveted prize.

Only, even as a child Rosalind had never liked being helped. She wanted to do everything for herself, earn every honor, every bit of praise, all on her own.

She wanted to choose her own husband, not have him led to her front door like a docile beribboned pony bought for a birthday present.

But she *had* chosen Craig! Rosalind thought

desperately. She hadn't gone out with him just because Mom wanted it, not like Penny had with John. So this wasn't the same thing at all.

So why did she feel so…so manipulated? So unhappy?

CHAPTER EIGHT

CRAIG HAD MARGARET KIRK'S cabinets ready for installation by the next afternoon. He almost called her, but caution held him back. He couldn't believe Rosalind would dump him now just because her mother decided he was the cat's meow again, but two dates didn't mean he knew every twist and turn of Rosalind's mind, either. Give it a week, he figured, solidify his position before he soothed his future mother-in-law's ire.

But the minute he arrived on her doorstep to pick up Rosalind that evening, he could tell Margaret's sentiments had changed. She was ready, figuratively, to clasp him to her bosom once more.

Taking his hand, she pulled him across the threshold. In the background Rosalind hovered. He didn't even get a chance to look at her.

Margaret still squeezed his hand as she gazed earnestly up at him. "Please tell me you'll forgive me. My daughter was right. Anyone can make a mistake. I'm afraid things have gone so smoothly to this point you'd lulled me into complacency! A different day I would have been more philosophical, but I was tired and hungry and—'' She stopped and said dramatically, "Enough excuses! Just say you'll accept my apology."

No didn't seem an appropriate answer, considering the circumstances. He did his best to be polite, and eventually Rosalind's mother let them escape. They went out the front door on a flurry of godspeeds.

"Have a good time! Don't worry what time you get in! I won't wait up!"

Craig didn't say anything until they were buckled into their seats in the car. Then he gave his head a dazed shake. "What happened?"

"She forgave you."

Her dismal tone made him uneasy. Surely, now that she'd gotten to know him, she wouldn't let her mother's approval influence her negatively? "You don't sound so happy about it."

Rosalind started. "What? Of course I'm happy! Wasn't I the one who told her she was being ridiculous?"

"Sure you were," he agreed.

"Well, then, why would you suggest I'm not pleased?" She frowned at him and repeated, "Of course I am!"

He thought the lady doth protest too much, but he only shrugged and said pleasantly, "Sorry. Where shall we go for dinner tonight?"

Evidently brooding, she said in a distracted voice, "I don't care."

Her mood seemed to improve after they arrived at Le Bistro, a faux French place he personally thought was kind of pretentious, but seemed to please Rosalind. The food was fine, he decided, but not as good as the crisp white tablecloths, snooty waiters and parchment menu made you expect.

Somehow the talk didn't flow quite as easily tonight, although he enjoyed Rosalind's company even when she was quiet. He steered the conversation to her plans for the grand opening celebration. She'd already ordered the wine, but hadn't quite settled on the music.

"I can't find a local string quartet. A pianist would be nice, but the store isn't big enough for even a baby grand, and I assume that would be more expensive, anyway." She gave a wry smile. "A couple of old fiddlers offered, but I didn't think their foot-stomping stuff would create the right atmosphere. So I'm still hunting."

Craig considered mentioning the band currently playing at a local bar. He'd heard them the previous Friday and thought they were damned good. Still, their notes didn't tinkle; they boomed. Probably their down-and-dirty music wouldn't create the right atmosphere, either.

He was pretty relaxed by the time he parked in the driveway of Rosalind's—no, Margaret's—house. This was the best part of the evening: feeling Rosalind shiver, hearing her tiny gasps, tasting her sweetness. He'd never had so much trouble keeping a grip on his self-restraint; something about her distinctive scent, her voice, her lips, drove him wild. He wouldn't mind fifty years' worth of nights with Rosalind. Nights like this: the bottomless black sky scattered with diamonds, the moon half-full and shimmery.

His car window was rolled down, letting in the warm night air. He smelled roses, maybe Rosalind, maybe real ones; he wasn't sure and didn't care.

In the silence after he turned off the engine, Craig slipped an arm around her shoulder and began easing her toward him. She came willingly. He bent his head. His mouth was inches from hers when Rosalind whispered, "It's dumb, but I wish my mother still hated you."

He stopped. "What?"

"I'm sorry." She gave herself a little shake and bowed her head, so all he could see was the crown. "I don't know what's wrong with me tonight. I should have stayed home and gotten out of bed on the other side tomorrow.''

A feeling of tenderness swept over him. His mother used to tease him when he was grouchy by telling him he'd gotten out of bed on the wrong side. Since his bed was up against a wall, the saying was particularly absurd, which was maybe why it always loosened him up a little, made him realize he was taking trouble at school or on a job or with friends too seriously.

"Hey, we all have bad days.'' He took her chin in his hand and tried to lift her head. When she resisted, Craig frowned. "Why the heck do you care so much what your mother thinks about me?''

"She picked out my sister's husband.''

Baffled, he stared down at the top of her head. "Does Penny have a bad marriage?''

Rosalind abruptly scooted away, back to her own side. "No, she's happy, which is what especially exasperates me. Doesn't she have any spirit at all?''

Now he was really confused. "She shouldn't like her husband because your mother does?''

Rosalind stared fiercely at him. "Well, why did she go out with him just because Mom suggested it?''

"I've barely met your sister and never her husband," he pointed out. "But if she's happy, what does it matter why she went out with the guy in the first place?"

Without answering, Rosalind veered onto another tangent. "I've always done everything Mom suggested. I don't know why. Yes, I do. Because she's usually right. But...oh, I don't want the same kind of life she thinks I should want! All *she* ever thinks about is security. I mean, Mom's always wanted to travel, but of course she wouldn't dream of dipping into her retirement savings to actually take a trip. The kitchen is different. After all—" her tone changed to mimic her mother "—it increases the value of the house." Rosalind threw up her hands. "But she won't take a real chance! I don't want to live that way."

Craig shoved his fingers into his hair and gave a sharp tug. Reality check. "Who the hell is suggesting you do?"

"She is!" Rosalind cried. "She thinks I should get married and buy a house and have a baby. Start a college fund. Probably forget the bookstore."

At last he was getting it. His eyes narrowed. "And she thinks I should be the father to your baby. The cosigner on the mortgage."

"Yes!" Her look beseeched him. "Now do you see?"

Yeah, he saw. Was this a good moment to ask her to marry him?

"Let me get this straight," he said. "Because your mother approves of me and introduced us, I'm the last man on earth you'd ever marry. No matter how you feel about me. Do I have this right?"

"Yes! No!" Rosalind hunched against the car door. "Oh, I'm so confused."

Craig was getting mad. Apparently the past couple of evenings didn't matter one whit to her. She was so hung up on some feud with her mother that what she felt for him would be thrown out the window.

"So your mother's opinion decides who you see and don't see?"

"No! That's exactly the point—"

"But it's what you're doing!" he bellowed. "I can't believe it! Here I thought I was falling in love with a woman, and now it turns out that underneath, she's still a girl rebelling against her mommy."

"That's not fair," Rosalind said miserably. "I'm just...well, at a point in my life where—" She stopped. "Did you say you were falling in love with me?"

He gripped the steering wheel with both hands, holding on so tightly his fingers ached. "Yeah, I said it. The point in your life where what?"

"What?" she echoed, then blinked. "Oh. A point where I realized that I've just been a...a puppet. Mom would encourage me to dream, but then she'd squelch any tiny step toward that dream. And I let her. So now I'm having to figure out which parts of my life are really *mine,* and which fit my mother better. Is that so unreasonable?"

"Are you saying *I* fit your mother better than I do you?" Craig asked, voice granite hard to hide his hurt.

"No! It's just that I can't help wondering...well, if she just pretended to be mad at you, once she realized why I wouldn't go out with you."

"Pretended?" Some demon didn't let him shut up right there, where he should have. He heard himself continue, "Next thing, you'll be saying *I* made the mistake on purpose so I'd tick her off and you'd go out with me."

"If you'd known, you might have!" Rosalind flared. She abruptly went still.

He should have filled the silence, but couldn't.

Her voice dropped to a whisper. "You did know. You asked me, and I admitted that I hated being set up by my mother. You *did* make a mistake on purpose, didn't you? A really, really big one."

Now he knew he should have gone with an inch, instead of a foot.

"Yeah, okay," he said loudly. "I admit it. I really liked you. I figured if your mother's opinion was the only problem, I'd change it. I thought maybe by the time she got over being mad, you'd have discovered you really liked me. Is that such a crime?"

Sitting upright, Rosalind snapped, "You have no idea how incredibly arrogant that sounds. I said no, you couldn't accept it. So what did you do but manipulate my mother and me so you could have your way. After all, you're so studly I couldn't help but 'really' like you, right?"

"That's not what I meant—"

"Oh, yes, it is," she breathed. "Well, guess what? You got caught. My mother is too nice to stay mad, and I'm too smart not to realize what you did. And here's news for you—she got over being mad, and I don't 'really' like you."

He couldn't help himself; he reached out and grabbed her shoulders. Under his fingertips he felt the tension humming through her.

"If you don't really like me," Craig said between gritted teeth, "then why did you kiss me until you were moaning?"

She wrenched free of his hands. "Maybe," she returned angrily, "I did 'really' like you then. Before I discovered what a skunk you are! And now I don't! I'll thank you to finish the job you contracted with me to do, and then get out of my life!"

Rosalind flung herself from the car, slammed the door and stalked up the walkway. Within seconds, she'd vanished inside.

Craig sat stunned. He felt as if a two-by-ten beam had swung loose and slammed into his chest. How had everything gone wrong so fast?

Maybe it wasn't everything—maybe Rosalind was wrong. Wrong for him. Maybe he'd let himself be led into a dreamworld by the delicious smell of apple pie. If she'd been the woman he thought she was, she'd be paving her own road by now, not tearing up her mother's asphalt.

And she sure as hell wouldn't want a string quartet and French wines at that grand opening celebration.

Swearing, Craig started the engine and flung the gearshift into reverse.

Get out of her life. Yeah, okay. He'd do that. Poorer but wiser.

CHAPTER NINE

THE FOLKSINGER'S VOICE hushed, his guitar strings quivered, murmured, died under his fingertips; and complete silence fell. The crowd clapped and hooted and raised their clear plastic cups of wine and beer.

From behind the cash register, Rosalind looked around with satisfaction but less pleasure than she had expected to feel at a moment for which she'd worked so hard. Lots of people had come and gone the past hour. Half-a-dozen women lined up to have books signed by a local romance writer. Another half a dozen had already paid for their purchases. The folksinger, a middle-aged man who spent his days driving a garbage truck and his evenings playing Seattle clubs, was a friend of a friend. He was so talented she didn't understand why he wasn't off in a recording studio, instead.

Somehow this opening celebration had evolved from the genteel occasion she'd envisioned to a party, complete with a keg of beer and an author known for her page-turning paper-backs, not for short stories in the *New Yorker*. And the evening was a success. Except—

The bell over the door tinkled; when a tall dark-haired man filled the opening, Rosalind's heart leaped. The next second, she saw that the man was a stranger, and the buoyancy evaporated.

Despite that awful night and the stiffness between them since, she'd really thought Craig would come to her grand opening. Didn't he want to see the result of all his work?

Apparently not, she realized, the heavy dull ache returning. Even if he did, hadn't she made clear he wasn't welcome? *Get out of my life,* she'd said. Well, he'd done that several weeks ago. Her mother's kitchen was finished; the last bookcase in her store anchored in place. He'd cashed their checks.

Despite her gloom, she summoned a smile for a friend of her mother's, who was heading for the door. "Thank you for coming, Barbara."

"I'll be back to shop for my fall reading later in the week." She chuckled. "When it's quieter."

Rosalind scanned the store. People wandered around chatting, munching hors d'oeuvres and browsing through the shelves. Everyone appeared content.

Rosalind lapsed again into brooding. She had been busy these past weeks, of course, almost busy enough not to think about Craig. About what he'd done and what she'd said. About what *he'd* said.

I was falling in love. In her most wretched moments she could hear the rasp in his voice. The disgust. The hurt.

She could hear what she'd thrown away.

Okay, he'd done something sneaky. But when in her life had a man pursued her the way he had? Why, he'd jeopardized his professional reputation just so he could take her out to dinner! And then she'd told him he was a skunk—an *arrogant* skunk—just because he'd believed she would like him. And she *had* liked him!

But she'd also told him the truth. Lately she'd been all mixed up. Maybe that meant she was immature, not ready for marriage and children. But wasn't it also true that a person's relationship with a parent kept evolving even when both were adults? Look what she'd accomplished here with the bookstore just because she'd reexamined her life. How did you reexamine your life without being a little unsure about some parts?

That thought made her mad again. Craig

hadn't even tried to understand! As if *he* was perfect! Putting her mother, an innocent bystander, through the disappointment and frustration of a long delay during her kitchen remodeling just because he was so sure Rosalind didn't mean what she said! She hated being subtly maneuvered into doing what someone else thought she should do. After putting up with it all her life from her mother, she wasn't about to let a man take over the role.

She gave a brisk nod. No, she'd done the right thing, even if it hurt. And it did hurt.

Eventually the crowd thinned and departed. Rosalind thanked the musician and handed him a check in an envelope. The caterer—another young woman trying to start a new career—took her trays of leftovers and departed. Rosalind closed up the cash register and exulted briefly in her first earnings. Her mother and Penny, who had stayed, joined her in optimistic contemplation of how much more she'd make this week and how that would grow as people heard about her store.

Then, with a sigh, Rosalind began picking up crumpled napkins and plastic cups decorated with lipstick and half-full of beer that had lost its fizz.

"You guys can go home," she told her sister and mother.

Apologetically Penny said, "Well, I think I will, if you don't mind terribly. Sarah wakes up so early. She doesn't care if it's a weekend."

Rosalind hugged her, feeling a rush of sisterly affection. It wasn't Penny's fault that she was so...docile. Happy wherever life plopped her. No matter how pretty or vivacious Penny looked, when Rosalind saw her she always thought of a gentle brown-eyed Jersey cow contentedly chewing her cud. But there was nothing wrong with being happy. Even if you let other people tell you *how* to be happy.

Rosalind glanced at her mother. Margaret Kirk was dusting her hands over the wastebasket and looking around with an expression of bemusement.

"What are you thinking?" Rosalind asked.

"What?" Her mother's head turned. "Oh, just how nice the place looks. How...established."

Maybe it was tiredness, maybe the ache under her breastbone, maybe the surprise in her mother's voice, that made Rosalind say sharply, "You didn't think I'd get this far, did you?"

"Of course I did!" her mother exclaimed. "I've never doubted your ability to accomplish whatever you set out to do."

All her confused feelings of these past months

boiled over. "Then why did you try so hard to keep me from setting out to do anything?"

Mrs. Kirk's stare met hers. Tension quivered between them. "What are you talking about?"

Recalling a list was no problem. She'd lain awake a million times making it. In this instance she'd skip the small stuff. Rosalind held up her hand and ticked items off on her fingers. "The swim team. I loved swimming. You gently encouraged me to stop."

Her mother made a small sound. "It took such time and money. I couldn't afford—"

Rosalind didn't—wouldn't—listen in case her anger got defused before she finished. Item two. "Running for senior class president in high school."

"I was afraid you wouldn't win, and I didn't want you disappointed."

Item three. "Majoring in history at the university."

Lines in her mother's face seemed deeper. "I only suggested you be practical."

"My job-hunting away from Perry Creek."

"WashTel is a top-notch employer," Mrs. Kirk said with dignity. "I was able to help you get a good position here."

"Opening the store."

This time there was a long pause. At last, very

quietly, her mother said, "You know it'll be a struggle."

"Is a struggle such a bad thing?"

"It can be." In her mother's eyes was a stark vulnerability Rosalind had never seen there before. "After your father died, life was a struggle. Believe me. You were little. You don't remember. Poverty is not something to seek out if you can help it. I have never done anything but try to help you avoid times as hard as I had."

"But I'm not in your situation!" Rosalind cried with passion. "I don't have two children. I'm young and healthy and...and able! Isn't this when I *should* take some chances? Or am I supposed to live in perpetual fear that I might end up poor like you were?"

Her mother flinched at Rosalind's bitterness. After a long, long moment, during which she never once allowed herself to look away from her daughter, Margaret Kirk inclined her head slightly. "You're right. I am a coward. Circumstances made me one, but I didn't have to let it happen."

Belated guilt squeezed Rosalind's chest. "Mom, you've managed wonderfully! I didn't mean that. It's just...I don't want to hurt you, but please, please understand that I have to try things, even if I fail."

Her mother came to her then, moving with a stiffness and fragility Rosalind knew had to be emotional and not physical. "Sweetheart," she said softly, taking Rosalind's hand in hers, "I have always understood. You're me all over again, which I suppose is why I tried so hard to steer you to safety. But I do understand. I want you to know that I'm proud of you and what you've accomplished here. If the business doesn't make it...well, at least you'll know you tried. Which is maybe what really counts."

Tears in her eyes, Rosalind wrapped her arms around her mother, who hugged her back. In that embrace Rosalind was conscious of an odd internal shift. For the first time with her mother, Rosalind felt like the adult she was.

When they awkwardly let each other go, both wiping away tears, Rosalind heard herself say forlornly, "Craig didn't come."

Mrs. Kirk's face held compassion. She showed no sign of surprise at what might have seemed a non sequitur. "I noticed. Did you two leave things so badly between you?"

"I'm afraid *I* did." Rosalind hesitated. "He...well, he did something that..." She stopped and took a deep breath. "Do you want to know what he really did?"

Mom nodded.

Rosalind told her.

A flood of expressions crossed her mother's face. "He made my kitchen cabinets too big on purpose?" she echoed.

The next second she made a hiccuping sound. In shock Rosalind realized that her mother was giggling. Although she pressed one hand to her lips to quell it, the giggle became a laugh that shook her entire body.

"Oh, dear," she finally gasped. "The thing is, I realized what the problem was, too, and *I* was thinking about manufacturing some excuse to be mad at *him.* Only, I hadn't thought of anything, and then he made such a monumental boo-boo. After a few days I could see how happy you were with him, so I didn't think it mattered anymore what I thought." She wiped streaming eyes. "What a creative fellow."

"Yes, but now he hates me!" Rosalind wailed. "He told me I wasn't a woman. I was a little girl still competing with my mother."

Her mother raised her brows.

"I know I acted like I was! Am. But I'm not!" Fresh tears stung her eyes. "I love him!"

"Then," her mother said firmly, "do something about it. But not—" she glanced at her watch "—right this minute. I trust that at 2:00 a.m. he's long since asleep. Let's go home," she said, tucking Rosalind's hand around her arm, "and go to bed ourselves. I'll come back with you in the morning and help finish up here. I promise."

Rosalind sniffed. "Thank you, Mom. But...but what can I *do?* I mean, after everything I said to him?"

"A nice straightforward phone message might be enough." Mom patted her arm. "Or you might go find him wherever he's working now. Tell him I've decided to despise him forever, so he's back in the running."

Her mother was asking her to have a sense of humor. To...well, be adult, she realized. And Mom was right. It *was* funny. The two women gave a wry laugh.

Tomorrow, Rosalind thought. Tomorrow was always another day.

"Mom," she said, "I love you."

CHAPTER TEN

CRAIG HAD FELT like a damned fool lurking out in the dark, gazing through the brightly lit bay window at the party inside like an orphan watching a family open presents on Christmas morning. He'd just wanted to see how it went. Hear the tinkling of some of those musical notes. See whether *cultured* folks actually showed up to sip wine and lift eyebrows at the fruits of Rosalind's frenzy of book ordering.

He'd had some vague idea she might need a shoulder to cry on if nobody came. No saying she'd want *his* shoulder—*get out of my life!* still rang in his ears. But nobody knew better than he did how hard she'd worked, how shaky her confidence was, how important the success of the bookstore was to her.

He really wanted this to work for Rosalind. So he wasn't sure why he'd felt hollow inside seeing her laughing and talking and working the cash register nonstop. Yeah, okay, she hadn't needed him. But he wasn't selfish enough to wish she had. Maybe it got to him, seeing that she'd thrown just the kind of party he'd hoped she would: good music, a popular author, friends, plenty of munchies. Even beer, however plebeian. He'd known in his heart that she wasn't the wine-and-string-quartet kind of woman. Not that finding out he was right did him any good.

A couple of times she'd glanced straight through the window at him. He'd have almost sworn their eyes met, but no flicker of recognition or surprise or annoyance registered on her face. She'd probably been unable to see beyond the window glass.

After about half an hour he'd given up and gone home, which was a 1920s-era bungalow, not so different from her mother's, in the old part of Perry Creek. He meant to fix it up when he had time. While he was dating Rosalind, he'd tried to see it as she would and really started making plans, but afterward he'd shelved the whole thing. He took a craftsman's pride in his work, but *he* didn't care if the old kitchen-cabinet drawers stuck or the cabinets had hardly any storage. He didn't cook much, anyway.

Tonight he flung himself into his recliner, but didn't reach for the TV remote control. He didn't even go back to the kitchen for a beer. He didn't want a beer, or some loud sitcom. He wanted the scent of lilies and violets and apple pie. He wanted Rosalind.

How could he have been so stupid? When she'd said that, about wishing her mother still disapproved of him, why hadn't he just mumbled something sympathetic? Maybe told her he understood, that parents could be a pain in the ass?

No, he'd had to tell her she was being childish. He'd even believed, for a few days, that she was. Until he had an argument with his own dad.

A family Sunday dinner was the occasion. Geoff, Craig's older brother, had just gotten a job as a high-school principal. Dad was bragging about how sharp Geoff was, which Craig didn't mind. The trouble started when his father pinned him with a stare.

"Bet you wish now you'd gotten that college degree, don't you?"

"Why should I?" Craig said, deliberately casual. This was a well-worn subject. "I'm doing fine."

Dad waved a fork at him. "College isn't just about making more money, you know. It's about expanding your mind. Using more than your hands."

That one got to Craig. He'd always been a reader. More so than Geoff. And he figured the kind of work he did required a hell of a lot more from him than skilled hands.

"I love my job. I'm good at it." He met his father's stare. "No, I don't wish I had a college education. Geoff's welcome to it."

He might as well have thrown down a gauntlet. Dad planted his elbows on the table and raised his voice. "So, what, you're going to tell your kids to skip college? Hell, maybe it doesn't even matter if they graduate from high school!"

Craig was ashamed to recall that, in the fight that followed, he'd yelled right back, "No, it doesn't matter! Not if they use their heads and find a job they like!"

He hadn't even meant it. Of course he'd encourage his kids to go to college. And they'd damn well better get a high-school diploma. He'd been a good student himself; just circumstances had kept him from going on—a chance at a job he liked. He didn't regret his decision. He did regret riling his father like that.

The truth was, he'd felt himself regress in age, as if time travel really were possible and happening right there at his parents' dining-room table. All of a sudden he was a teenager again, resenting being told how great his big brother was, wanting reassurance himself that he was doing okay.

After stomping out the front door and letting the screen door slam, Craig had stood on the front porch breathing hard. He'd never realized before how childish he could be when he had to deal with his father.

He'd immediately thought about calling and apologizing to Rosalind, but he'd doubted it would do any good. She wasn't just mad about what he'd said; she was mad about what he'd done. Which was, even he had to admit, pretty underhanded.

So he hadn't called. He kept hoping *she* would. So far, no cigar. She hadn't looked as if she was missing him tonight, either. One man had wrapped his arm around her shoulders as if he'd had a right, even kissed her on the cheek. By now, she was probably seeing someone else.

Profoundly depressed, Craig went to bed. Feeling no better in the morning, he headed off to work, where one thing after another went wrong. It culminated with a long wrangle with a customer who didn't want to pay his final bill, claiming the work was shoddy. Craig didn't do shoddy work.

Tired and grumpy as hell, he went home. Tonight he would have a beer. Maybe six of them.

He almost didn't listen to his phone messages. After the day he'd had, they couldn't be good. A reluctant sense of duty made him push the flashing red button. Someone might need him.

He sat at the kitchen table, untied his boots and peeled off sweaty socks while Geoff's voice said, "Hi. Mom says you and Dad went at it again. She's fussing. Why don't you give her a call? Which isn't why *I* phoned. I wanted you to be the first to know Jenny and I are going to have a baby."

Well, hell. That was something. They'd been trying for years. He'd call this evening and offer his congrats.

The machine beeped, went on to the next message. In the act of stripping off his T-shirt, Craig froze.

"Hi." Rosalind's voice was small, hesitant. "I just wanted you to know that I've been doing some thinking, and Mom and I have talked. I've realized I really want her to dance at my wedding." Click.

The machine fell silent. Craig stared at it. What in hell...?

She wanted her mother to dance at her wedding. He frowned in concentration. Was that like having someone dance on your grave? A triumphant spit-in-your-eye kind of thing?

Nah. She meant dance versus...sulk? Stay

away? She wanted her mother happy at her wedding.

Hope took a leap from his stomach to his chest, leaving him out of breath. Did that message mean what he thought it did?

He'd never taken a faster shower in his life. He yanked on clean jeans and swore as he dug through his sock drawer in search of a pair. A comb through his hair, a T-shirt that wasn't too wrinkled, and he tore out of the house.

Rosalind's car wasn't in front of her mother's house. Instead of knocking, he drove to the bookstore. After seven o'clock it was closed, but lights were still on in the office/stockroom. He circled the block, parked in the alley and knocked on the heavy steel door that was her back entrance.

After a long silence it opened a crack. She had the sense to leave the chain on, he saw.

"Yes? Oh. Just a minute."

Heart drumming, he waited while she closed the door again and took the chain off. The glimpse of half her face hadn't been enough to tell him if she was ready to fall into his arms.

The door swung open and he still wasn't sure. She stood there looking at him, expression unreadable.

"I was an idiot," he said, stepping across the threshold and pulling the door shut behind him.

Rosalind didn't let him finish. Tears sparkled in her eyes. "No, I'm the idiot! I was…falling in love with you, too, but I was so focused on what my mother wanted that I ruined everything! I'm sorry! Will you forgive me?"

"If you'll forgive me," he said roughly. He held out his arms. "God, I missed you."

She flung herself into his embrace. He enfolded her, buried his face in her hair and inhaled the scent of lemon, like the lemon-meringue pie his mom made once in a blue moon.

"This is probably too quick," he whispered, "but will you marry me?"

Rosalind looked up, laughing, although her cheeks were streaked with tears. "It is too soon, but…yes. Oh, yes!"

Her mouth was incredibly sweet. She melted against him, just the way he'd remembered, and after a bit she made that little moaning sound that drove him so crazy.

He had her back up to the wall and was gripping her buttocks to pull her more tightly against him when sanity tapped him on the shoulder and said, *You really want the first time with the woman you love to be like this?*

"No," Craig muttered, and slowly eased

away. Despite the sharp ache in his groin, he reveled in the look on her face: the cloudy eyes, the pink cheeks, the trembling full mouth.

"Are you sure," he said slowly, "you're not going to mind having your mother notch up another success on her matchmaking scoreboard?"

"Mother?" Rosalind looked dazed.

Pleased at his effect on her, Craig said, "Yeah. You know. The woman who raised you."

"Oh." She pressed her hands to her cheeks. "My mother."

"Yeah," he repeated patiently. "Her."

Reality thumped back; he saw it in her eyes. She made a face. "I'll probably mind sometimes. And, yes, that *is* childish."

Ruefully Craig said, "We're all childish where our parents are concerned. Remind me to tell you about the fight I had last week with my dad."

"Really? Oh, Craig, I'm sorry."

"Not that big a deal. It just…made me think."

She bit her lip. "I…I have a lot I should tell you."

He shrugged, kissed her again, but lightly this time. "I'm starved. We can talk over dinner." Then he grinned. "As far as your mother goes, I figure you've just come to your senses. Realized that someday you'll have kids of your own."

She tilted her head to one side. "And?"

"Hey, you'll want them to think Mother knows best. Right?"

A delicious cascade of laughter loosened the last knots inside him.

"In this case," Rosalind said with wrinkled nose, "Mother did know best. And, oh, how it pains me to admit it!"

"MAY I HELP YOU?" Rosalind asked in her best bookstore-owner voice.

A rather sweet-looking man, balding, maybe a few years older than her mother and not a whole lot taller, was scanning the travel section. "No, no," he said. "I'm just an armchair traveler, about to become more. Only, I haven't decided where to go for this first trip. So I thought I'd add to my collection of travel books."

"Do you like pictures or words?"

"Oh, words, by all means."

"Have you read this?" Rosalind reached past him to pull out a book about Greece that her mother had extolled. "I understand this one is excellent." She touched another spine. "This is a good one, too. Not that you'd want to go to Afghanistan right now."

"Ah, but thanks to the printed word, I can go there without endangering myself." He took the book. "Have you read it?"

She explained about her mother's fascination with foreign lands. "She's the one who reads these books. To tell you the truth, I'm very happy in Perry Creek," she admitted. "I'm to be married next month."

He congratulated her and they chatted some more. He asked questions about Rosalind's mother, which she answered willingly. His wife had died of cancer three years before; she was one of the reasons he had never indulged his desire to travel.

"Helen had a delicate stomach. Any kind of spicy food made her ill. And she was rather shy." He smiled. "A very nice woman, but not...adaptable. Adventurous."

He hardly looked like the adventurous type himself, which didn't mean a thing. It wasn't as though he was likely to climb Mt. Everest. Strolling the streets of Rome would probably satisfy him.

Rosalind eventually left him to his browsing. When he finally came to the cash register, he had a stack of books that had her mouth dropping open. "You want *all* of those?"

"It's not as if I don't have plenty at home," he admitted. "But I'm something of an addict."

"The library..." she felt compelled to suggest against her better business instincts.

"Oh, I can afford to indulge myself." He smiled. "I'm an orthodontist."

A respectable profession, plenty of money, and wanderlust. Plus he was single. The idea was born.

Rosalind almost pulled it out by the roots, so to speak. After all, he wasn't her mother's type physically. Mom thought Tom Selleck was handsome. She liked men big, masculine, bold. She had always tended to pick out the salesman type for Rosalind.

On the other hand, Rosalind thought, Mom never had remarried. So maybe—a wicked smile spread across her face even as she began ringing up the books—maybe Mom just didn't know herself. Why, maybe she, Rosalind, could choose a better prospect for Mom than Mom could herself.

Truthfully Mom had probably given up long ago. Rosalind could just imagine it: when her year of mourning had been up, friends had begun presenting potential second husbands. Then, of course, there'd been the gems she'd met at work. Mom had doubtless gone through exactly the same thing *she* had.

"Do you find my profession amusing?" her customer asked stiffly.

"What? Oh, no, no!" she hastened to assure

him. "No, something you said made me think about my mother."

His face relaxed. "She sounds as though we'd have a great deal in common."

"Yes, I was thinking that myself." Rosalind typed in the inventory number for the second book. "In fact," she said diffidently, "my fiancé and I are having Mom over for dinner tonight. I'm sure she'd love to talk about Athens and Beijing, instead of wedding plans. Is there any chance you'd like to join us? Considering your total—" she told him what it was "—I think I owe you a dinner!"

He agreed with what she regarded as promising eagerness and left after she'd set a time and given him directions.

Yes, Rosalind mused, Mom simply hadn't known what she wanted. Mr.... Rosalind glanced at the check, her delight buoyed by more than just the number of zeroes under the amount. *Dr.* Charles Jenkins would be perfect for her mother. She just needed a little help seeing that.

And turnabout *was* fair play. Right?

Dear Reader,

Happy Mother's Day!

When Harlequin asked me to write a story for this anthology, I was delighted; the relationships between parents and children fascinate me. What's more, my mother is my best friend. So what did I choose to write about? The tension between mothers and daughters, and the evolution of that relationship from parent-child to friends. And, boy, do I remember it well! In particular, I focused on that moment when a young woman realizes that becoming like her mother isn't, after all, such a terrible thing.

My own mother read every word even before my editor did. She laughed, critiqued, nagged and encouraged. As every mother should. As I, of course, will do for my daughters.

I only hope that my daughters and I are as lucky as Rosalind and her mother, and as I've been with my mother; I hope that when their growing up is done, we'll be best friends.

And I wish the same for you, with your mother and daughters. After all, only a mother can see right through her daughter. And Mother always knows best. (Dare I say?)

Best wishes,

Janice Kay Johnson

SOUL KITCHEN
Margot Early

I made up rhymes in dark and scary places,
And like a lyre I plucked the tired laces
Of my worn-out shoes, one foot beneath my heart.

—Arthur Rimbaud, "Wandering,"
translated by Paul Schmidt

CHAPTER ONE

Touch Me
Venice Boardwalk

GABE LUCERO heard the sailor ask Dany to come with him around the world.

It happened outside Venice Rollerama, at the boardwalk skate-rental booth, on a sunny April afternoon when the breeze raised whitecaps in Santa Monica Bay. "I talked to Jake," said the sailor, shifting his weight. "Want to come with us? Sail around the world?"

Sound carried on Ocean Front Walk. The rhythm of a reggae band playing near the permanent umbrellas where the homeless gathered. The whisper of in-line skates on concrete. The sales pitch of Wise Man, one of the boardwalk winos, trying to hawk a toy record player he'd found in a Dumpster. The rattle of the tow-chain pulling The Gondolier up its track. Then the hollow screams of passengers as the roller-coaster train eased over the peak and began to drop from eighty-six feet. And the music from the rink's outdoor speakers. The Doors. Almost always. Beyond the boardwalk and the lifeguard stand, waves hit the beach, and Gabe could hear them, too, if he listened.

But none of the sounds of Venice muted the words spoken by a man twenty feet away at the skate-rental booth.

Gabe leaned on a stepladder, hot-gluing missing beads to the mosaic that arched around the double doors to the rink. The doors led into the land beneath the roller coaster, into the oldest rink on the coast, Venice Rollerama—or, as the perennially altered sign proclaimed, "Venice IS Rollerama."

Want to come with us?

He had to look down and over at them.

She had left the booth and was hugging the guy's neck, kissing him. Making out with him.

Turning to sit on top of the ladder, Gabe watched. He liked to bend over women the way that guy was dipping his head over Dany's. He liked to feel a woman's tongue. He saw Dany's bourbon eyes in his mind and heard her clear voice with poetry on her lips, words as unsubtle as gunfire. The April breeze stopped, and his blood ran. Repositioning his arm that held the glue gun disguised the problem. When Dany stopped kissing the guy, when her eyes suddenly saw *him*, Gabe said, "That's disgusting. Why don't you kids take it somewhere else?"

The sailor had his arm around her.

Keale. That was his name. Keale Johnson, from the big island. Hawaii. He was staying at the marina, building a ship in a boatyard behind the racetrack. Dany was down there a lot.

Dany was leaving Venice with Keale, in that ship, on that trip around the world; Gabe had heard it first.

He returned to the mosaic, fitting a bright yellow bead into a *t*. Psychedelic lettering formed the words "There are things known and things unknown, and in between are the doors. —Jim Morrison, 1943-1971." The owner of the rink, Dany's mother, had commissioned the mosaic three years earlier and asked for a touch-up this year. Some beads had been stolen; others had been knocked off.

There was a low wolf whistle from the boardwalk, and Pooch, 1997 Queen of Venice Beach, skated past, wagging his fingers at Gabe.

Gabe smiled tolerantly and faced the beadwork again.

Want to come with us? Sail around the world...

He could have Dany himself, like picking a dandelion. But dandelions had a way of taking over. Dany was a weed—that strong, that wild, that pervasive. You didn't let her tongue in your mouth unless you wanted her to spread inside you.

Gabe preferred annuals. Polite, inoffensive pansies and zinnias who respected borders and never popped up uninvited, season after season.

There was a creaking from nearby. He wasn't the only painter on Ocean Front Walk today. Workmen were whitewashing the timber frame of The Gondolier, the roller coaster. Painters worked high on platforms dangling from cables above Rollerama.

The train trundled by, whipping around a curve, passengers screaming like a choir's single note.

Gabe leaned into his work. Focused.

HOLLOW. DANY FELT HOLLOW. Flat.

This was the chance she'd been waiting for, to get out of Venice and find the kind of life she wanted, the kind of life any thirty-one-year-old Venetian spinster should want. A wonderful man inviting her to sail around the world. It should have been an ecstatic moment, and she'd known how to react, and she'd behaved that way, throwing her arms around Keale.

The Gondolier rumbled past over her head with a deafening roar and the smell of electricity, diesel fuel and hot metal.

When it had passed, Keale said, "Want a coffee?"

Common Grounds, the café, was two doors down, just beyond Mr. Dark's Tattoo Parlor.

"Thanks."

He let her go and didn't ask what kind of coffee she wanted because he knew. His blond head and tall body merged with the traffic on Ocean Front Walk. He was blue-eyed and bearded and perpetually suntanned and sexy, and he was also trouble. Dany knew he'd managed to get fired by the National Park Service. He'd caught poachers in Hawaii Volcanoes National Park and had split the pig with them, hosted a luau at park-service housing. She'd gathered he didn't hold jobs long. But now he was shipbuilding, and he could take her away from Venice.

This time she was going.

She watched Gabe glue another bead into the mosaic over the doors. On the nearest wall was a mural of The Doors' first album cover, and across that was a red spray-painted scrawl: "JIM MORRISON SLEPT HERE." Every year anonymous hands retouched it. Gabe swore he wasn't the one who did it—though he'd written it the first time, long before he'd painted the mural. Gabe painted and beaded murals all over Venice. He'd been a public defender until four years ago, when repeated absences from work had cost him his job. The reason wasn't flakiness. It was heart, a loyalty and love that sweated from his pores and drove his every action—devotion to his brother and sisters. When they cried out, he was there, to help deal with the death of a friend, a gun at school, a freak-out in the vice principal's office. He never let them down.

It was a good quality in a man. Gabe was dependable.

Unfortunately he was also untouchable, like fire. Dany had never dared thrust her hands into the flame. Gabe could melt her, bind her to this place, the way touching another kind of fire had bound her mother here in April 1966.

Anyhow, he had never shown interest in Dany. They'd been friends for more than twenty years, yet had never so much as held hands in the skating rink. He'd never let his arm brush her shoulder or his thigh touch hers as they sat side by side while the Gondolier shot down the big drop, rumbling, rattling, shaking their bones. He'd never touched her as they floated on surfboards near Redondo or Hermosa Beach. Even dancing with her at street parties on Ocean Front Walk, even when she was staggering drunk enough to run off with Wise Man, Gabe had never touched her.

She doubted it was because *he* feared getting burned.

At twenty-one she had married another man, moved to Laguna Beach. By twenty-four she had alienated her husband and his family. At twenty-six she'd wound up back in Venice, and in the five years since she'd taken lovers—the kind you could get in Venice—and Gabe had never touched her.

The skate booth provided shade while she waited for Keale to bring her double cappuccino. She wandered in poetry and song, and she jotted down lines, toying with them in a spiral notebook.

The mast holds when the wind blows.
Who wants to be the mast?
Even the mast bends or breaks.
Without bending, I'd be breaking.
No one knows
how the mast holds when the wind blows.

Three adolescent girls licked ice-cream cones on the beach outside Mr. Dark's Tattoo Parlor. They showed up every day, in miniskirts and stretch tank tops, to watch Gabe glue beads to the door arch, touching up the mosaic. They were not art lovers, unless you called Gabe art.

Dany checked her watch. All the rental skates had to be turned in by five-thirty. Rollerama never opened till sunset. Then skaters and people who wanted to see the bead murals inside paid their four dollars and poured inside. Janis Joplin gave you a piece of her heart, and Grace Slick wanted somebody to love. The Doors loved you two times—no, a million times. Every night was Doors Night at Rollerama and in the life of Dandelion Morrison Wilde.

As Gabe stepped down off the ladder and squinted at the mosaic, Dany tried not to stare. His black hair dragged below his shoulders. He was long and lean and muscular. He had made it to adulthood in a bad neighborhood a half mile from the beach. His mother was a full-time alcoholic and junkie who supported her children and her habits any way she could. His father had been a Caribbean sea snake with a penchant for young boys. His oldest sister had eaten a bottle of Tylenol when Gabe was nineteen.

Now his three surviving half siblings came in and out of Gabe's apartment with the freedom of cockroaches, and he would never leave L.A. until they were grown, and maybe not then.

His arms always drew Dany's eyes. He was built as a man should be. She'd seen him in suits and ties when he worked for the county. Since he'd been fired, a slender gold hoop had appeared in his left ear, and now he lived in loose tank tops and various pairs of baggy shorts, athletic socks and running shoes.

The bending mast has stays
and what are mine
and why not fall
and wet the sail in the sea
and drift until I drown?

He picked up a plastic mug she knew held a cappuccino from Common Grounds. Shutting the notebook, locking away the personal and private, Dany slipped out of the skate-rental booth to straighten the crocheted bikinis hanging on hooks from the edges of the booth. They were made by women in Bali, and Dany bought them from her mother's lover, who made annual runs to the South Pacific and beyond; she sold them for sixty dollars each. It was just one of many ways she fed her Escape Account.

Now that hoarded money would come in handy. Keale was taking her away, and she tried to imagine it, tried to imagine really leaving this place, her mother's place, a discarded era of protests and assassinations, the renaissance of a disturbed world. Keale would fish for their dinner, and she would cook it, and they would become lovers. He had poetry in his soul, and it was the uncomplicated kind.

He was about twenty IQ points less than what she wanted, but beggars couldn't be choosers.

"That was pretty romantic, Dany. Going to sail away with him?"

Gabe was emptying the dregs of his plastic mug onto the concrete, dribbling it over spots of dried chewing gum. He squinted up at the two platforms dangling alongside The Gondolier. The painters sat on one, eating. A man waved down at them, and Gabe waved back. Wooden saw-horses blocked off the area below the platforms, and Dany sat on one of them and tore at a loose thread on her baggy cutoffs.

"Yes, I am." The shadow of her hair on the concrete was the shape of a mop. Just the day before, she'd gotten new blond foil highlights. They were the only thing that stopped her from looking just a little too much like the dark-eyed, staring, hollow-cheeked man in the mural behind her. She thought maybe Keale had asked her to go with him because of her new hair color.

"I await this with interest. I think he'll enjoy having you along."

She glared. "He'll love it."

"Like I said." Gabe changed the subject. "Playing tonight?" Besides helping her mother

with the rink, Dany waited tables at the Whole
Earth Café and played music at Common
Grounds and other coffeehouses and bars in Ven-
ice.

Before she could nod or shake her head, someone shouted and Gabe glanced up.

His hand locked on her arm like a burning
band and yanked her staggering over the hot
boardwalk. She slammed against the salty skin of
a body builder, almost killed an in-line skater,
tripped and landed against a worn cotton tank
top, against smooth dark olive skin, her nose
against the underside of his jaw, her lips smashed
on his throat. Touching... Oh, touching.

Touching Gabe.

A violent clanging bang shook the concrete as
the platform hit, and white paint geysered up like
an explosion, spraying Jim Morrison's face, blot-
ting out the hollow cheeks but not clouding the
burning brown eyes. Eyes like Dany's.

A tingling heat singed her skin. The hands on
her bare arms were disembodied, hands she
knew. Holding for a long time.

He's touching me.

He wasn't in a hurry to let go, either. Maybe
he didn't know what he was doing to her. Maybe
he'd never known.

He was behind her. She couldn't see his face,

but when he said, "Hi," she knew what he meant, the only thing he could mean.

He'd just acknowledged her as a woman. As far as Dany knew, that had never happened before. Or perhaps this was the first time he'd wanted to reveal it. But if so, why?

Swallowing, she eased away.

I imagined all that.

Only the crashed platform was real. No one had been on it.

Thanks to Gabe, no one was under it.

"Looks like a lawsuit," said a voice behind them, and there was the giant who had been a sometime shadow in Dany's life, her mother's paramour, Jake Donahue.

The other platform cranked slowly down to the ground while Dany hurried behind the skate-rental booth. She nodded to Jake and found Gabe's eyes.

She had imagined nothing.

Jake's hair, a thick froth of auburn mixed with gray, showered all the way to his waist. An elastic gathered the mass in a loose ponytail. He fished for a cigarette from a pack in the pocket of his T-shirt and wandered to the fallen platform to examine it before he cast glances between Dany and Gabe.

Dany found things to straighten behind the counter. *Great time for Jake to show up.* Keale

Johnson was working with Jake. The Blade Institute, a marine-research institute out of Santa
Barbara, was sponsoring the trip. Since Jake was
supervising the project, Keale had asked Jake if
Dany could circumnavigate the globe with them.

Jake had known both her and Gabe since they
were kids. *Okay, so he saw us looking at each
other. So what?*

A single touch. A single word.

But minutes later, when she spotted Keale returning with her coffee, Dany could still feel
where Gabe had touched her, where his hands
had grasped her arms. She wondered if it would
be like a sunburn, if it would start to hurt that
night, and she thought it would.

KEALE WALKED HER down to The Canal that
night. She was playing in the bar, a one-woman
band with a Gibson 160-E and her own repertoire. She played as Dandelion Wilde and never
wasted an opportunity to remind her mother that
Jim Morrison hadn't played an instrument. Jenny
always said, *He was a poet,* scoring the last point
because Dany was a poet, too. Escape held no
luster beside the integrity of art, of reaching for
the stars, of clinging to sincerity. On the drunken
nights, she was as proud as Jenny that Jim Morrison had quit music lessons when he was still a
child.

"Want to come out to the marina tonight?" Keale asked.

He slept on Jake's Chinese junk, the *Lien Hua*, down at Marina del Rey.

"Um..." *You're leaving this time, Dany. You're really going, really getting out of here, and you'll be stronger and better and happier for doing it.*

They passed an old woman—Miss Buffy—looting garbage cans. Dany started to greet her, till another sight stilled her tongue. Ginger and Celeste. Hunting the same turf. Ginger saw Dany and immediately pretended she'd just been passing through the alley. She grabbed her three-year-old daughter's hand and said, "Let's go, honey."

Dany had waited on Ginger and little Celeste at the Whole Earth Café when they came in and ordered a single cup of coffee so they could use the clean rest rooms. Ginger's was a story Dany didn't know. She just knew that the blonde had a pretty smile when she looked at her daughter. And that they bathed in the boardwalk showers every day.

She'd never seen them digging through trash before.

Before she could think what to do, they were gone, out of sight around the corner. And Dany had to get to work.

Not my problem. It was the mantra of Venice; it had to be, or you lost your mind.

Keale cleared his throat, and he had seen them, too. "You were saying."

She remembered what she had to explain. The subject had lost urgency. "I didn't mean you to read anything into that kiss."

What passed for silence in Venice fell between them.

"That would be presumptuous of me. You only shoved your tongue down my throat. Which I enjoyed, by the way."

She granted him a few more IQ points. *She* was the fool, for caring that Gabe Lucero had touched her, however briefly. "My name is Dandelion Morrison Wilde, and I'm an alcoholic."

"Jake told me."

Keale Johnson was a good guy, who had invited her to sail around the world with him. This was her chance to fall in love with someone more respectable than the guy on the third floor of Gabe's building—Kevin Who Keeps Snakes—or Howie the Body Builder or Mike the Lifeguard, whose only real drawback, if you saw it that way, was his bisexuality. The Men of Venice.

Keale cracked a smile as they passed the Whole Earth Café. "Jake thinks it's genetic." Her alcoholism.

That wasn't remotely funny.

They'd reached The Canal, and Dany paused. With the hand that wasn't holding her guitar case, she touched Keale's bearded jaw. "I'll go on your sailing ship. But let's not risk our minds, all right? I'm much too mean for you."

His sea-colored eyes became interesting. "No one's ever said that to me before."

KEALE STAYED through her first set, then left. Everyone was watching a baseball game, but Dany demanded their eyes and ears.

> We settle for lies.
> We settle for less
> until there's nothing left to lose.

She chanted the words between chords, between pulses of water music.

> Childhood dreams and fairy-tale frogs,
> I swam the moat,
> and the prince escaped
> anyhow.

She played and sang till two o'clock, bar time, then walked home alone, afraid of nothing. If anyone touched her guitar, she would kill him.

There were two ways into the rink—the alley and the front doors. Drunks owned the alley tonight, weaving, falling, profane and pushy, alien even to each other. No Ginger and Celeste. *They must have a good place to sleep.*

On the boardwalk side of the rink, Wise Man, in his pink plastic raincoat, ducked into the recessed doorway beneath Gabe's bead mosaic to take a leak.

Dany stepped back, into the shadow of the Tilt-A-Whirl, and waited for him to finish and go away.

At her back, beyond the boardwalk wall, the ocean swayed, casting its breaths on the shore. Though the looming neon sign for The Gondolier—which pictured a wild Italian canal driver in a cockeyed hat—still burned over the boardwalk, the roller coaster itself was dark, skeletal, one train frozen on the tracks like a caterpillar caught out in winter.

Wise Man zipped up and swaggered off, past Mr. Dark's Tattoo Parlor, past the Common Grounds Café, toward the permanent umbrellas and benches crowded up against the boardwalk wall—the gathering place for the homeless, the drunks and the junkies of Venice Beach. As Wise Man joined the rough dark group clustered in the night shadows, a woman bellowed righteous obscenities. Another screamed back.

Ginger wouldn't be there. She was different.

In the night a figure stepped out onto a balcony

of the apartment building across from the umbrellas. He was shirtless, lean and long, and Dany
counted balconies and finally waved. He rested
his hands on the railing, and the wind from the
sea blew his hair, black as raven's wings in the
night. She thought he watched her, but he didn't
return her wave, and the distance between them
was three floors and hundreds of yards of desire,
all hers.

That ''Hi'' had meant nothing. She sang
softly, to herself.

Childhood dreams and fairy-tale frogs,
I swam the moat,
and the prince escaped
anyhow.

As Dany picked up her guitar case and crossed
the boardwalk, an in-line skater emerged from
the shadows, flying on concrete. She couldn't
have dodged him if she'd wanted to, but the
phantom shape easily curved around her, his
headphones blaring, before he vanished in the
night.

The doorway reeked. Scooter, the skate repairman, hosed down the pavement each morning, bitching every time. As Dany thrust her key
into the dead bolt, careful to touch nothing, foot-

steps kissed her heels, and she half spun from the door.

"Hey, bitch." It was one of the women from the umbrellas. Rhonda, with filthy blond dreadlocks, skinned-knee jeans, bare feet and tracks on her bony arms glinting red under that neon gondolier. A junkie. Dany knew them all, their names and their habits and some of their stories, because they were there every day, just like the ocean. Rhonda swayed, clutching a bottle in a paper sack. "Hey, bitch, you tell 'em Rhonda said so. You tell 'em that."

"Sure."

"Don't mess with Rhonda. You hear?"

The key turned, and the door gave, and Dany sensed her mother's pit bulls behind it.

She used the bottom of one high-top sneaker to push the door open enough that she could get in without touching anything.

"That bitch wanted my man! Nobody messes with Rhonda. You tell 'em Rhonda said so."

"Okay. Good night, Rhonda." Dany withdrew her key, slipped inside, into a darkness colored by the pinball machines and video games in the corner near the refreshment stand. The row of round lights, the snack bar's all-night circus lights, gave off a phosphorescent gleam, animating the nearest pictures on the walls, the bead murals that brought tourists and skaters off the boardwalk and into Rollerama.

Jimi Hendrix.

Bob Dylan.

Janis Joplin with the word "pearl" scripted beneath her...

She could smell the fresh popcorn from the session earlier that night. Her mother always left a key in the lock on the inside, and Dany turned it now, securing Rollerama. As she did, something growled from feet away.

Shit. "Hi, Bingo." Pit bulls were the finest dogs in the world, with the single exception of her mother's newest pound puppy, selected by Scooter, like Jenny's other dogs. "Cool it, all right?"

The door beside the skate shop opened a crack, and light sprang over the snack bar and into the rink, a long tunnel of light.

"Dandelion?"

The growl again. Dany heard saliva puddling on the floor.

"Bingo, cool it," said the same voice.

Dany slowly turned, and there was Jenny, her curly long hair spinning down past her shoulders, hazy in rainbow fog from the games. The lights seemed to shine through her long gauzy skirt, too, lighting the edges of her bare legs. Patchouli and cigarette smoke followed her like the scent of a flower's petals. It was hard to believe Jenny was fifty, until you took in the fact that she'd never heard of Alanis Morissette or even Madonna.

"Hi, Mom."

Dogs snuffled at Dany's feet, sniffing her jeans and sneakers.

As Jenny double-checked the door, Dany suggested, "Do you think an electronic alarm system would keep them from using our doorway as a toilet?"

Jenny just looked at her, and Dany reflected that her mother had never *seen* a vagrant urinating in the rink doorway—or a three-year-old and her mother dining from trash cans—unless it had happened before July 7, 1971, the day the world had learned Jim Morrison was dead and the day Jenny had decided never to leave the rink building again.

"How did it go?" said Jenny.

Playing at The Canal. Did her mother hope Dany was on her way to a poet's immortality? That someday she would tell the world she was Jim Morrison's daughter?

Not a chance. She lived in Venice, but other than that she wasn't crazy.

"Fine." *I'm going away, Mom. This time I'm really going and I'm not coming back.*

She couldn't say it at two in the morning.

When she said it, tomorrow, she knew what would happen. Jenny wouldn't so much as look sorry. Instead, she would reach for her cigarettes. Smoke and study Dany and finally encourage her, the way you encouraged a friend who had more problems than you could fix.

Talking around each other. Living in shaky peace until it became too much, until it exploded some morning or night and Dany said the things she really felt and Jenny just looked at her, like, *What do you want me to do about it?* Just looked at her, like, *And then?*

Dany knew what to do then. There was always a certain route to joy. A quick and liquid route.

Yeah, you try that, and you'll blow this chance, too. You have to keep it together this time. She couldn't let the mast bend so far, couldn't let the sail fall in the water.

This time would be different.

It had to be.

IN THE APARTMENT, in the kitchen with its bead murals—the one over the sink that read "SOUL KITCHEN"—the other over the stove of *him*— Dany stood motionless, imagining the corner of her closet where she stashed a bottle of Jack Daniel's, for emergencies. Jenny had never been a drinker, and she didn't approve of her thirty-one-year-old daughter drinking. But Jenny had turned in, and her daughter always did as she wanted, anyway.

This was a good night for a drink. Dany could still feel where Gabe had touched her. It was like a sunburn, as she'd thought it might be.

Don't do it.

She could stop after one drink. She possessed the willpower. Each drink was a choice, and she could stop.

She often didn't stop, but she could if she wanted.

She could let the mast bend just a little; if it didn't, surely it would break. Surely *she* would.

Irritated, she let her eyes hunt out the details of the apartment's front room——the kitchen blending into a small living room. Incense burner on the coffee table. Albums stacked against the edge of the couch. A black-and-white signed photo of Jim Morrison. Glass doors opening onto a private deck, an impenetrable square where her mother waited for the sun.

She peered down the hall. Light shone beneath Jenny's door, then went out.

Dany made her way to her room. Leaving on a ship with Keale Johnson was a good reason not to drink. But tonight it wasn't good enough. She carried the bottle back to the kitchen and poured herself a shot in a glass supposedly purloined from the Whiskey à Go Go in 1966. Maybe *he* had touched this glass. One shot. Then another. Then another. *Oh, yes. Better.* She tried to blot out what she'd witnessed earlier on the way to The Canal. Ginger and her baby.

I have to get out of Venice. She was wasting her life. She'd never meet a good man here, never get married and have kids. She would just get old. Keale Johnson was her last hope.

The bead mural gazed with starry brilliance, bigger than life. "Well," she said to him and she took the bottle and her notebook out onto the enclosed deck, the tiny area surrounded by board-and-batten fence and chain-link that reached up eight feet farther. She climbed onto the roof, beneath The Gondolier. The night rocked with the ocean. Shapes shifted in the shadows, and she peered at each one for a long time before deciding she was alone.

Clutching the bottle, paper and pen, she teetered over to where she could see the loading platform for the roller coaster, where the trains took on their passengers. A guardrail protected the people in line from falling to the concrete eight feet below, though eight feet was not a long way to fall.

Just far enough to die from a fall.

Dany drank, and the whiskey made her happy. It wouldn't last—tomorrow's grief was a storm just offshore—but tomorrow was illusion, tonight real, her finest possession. *I love all my nows. I live all my vows.*

Hands closed on her shoulders.

She shuddered and stumbled, and he caught her as she swayed at the edge of the roof, above the loading platform. Jack Daniel's sloshed on her denim jacket and cropped sweater. "Shit!"

Touching her. Twice in twenty-four hours.

"Be glad it's not someone who wants to hurt you."

"Like you care." *You didn't wave.* From his balcony.

"What are you doing?"

"Having an identity crisis. As long as I'm not too far from the umbrellas, I know who I am. As long as I'm not too far from the artwork of my talented friend, Gabe Lucero. His older stuff, that is." Meeting his eyes, she sucked on the bottle. Swallowed. He hadn't put on a shirt, and she said, "Boy, I bet Pooch is wishing for *you*." Incautious. She'd never wanted him to guess how she felt.

Oh, but she wanted that "Hi" to have meant something.

Gabe grabbed the front of her jacket as she took a step backward, almost off the roof. He moved her away from the edge and released her.

She sat on the roof, legs swinging in space, and set her writing tools beside her. This time

Gabe didn't interfere, and when he saw the bottle go to her lips, he shut off the part of him that wanted her to stop, that wanted her sober. The part that came from wishing time after time that another woman in his life would not take that drink. *Why did you come out here tonight, Gabe?*

A hard-on from a stepladder. Another when he'd grabbed her as the platform fell. A man asking her to sail away, around the world.

He could keep his distance, driven off by her scent. He hated the smell of whiskey as much as he hated all the cheaper fixes, the cheapest a drunk could find. It should have killed his lust, and someday it would.

"Why are you drinking?"

Dany considered. She was going away. She really was. Why not tell him? "I *burn* for you, and you touched me today for the first time ever. I'm drinking to forget, so don't worry. I will forget, and then I'm getting out of here with Brad Pitt's little-known identical twin, Keale Johnson." There. She'd said it.

Overhead, The Gondolier cast long shadows. The shadows had always been there, through all the years Gabe Lucero had never even kissed her.

Drunk, she tried to remember what he had asked, *if* he had asked something.

"What's your mother going to do?"

"Maybe she'll step outside and smell the beach tar." Dany scooted along the roof edge until she could see the loading platform of The Gondolier. Standing, Gabe could see it well. Some memories were clear as film clips, even when you didn't want them to be.

For him, one of those memories was of a night he and Dany had shared when they were just kids, eleven and twelve. He never drank to forget. Neither did she. There was no why to Dany. Only *why not?*

He wanted nothing to do with her.

He wanted her to get on that ship and go, and there was only one problem.

I burn for you.

She shouldn't have said that—unless she wanted…this.

He crouched beside her, took the bottle and set it away, and her eyes became large, going from his face to his hands. Gabe watched his hands, too, watched them hold her shoulders and ease her onto her back at the edge of the roof beneath the roller coaster.

"That trick you were doing with your tongue earlier today."

She couldn't quite breathe. Only say one word. "Yes."

"I want to try something. Let's call it an experiment."

She'd get burned. But it was much too late. His hands held her down against the roof, and his leg pressed between hers, jeans rubbing, thigh and knee seducing. A cry in her said, *stop, stop, stop,* but another part wanted to know much more. Long fingers threaded in her hair.

Her mind swam against his, the way two people could do when they'd spent childhood playing games together, pretending they were characters in a Ray Bradbury novel, navigating Cooger and Dark's Pandemonium Shadow Show. When they knew that evil carnival for life.

His mouth fell warm on hers. His tongue stole her spirit, though she only noticed later. He clasped her head, as though he loved her mind, too. His eyelashes were beautiful, swimming in ocean-pulsing darkness beside her eye.

They stopped kissing, and his head was against hers.

"I'm going to burn up." She'd swum the moat, and she'd caught him. This was what it was like. This was what she wanted most. "I always knew if you touched me I would catch fire."

"Too late."

"I won't stay. I won't spend the rest of my life listening to the Doors and dealing with a mother who's never seen an automated teller." *I won't even stay for you, because I know this is just a moment. I've never deserved more or I would have it now.*

"I don't care if you stay or not. As long as you don't go now." He smiled, his respect for her miserly and vicious.

He didn't seduce her, and even the condom he had with him was an insult. It was all very deliberate, getting only as much clothing off as necessary, thrusting inside her with the creaking frame of The Gondolier above and the neon light from the sign casting one long pulse of color over them.

Dany bit her lip at the violence, at how difficult it was, at how he didn't come into her in one thrust but in many, and she wanted it just that way, like a painful life in which your mother insisted that your father was a dead rock star, a lost poet, one of the immortals. Then the pain was gone, there was just roughness of tar paper and Gabe inside her, fire, this part of his body and part of his soul that she had never known and still did not. She cried out softly, and he found her mouth, and his tongue stole the rest of her.

"Please." *Help. I love...* Her eyes shut. *Please. Forever.*

"I can lick you, too. Have you ever imagined me licking you? I think you have."

No, no. No. "Yes." Licked by fire.

"Ask me, and I will."

"Forget it. I'm not going to beg you." Pressing closer, opening more. *Gabe. Dammit, Gabe, why did I have to learn what this is like?*

She would die of the knowledge, in increments, in hours and days of wanting.

He moved. Slowly. Friction could ignite tinder.

"I'll never get over this," she said.

"Too bad."

"Stop." Moaning. The roof shivered, and she saw the roller-coaster track spiraling into the ocean mist and water sky. He shook and burned over her like a flash fire.

When the last flames died, she smelled tar. The roof had scraped her butt.

He didn't help her dress. They dressed alone like two separate beings with a shared history of shame. She didn't wonder what it would be like to sleep in his arms, because there couldn't be that kind of future for them. It had to be sex under a roller coaster, love on rooftops. Fire could travel fast and burn out, and the only tomorrow on Venice Beach slept on the dirty benches beneath the umbrellas.

She finished buttoning her jeans, gathered up her unwritten poems and glared at him under The

Gondolier's pink-and-green light. "I'm leaving. I *am* going now."

He bent over, picked up the bottle of Jack Daniel's and handed it to her.

"Then don't forget this."

It's harder than it looks
To stand still for days
Only hours at a time
Utterly immobile
Thinking of motion
Of flight
Of dancing

Of even falling
Just for kicks

But still standing
Still

—Dandelion Wilde, "Waitress"

CHAPTER TWO

Take It As It Comes

SHE COULDN'T SLEEP. She had been used by the man she'd always wanted more than any other. She had known he didn't love her, and she had pretended that he might. To cry would be to forfeit her pride—the only thing she hadn't given him. She wrote poetry instead.

It stopped her from putting on skates and heading for the marina to see Keale. She stopped herself from finishing the bottle of Jack Daniel's. She could write drunk, of course. But she poured out the whiskey because she knew she had to get sober and stay sober if she wanted to leave on that schooner.

She wanted to leave very badly.

In the morning she wasn't hungover, just tired. Before dawn, she found Jenny feeding the dogs on the deck, enclosed by the high fence, the fence that hid Ocean Front Walk and the alley and any sign of the year 1998.

It wasn't light yet, and Jenny squinted at her while Doris, John and Bingo went after their food, tails wagging. "Were you on the roof last night?"

"For a while."

Jenny nodded as though she knew everything.

Jake was in town. He didn't spend every night with her mother at the rink, but he stayed often. "Did Jake sleep over last night?"

"He's inside. Why?"

"No reason." Except that Jake had seen the looks between her and Gabe yesterday, and sometimes Jake saw other things you didn't expect. *Forget it.*

She had to go to work. Had to give two weeks' notice at the café, in fact, because the schooner was that close to being in the water. Tucking her bathrobe around herself, she tossed back her hair and said, "Mom, did Jake tell you I'm going with them?"

"He said Keale had asked if you could go." *And now,* her eyes said, *I see you are going.*

Stepping around the dogs, Jenny headed back into the rink apartment, and Dany followed, escaping the alley smells. Garbage and urine and vomit. *I'm leaving this place forever.*

We settle for lies.
We settle for less,
till there's nothing left to lose.

The apartment seemed particularly dark, the flicker of Jenny's lighter very bright.

Dany was glad her mother had given up "experimenting with drugs," even if she hadn't given up on anything else to do with the sixties. She'd tuned in, turned on and dropped out, all right. And every word of advice she'd ever given her daughter was colored through the filter of her religion, which was that twentieth-century renaissance.

"You'll have to rely on Scooter, I guess." Dany tried to imagine her mother getting along with only the skate repairman to shop for her groceries, to bring her used books and walk the dogs. Of course, that was how it had been when Dany was married and living in Laguna Beach with Brett Hetherington of the sunscreen Hetheringtons—the people who made waterproof AmFib, with a sun-protection factor of eighty.

Jenny would get along, as she had in the past.

And she wouldn't rely on Scooter. Dany knew who had come through in the past for her mother, the same way he came through for the old people in the apartment building he managed. Gabe.

In her kimono, a gift from Jake, Jenny crossed the small living room to the stereo. An album rested on the turntable, and she switched on the console and set the needle on the record.

Waiting for the Sun. It opened with ''Hello, I Love You.'' Dany longed to drag the needle across the album and turn on the CD player, instead—the Indigo Girls, Nirvana, Shawn Colvin, The Minutemen. Even the Bee Gees would seem modern.

''Do you want to talk about it?'' she asked her mother, competing with *his* voice.

Hello, I do not love you, and I can't stand this lie, this lie we live.

Jenny turned, drew on her cigarette and exhaled. With her slender body and her long hair, she still resembled the girl she must have been at nineteen. Pretty and Venice savvy. "What's to discuss?"

"Will you eat? Or will you live on cigarettes and Pepsi?" *I wasn't going to ask these questions. I wasn't going to care.*

"Dandelion, I'm a grown woman. Don't worry about me." Thoughtfully she added, "Keale's a nice guy. Going with them might be just what you need."

"I don't *need* anything." *I speak with music and words. I am the daughter of an unknown father.* She ached, tight, her mouth tensed and ready to let loose a shocking stream of rhetoric, proclaiming her dark completeness.

Jenny laughed, low and husky. She had a wonderful voice, a wonderful voice saying, "I didn't mean anything, Dany. If you want the truth, I *don't* think that sailing around the world is something you need. I think everything you need is right inside you."

How had this become a conversation about her? She was trying to make sure her mother would be all right in her absence.

But Jenny was confident, and Dany knew her mother really would be fine when she left. She's always known it.

Nothing was stopping her from going.

Nothing stood in her way.

Except that going would be less. Settling for less, again.

"You know, Mom, I wouldn't have to go if you'd just admit one thing, one thing so I don't have to spend my life insane. The AmFib king was never even a prince, but it's miraculous that I found even *one* man crazy enough to spend his life with a woman whose mother listed Jim Morrison as the father on her birth certificate."

"I've told you I didn't have the money for a paternity suit. It seemed like an easy solution, and it was."

Dany wanted to throw something. "I am *not* his daughter! That would be a joke, except it's not funny. It's awful. It's embarrassing."

Her mother was giving her that look again, the look that meant, *What do you want me to do about it?*

Tightening the belt on her bathrobe, Dany headed over the doggy carpet and down the hall, crashing into Jake Donahue. She'd forgotten he was around.

He flattened against the wall, letting her pass, and Dany said, "You're part of it. You're culpable."

"You're wrong."

She wanted to kill him and her mother both— Jenny for the things she'd done, Jake for understanding why she'd done them, for sharing the way Jenny saw the world.

HER UNIFORM for the Whole Earth Café was brown, a real waitress uniform, a vintage look that was supposed to give the café some kind of retro authenticity. The uniform was polyester, and she hated it, and as she dressed she reminded herself that she was as good as gone. The dogs followed her from the apartment to the rink and to the doors. Scooter hadn't yet arrived as Dany let herself outside.

April sunshine almost blinded her with its soft glow. She liked Venice best in the morning, when the low sun bounced light off the water and dyed the foam pink, and the boardwalk almost seemed clean. Immobile figures sprawled on benches beneath the umbrellas like fallen party decorations. The breeze lifted a lock of hair, and its owner, man or woman, never stirred. Miss Buffy wandered along the boardwalk wall, her belongings amassed in a supermarket shopping cart.

"Hello, Miss Buffy."

"Good day, good day," answered Miss Buffy.

Dany scanned the beach and boardwalk. No Ginger and Celeste.

Where did they sleep? Had Celeste cried herself to sleep, hungry? Once Dany had given the baby—she thought of her that way—a stuffed dog from one of the vending machines in the rink. While Celeste giggled and put it in her mouth, Ginger had smiled warily.

The Tilt-A-Whirl, the carousel, the Tarantula, stretched their black shadows westward. Jack from Mr. Dark's Tattoo Parlor swept the board-walk in front of his window, getting up some broken glass. He owned the Tilt-A-Whirl and the Tarantula, and he wanted The Gondolier, which was owned by a movie producer who hadn't yet figured out how to turn Venice Beach into family entertainment.

The street vendors and peddlers were already setting up for another day of commerce. Gabe slouched on the steps of his building in torn gym shorts. He'd been in the water already and was drinking coffee.

Dany looked at him and shoved her middle finger up through her bangs.

He grinned. "You say when."

His reply, like her gesture, tarnished the beauty of her feelings, the sheer vibrance of the pain of love and of being alive.

As though he felt it, too, his expression changed, and when he got up from the steps her heart pounded. In her uniform, she was already past her prime, a woman who would grow old waiting tables at Venice Beach, complaining about the high crime rate, wishing for a husband and three kids, everything she'd blown when she was younger and prettier.

Everything she'd blown because she couldn't have them the way she wanted, which was with Gabe.

"Dandelion."

A drop of salt water from his hair landed on her forearm.

She kept walking.

"What did I do?"

She stopped. She should deal with him, get it over with. Into his dark eyes, she enunciated clearly, telling him exactly what he'd done.

"I liked it," he admitted. "So did you."

"I'm sensitive. You took advantage of me."
And I'm in love with you.

She'd need a whole case of Jack Daniel's to be that honest. Anyway, she wasn't doomed to be a Venice waitress till she died in front of the TV after another day on her feet. She was going away. She was going to sail around the world with Keale Johnson.

She met Gabe's eyes. "It didn't happen. All right?"

"I beg your pardon?"

"I want to forget about it. Let's just say it didn't happen."

"Hey, mon. Hey, queen of the rink." It was Wise Man, coming past, ready to interrupt.

"Hi, Wise Man." Gabe never took his eyes from Dany's face.

The homeless man said, "Uh-oh, shouldn't have done it."

Dany growled, "Stay out of it."

Wise Man walked on, laughing. "Have it your way, queen of the rink."

Gabe blocked her path, and his arms were rippling strong, his shoulders touchable, his skin intoxicating.

"What is it?" Dany demanded. "That I'm suddenly blond?"

"No."

His hands were in her hair, there on the boardwalk, his mouth against hers. Kissing Gabe, first thing in the morning, on Ocean Front Walk, like a declaration of love—or war. *I'm going to get left in a big way. Dammit, he's going to break my heart.*

His tongue against hers was gentle, not like the night before.

It was tempting to flirt, to say, *I'd almost think you don't want me to go.*

The pretense of lightness was despicable to her.

It was spring and morning, and the ocean was just yards away, and it was in his hair, too. A life squandered on Venice Beach looked sweet. The carnival had just come to town, and it was brand-new and exciting, and she wanted to ride the roller coaster and feel her stomach lift out of her body on the big drop.

The carnival was Gabe Lucero's eyes, and he was The Gondolier.

"Not only did it happen—" he smiled down at her "—it's going to happen again."

This was what it meant to feel her heart race. The warmth and heat and melting of love. She hated it. She would sail away from it, with bent mast.

He said, "I'll see you when you get off. I'm working on Mr. Dark's."

The Tattoo Parlor. Painting a mural. When Dany and Gabe were children, Jenny had read to them from Ray Bradbury's *Something Wicked This Way Comes*. They were ten and eleven when they began pretending to be Jim Nightshade and Will Halloway creeping around Cooger and Dark's Pandemonium Shadow Show. They'd loved that the boardwalk had its own Mr. Dark— Jack, the owner of the tattoo parlor. They would

ride the carousel sitting backward on the horses,
pretending they were getting younger, ride it forward and pretend to be twenty-one, that magical
age when life began.

Dany tried to remember what Gabe had looked
like back then. But all she could remember
clearly was how Terry Vashon, Gabe's father,
had looked after his head hit the concrete below
The Gondolier's loading platform.

When Dany came along, Vashon had been
fumbling with his fly with one hand and holding
Gabe with the other. The Gabe Dany couldn't
remember, the child Gabe, had stood there in
some half-passive resignation and she had come
upon it, and it was the kind of thing where you
just walked away. Except that when Gabe had
seen her, he'd tried to run, and she'd done what
friends do and thrown herself at the scary man
who ran the roller coaster and who she knew was
Gabe's father, even though no one had ever said
so.

It was another thing she could recall clearly.
A big and agile man falling backward over a railing, unable to catch himself, unable to stop at all.

Later, when she and Gabe were skating alone
in the rink after hours, quietly terrified, keeping
their secret of walking away from the dead body
of the father who didn't give a shit about him—

after Gabe had cried and told her he hated her, that she was a stupid bitch—*You killed him!*—she had asked Gabe if Terry Vashon had done that to him before.

He had said *no,* and it was a lie.

She thought he would tell her the truth now if she asked, but there was no need to ask. Last night he'd said, *Why are you drinking?* If he'd stayed till morning, he might have the answer. Exhibit A: Jenny. *I drink because my mother has never been able to give me real-world advice, just the platitudes of her era, the words that ought to work.* Gabe would disagree, and the argument wouldn't be worth her breath. Hours had passed since he'd asked the question, but addressing it might lift her in his eyes. "I think I drink because it makes me like him."

No need to define "him." Gabe had painted two murals of him for her mother.

"I think," Gabe said, "that you drink because you *are* like him."

She laughed.

He did not.

IT'S GOING TO HAPPEN again.

She wanted it to happen again, wanted it so much that she mixed up two orders, something that *never* happened. In the midst of her daydreams, she looked up, and Ginger and Celeste sat in her section.

Dany bit her lip, hustled toward them.

Everyone's hair was brushed. Celeste's was corn-silk white, Ginger's dark blond. They were dirty, though; it was just too hard to keep clean when you were fighting for your life, when you had no home.

With a glance at the counter, at her other tables, Dany slid into the booth across from them. "Do you need money?"

Ginger's eyes asked what Dany would want for the money.

It was a look you pretended you didn't see. It was too lonely to feel like the last decent human being in Venice. Dany knew she *wasn't* that and wasn't better or worse than her neighbors.

The good were good here, like anywhere else.

She said, "Coffee? Are you a vegetarian or anything?"

"Anything," said Ginger, white-faced.

Dany scrawled down an order—the breakfast special for Ginger, oatmeal and juice for Celeste. The baby was cranky, rubbing her eyes, her T-shirt filthy.

"This is on me, so don't worry." That she might be cheating the café. Dany didn't meet Ginger's eyes. "If you tell anyone, I'll never forgive you." You couldn't start helping people in Venice. Everyone needed...

Dany went up to the counter and put in an order. The cook lifted his eyebrows.

"I don't want to hear it."

"Hear what? AFDC gives five hundred dollars a month to a woman with a baby," he said. "You ever tried to rent an apartment with that?"

"Obviously not," Dany snapped. "Do I look like a welfare mother?"

When she brought their food, she left forty-six dollars on the table, all the cash she had with her, maybe enough to buy herself a good night's sleep. Ginger's hand snaked the money from the table. "Thanks."

Dany did not feel better.

HER SHIFT LASTED till two, till after the lunch crowd, and then she was out on the boardwalk again.

She didn't go right home.

To get there, she would have to pass Mr. Dark's Tattoo Parlor and see Gabe on a ladder, painting a mural.

Instead, she removed her shoes and went to the beach. The sand hurt, like walking on hot coals. Pooch was throwing a party, guys smearing his back with suntan lotion. One of them was the lifeguard she'd dated.

She tried to remember Laguna Beach, and what she remembered was Brett's family reunion, when she'd gotten drunk and gone skinny-dipping in the ocean in front of his parents' home, then danced naked through the shallow breakers. She'd dressed herself in wet seaweed and posed, like a sculpture, in the foam until her husband had come to get her.

He had said, "I hate your guts."

She had answered, "Let's get a divorce."

Dany had changed since then. She considered Keale Johnson's feelings more deeply than she ever had her husband's.

Keale would get over her. He'd have to, because Gabe had said, *It's going to happen again.* He'd said, *Love me two times,* and she would.

She would stay in Venice until he'd loved her all that he would.

She walked east, carrying her shoes and socks, her bare feet in the cool water. Glancing toward the boardwalk, she saw Wise Man balancing on the wall with an egg on his head while his gang cheered. Beyond the wall, street performers in striped union suits turned handsprings and round-offs.

The sun warmed her shoulders through her

polyester uniform. She felt dirty from waiting tables.

Up above the high-tide line, a dwarf kissed her body-builder boyfriend.

To tell Keale she wasn't going... It didn't mean, of course, that she'd never leave Venice Beach. Wasn't that what she'd saved for? She still had her Escape Account. She could cash it out tomorrow and go wherever she wanted.

It was just that never again would there be a ship and a handsome man with turquoise eyes. Keale really liked her. It was a chance at love, and instead, she wanted a man who'd screwed her underneath the roller coaster, a man who probably didn't recognize marriage as a worthy institution because, like her, he'd never known a happy couple.

Think what you're doing, Dany. If you stay...

It couldn't work with Gabe.

But did that matter?

She was *alive*. Today she was alive, and she *felt,* and she felt because of him, and she could not let it go, she could not will it to stop, and she would not, because it would be a kind of suicide. She would feel each second of it.

It was love, and she wouldn't settle for less.

"One should always be drunk. That's all
that matters; that's our one imperative need.
So as not to feel Time's horrible burden that
breaks your shoulders and bows you down,
you must get drunk without ceasing.

"But with what? With wine, with poetry,
or with virtue, as you choose. But get drunk."

—Charles Baudelaire, "Get Drunk!"
translated by Michael Hamburger

CHAPTER THREE

L.A. Woman

IN THE BOATYARD behind the racetrack where the
horses ran, in the shadow of the schooner, she
said, "I've decided to stay here."

Keale's workingman hands rested on his hips,
above his sagging tool belt.

"What's going on? Your mom?"

He knew Jenny didn't leave the rink. It was
one of the first things Dany had told him when
they'd met two months earlier. He'd nodded and
hadn't treated Jenny oddly when they were introduced during one of the sessions at Rollerama.

Dany shook her head. She was sweaty. She'd pedaled her one-speed Schwinn to the marina. Her driver's license…well, it was history, gone the way of her marriage.

At least she'd managed to leave the boardwalk without seeing Gabe. It was superstition. Fear that if she saw him before she threw out her escape key, threw away the chance to leave on the schooner, he would say he didn't want to make love again, after all.

"It wouldn't be fair to you," she told Keale. "For me to go."

"Ah." He surveyed the curved wooden side of the almost completed schooner. They were going to haul it to an airplane hangar tomorrow, for finishing.

She knew that he knew there was someone else.

"Thanks for asking," she said.

"The invitation is open." Blue eyes traced her features. "Always."

"You really would have hated being at sea with me. I'm a very difficult person."

"So Jake's told me. I was looking forward to it."

He was cute, and she knew from the way he talked about his family that they were all sane and sober and loved each other.

She knew, somehow, that she wouldn't fit in and that it wouldn't be like Brett's family, who had simply found her appalling. Keale's family would be hurt by her, would hurt for him.

"I've got to go," she told Keale. "Thanks. Thanks for everything."

She was halfway to the gate of the boatyard, where she'd parked her bicycle, when Keale caught her by the shoulder. "Dany. I really like you."

"You *really* don't know me."

And she left.

WHEN SHE MADE IT back to the rink, there was no ladder in front of Mr. Dark's, just a half-painted mural. A teenager named Kelly was at the skate-rental booth. She must have seen Dany checking out the painting.

"If you're looking for Gabe, his brother came running up a while ago, and they both took off."

Dany tensed.

It had been more than a decade since she'd come into the apartment one afternoon to find her mother and Gabe sitting on the couch. Gabe had been crying, Jenny rubbing his back. It was when his sister had eaten the Tylenol. It took several days for her to die; in the hospital, they could do nothing.

Jenny. He always turned to Jenny—and wouldn't turn to Dany to save his life.

She scanned the passersby on the boardwalk, hoping to see Gabe and his skinny teenage brother, Jeremy.

"Thanks," she told Kelly, and went inside to find her mother.

Jenny was working with her longtime DJ, Thomas, on the sound system, the dogs gathered around her feet. "Try it now," she told Thomas.

"No, it's not right."

"You could switch to CDs," Dany couldn't resist hinting. Rollerama ran on vinyl only. "I'll even lend you mine."

"You need something, Dany?" Her mother looked tired.

Tired of me. Tired of my drinking and complaining.

Dany set aside the thought. Her Thirty-Year War with Jenny could be won another day. She grasped her mother's wrist and dragged her toward the closed snack bar. She repeated what Kelly had said.

Jenny's eyes slanted to the side and down, thoughtful. She searched her daughter's face. "Where have you been?"

Dany still wore her uniform from the Whole Earth Café.

She wasn't ready to tell Jenny that she wasn't leaving. "I was with Keale. Do you need me tonight?" She wasn't scheduled to play anywhere.

"If you could work the skate shop, it would help." Jenny gnawed her bottom lip, then scrutinized Dany again. "Are you going to Gabe's now? Maybe you can help."

"Let me have a shower first."

Jenny's lips twitched.

"What?"

"You're running away with Jake and our friend from Hawaii, and you went down to the boat in your uniform. Gabe has an emergency, and you want to wash your hair."

Embarrassed, Dany muttered, "Well, Gabe *isn't* an emergency. That's why I'm having a shower." An idea occurred to her. How many times had Gabe wound up in Jenny's soul kitchen, getting a good meal and a story before he fell asleep on the couch? When a woman gave out that kind of love to an urchin, it gave the urchin a hold on her heart.

Knocking some spilled popcorn off the counter of the snack bar, Dany spoke to her mother's bare feet, her swirling gauze skirt. "Maybe *you* should go. You're like a mother to him."

"He has a mother."

But Dany caught Jenny looking toward the

crack of light between the rink's double doors. Wistful? No such luck. Her mother was placid, content to exist in Rollerama like Willy Wonka in his chocolate factory.

"Don't you ever want to see what's out there? Don't you ever want to swim in the ocean again?"

Peaceful, Jenny shook her head.

"Why not?"

"Love."

Dany resisted these conversations—and the notion that her mother's obsession with Jim Morrison had anything to do with love. There were arguments, but she hated giving them, because arguing meant... Well, it dignified the thing Jenny claimed, the thing Gabe had spray-painted on the wall of the rink. *Jim Morrison slept here.* It dignified Jenny's corollary: *And I had his baby.*

But Dany never kept quiet. "He was a nihilist, and he was not a *loving* person. He wouldn't have valued your becoming a rock-and-roll priestess on his behalf. He valued hedonism. You're talking about a man whose personal imp was the size of King Kong. If you want to celebrate his life, you should get out and live. Find the next whisky bar. Cause mischief."

Jenny's look was ironic. "I think you do enough of that for both of us." Jenny hadn't mentioned that Dany had been drinking the night before. Dany hadn't thought she'd guessed. Her mother drew a cigarette from a pack in the pocket of her gauze skirt. "Why don't you go take care of Gabe?"

The question was almost a dare.

"After I wash my hair."

In the shower she told herself that there was mercy in the world, that no one else in Gabe's family had crossed to the other side, as Jenny would put it. Everything was okay. It had to be.

She got out, dressed in cutoffs and a tank top. Her hair tumbled in loose wet curls around her face as she stood before the bathroom mirror. Soft features. Brown eyes. She sucked in her cheeks, and the face looking back scared her, the way something inside her scared her—and strengthened her. It was steel, that thing. It did not bend like a mast but insisted on only one truth. Sincerity.

On impulse, she grabbed the Gibson in its case and took it with her as she headed for the door to the alley.

THE BUILDING WAS CLEANER than most, thanks to Gabe. It was safer, too. An American Gothic senior citizen and his wife came down the stairs as Dany went up; she never trusted the elevators in these places.

"Hello."

The man tipped his hat to her. His wife mumbled and clung to his arm.

A sign on 312 read MANAGER. Someone had etched "Angel" on the door. Gabriel. She'd never been inside.

Dany knocked and listened.

Footsteps.

Her heart took off. *He's here. He's here.* How would he take her showing up unannounced?

The door opened. Gabe, in baggy plaid shorts. Beyond him, his half siblings sprawled through the front room and out onto the balcony. The little sister in the torn chair by the glass doors, Magda, had tear streaks on her face. Jeremy leaned on the balcony railing yelling at someone below.

Gabe didn't ask her in.

When she realized he wasn't going to, she backpedaled through the muck of rejection. "Sorry. I didn't mean to interrupt."

He saw her guitar. "Going to work?"

"No. I just…thought I'd come by. I'll…see you later."

He only nodded.

Can I help?

But he had closed her out. He didn't meet her eyes. He was involved in whatever was happening on the other side of the door.

She told herself, *It's not personal.*

Even though he didn't close the door till she turned away, it was as if he'd closed it in her face. She navigated the stairs, avoiding trash she hadn't seen before, noticing a hole where someone had put a fist through the wall. Why didn't he treat her as a human being who could care?

Nothing ever changed. He turned to Jenny but not to her.

He does not love me. He never will.

The winos had gathered on the steps of his building, and Wise Man gave her a deep courtly bow. "It's the queen of the rink. Play us a song, queen of the rink."

Why not?

She scouted for a semiclean bench. Crossing to the boardwalk wall, she cast a smile over her shoulder at the characters on the steps, and they spilled after her. She opened her guitar case and clasped the Gibson. It was more of a collector's item than anyone knew, but that was her secret. Hers and the guitar's.

She couldn't plug in here, though the instrument had pickups.

She kicked off her sandals and rested her butt

against the boardwalk wall. She picked out some blues chords, sang "Motherless Children."

As Jenny had said, Gabe and his brothers and sisters weren't motherless, except when alcohol and drugs made their mother absent. She lived in ever-changing apartments in a nearby housing project, and her children—all but Gabe—live with her. Dany had met her once, and her face haunted Dany like a mirror of the future.

Rhonda wandered up to the little group and said something to George, one of the winos, and he said, "We're havin' some music appreciation here, Rhonda. You shut up."

"Hey, don't tell me to shut up, asshole!"

Dany sang on.

Some tourists stopped, and one of them dropped a dollar in her open guitar case. Miss Buffy pushed her cart up to the umbrellas and settled her weight on a bench.

Where were Ginger and Celeste? Dany hoped they were gone. But forty-six dollars wasn't enough; they needed a miracle.

As she strummed the last chord, her mind on her own mother, a mother who wouldn't come outside to hear her play, Wise Man said, "That is so pretty. You play so pretty, queen of the rink."

She tuned again, then picked out a melody in

a minor key and chanted a harmony against it, her voice crowd-reaching and powerful.

Look inside you for the lies.
Look inside you for the fear.
We settle for lies.
We settle for less
till there's nothing left to lose.

People stopped and listened. Dany didn't need them, but they needed her—and she needed that. She played a traditional next.

Make me down a pallet on your floor....

Wise Man sang with her, harmonizing, and Dany could smell the street smell of him. She should keep a careful distance if she didn't want Wise Man howling at the rink doors in days to come.

Another of hers, "More of My Blues."

It's gonna be okay when the sun comes up.
It's gonna be okay, 'cause the night will end.
In the day, it all looks different.
In the day, it all looks right again.

She could sing and not think about having told Keale she wasn't leaving and not feel how she'd felt when Gabe had shut the door. Once, she glanced up at the third-floor balconies until she found his.

Jeremy was still out there and staring right down at her with the intensity of a fourteen-year-old. He was like Gabe in that you couldn't tell what he was thinking.

Someone else put money in her guitar case, and Miss Buffy bent down to collect the bills.

"Don't even think about it," said Dany. Helping Ginger and Celeste had been an exception. She had to keep her Escape Account fed and full.

Miss Buffy chuckled and scurried on.

A handsome black man with dreadlocks paused nearby. He raised a guitar case and lifted his eyebrows.

Dany nodded, and a few minutes later they were playing Bob Marley songs, and he sang while she harmonized. One of his band members strung an amp from Gabe's building, and Dany plugged in.

As people began dancing on the boardwalk, in singles and unlikely pairs, she spotted Ginger. She held Celeste in her arms, singing to her child as they rocked to the music.

The sun beamed on smiling faces, on boardwalk happiness, and Dany tried not to imagine where Ginger and Celeste slept at night.

The sun sank lower in the sky, and when she looked into it she saw his silhouette, farther down the wall. He had his arm around Magda, his youngest sister, the one who'd been crying. She was eleven, the age Dany had been when Terry Vashon died.

You told me to get lost, Gabe.

After the song, she unplugged, thanked Green Mon and Joshua, his drummer, and packed up her guitar, pocketing a third of the money and leaving the rest for them. As she cut through the crowd, heading home, tired again, she hoped she would feel a hand on her shoulder, Gabe stopping her.

Instead, she smelled unwashed bodies and suntan lotion, and by the time she tripped over a tube of AmFib on the concrete, she knew he had not followed.

MAGDA SAID, "She left because of us."

Gabe didn't answer at once. Magda and Carissa and Jeremy had known Dany for maybe five years, ever since she'd come back to Venice. None of them liked her particularly.

He'd never given them a chance to like her. She was an alcoholic. They came in all shapes and styles. Her style was sudden out-of-control, personality-altering drunks. The other night hadn't been one of them. She'd been sidetracked by sex. No, when Dany lost it…

The question was if you could live with it. If you wanted to.

Gabe didn't, and he didn't want to bring her into the already disturbed lives of his brother and sisters. Magda's face was still tear-streaked. She was the only one of them who was still really sensitive. Jeremy had shrugged, said, *Magda, it's nothing.* Carissa had said, *So what?*

But Magda had lost a best friend.

And Gabe's mother was edgy, and her children had sensed that she was about to let loose, and they'd left.

"She doesn't like us, does she?" Dany. Magda drew in the sand on the concrete with her big toe, the nail painted with blue polish. Reggae still blared beside them.

"That wasn't about you. It was about me."

His half sister squinted up at him. None of them had the same father. It didn't seem to matter. Because when their mother was maternal, she was a good mom. For some reason they clung together tighter than most full-blood siblings.

"Can we stay tonight?"

"You can always stay."

"Can we go skating?"

He hesitated. That morning he'd told Dany it would happen again. It had seemed certain, until Jeremy had run up to him beneath the ladder. *Magda needs you.*

The inappropriateness of Dany's having a permanent place in his life, as his partner, had been clear then.

Well, he couldn't avoid her. Venice was too small.

He'd have to smooth things out, put them back the way they'd been.

Except, sometimes, that wasn't possible.

"Sure. We'll go skating."

SHE WASN'T GOING to drink. Drinking *would* make it better, but she wouldn't do it. There was something about living near the umbrellas that occasionally made her stop and think. *That could be me.*

And something about the past twenty-four hours had made her feel disgusted.

She entered the apartment from the alley and was glad not to meet her mother. Jenny had sent her to Gabe. *And every time I try to help Gabe, this is what I get. A door shut in my face.*

True, she didn't try often. He didn't want support or friendship if it came from her.

He told her she was like Jim Morrison, a poet and an alcoholic, as though it was a compliment.

As though art was the highest thing, after all—and it didn't matter whether you loved and were loved in return.

She went into the bathroom to wash her face, and her face gazed back at her from the mirror. She sure didn't look like her mother.

In her room she dressed for the evening session—a denim, button-front skirt and a fitted red-and-black blouse edged with intricate embroidery, sparkling with strategically placed mirrors to ward off the Evil Eye that was ever present on Venice Beach. She put on makeup and her skates—red custom boots with black wheels and metallic laces. When she was dressed, her next thought was to pour herself a drink. Her earlier resistance faded. There were not so many things she loved that bacchanalia came low on the list.

It came high. Very high.

She went to the kitchen for a glass of ice and returned to her room for the Jack Daniel's.

Minutes later she was happier.

She started to take her glass through the door into the rink. Jenny appeared in her path, coming the other way. She saw only the glass.

In her tie-dyed skirt and Indian blouse, with

beads hanging around her neck, she shook her
head. "No. No alcohol in the rink."

"I'll drink it before I go in." Dany tried to
keep her smile sweet.

"You won't go in. You can drink or you can
work. Take your pick."

Dany met her mother's eyes and sipped from
her glass, then sat on the couch and crossed her
legs. "Okay." She would drink; Kelly could run
the skate shop. Or Jenny could, since she loved
the place so much.

Her mother sighed and headed down the hall
toward her bedroom.

Dany finished her drink and got up to make
another. She drank half, left the rest for later and
went out to the rink. The session was just beginning. The rings of pink and green circling the
edge of the ceiling were lit, the mirrored ball
spinning. It was Doors night, and Thomas kicked
off with "Break on Through."

Ray Manzarek's organ pulsed in her veins with
each stride. Jim Morrison shouted and crooned,
bringing the news like an ancient Greek.

Dany sensed smoke in the air, and when she
came around the floor, she saw the four of them,
with their dark good looks, their fire. Paying.
Asking Scooter for skates. With a three-turn,
Dany flipped her back toward Gabe's eyes.

"Hello, I Love You" was next, and Jake and Keale Johnson were coming inside. She nodded but steeled herself. She was done with Keale. She wasn't going to hurt anybody. She was going to be alone.

She was going to be okay.

She wasn't going to end up under the umbrellas.

She had poetry, and that was enough and all she had to lose.

GABE'S EYES felt too dry, too hot, as he watched her long legs, crossing one over the other, gliding to the beat of "Twentieth Century Fox." Jeremy was already out on the floor, skating backward, weaving between the other skaters. Magda and Carissa waved to their friends.

Keale Johnson and Jake walked by. Jake said, "Hey, Gabe."

"Jake."

Keale laced up a pair of rental skates while Jake talked to Jenny by the music stand.

Dany twirled on the floor in a sit-spin. The roof shook as The Gondolier swept overhead, the sound of the roller-coaster train blending with the Doors.

"Couple skate," said the D.J. "Skate slowly and carefully please."

"Light My Fire" played through the speakers.

Gabe reached her in a few strides, caught her hands and turned her. She'd been drinking. His stomach twisted, and he could only look at her glassy brown eyes. They were staring dark, committed to Dany's rules. She never gave a nod to any others.

Her hands were dry in his, not holding tightly. He saw her shape beneath her blouse. Skin showed between the hem of the sweater and her low-waist skirt. He touched her waist, her bare skin, because it was Venice and the rink and nighttime, and she was drunk, and he'd never live with that habit but he would take advantage of it.

"This singer," said Dany.

"Yes?"

"He's my father."

Gabe hoarded his feelings, saving them for someone he'd never met, for an annual who would respect his borders and never tempt him to cross hers. "There are people who want everyone to be the same. Then there are the rebels, who'll never let that happen. Your mother is one of them."

"I hope everything is okay. With your family."

"Magda's best friend moved to San José."

She looked relieved, and he tried not to think about that, about Dany worrying, Dany caring.

"Light My Fire" was a very long song.

His fire was lit.

He didn't concern himself with the welfare of her heart; she didn't need him to. He dipped his head to hers, to seduce her. "Want to make love tonight?"

Her head went back, and those dark eyes flashed at him, and it was like the crown of a dandelion blowing seeds all over and through him. Her smile was reminiscent of the mischievous smile of a dead rock star. "Yes."

She sang with the next song. "I Looked at You."

He kissed her there on the rink floor and let his tongue touch hers.

There was no turning back.

The things I want
I cannot have
The things I have
I once wanted.

I make a trade
Like stolen horses
My life
For memories of yours.

And your memories
Remember me.

—Dandelion Wilde, "Charity Auction"

CHAPTER FOUR

End of the Night

THEY SKATED TOGETHER all night to the Doors, to his voice. She left her glass of whiskey in the apartment. Now—*now* there was something to lose.

Keale stayed only long enough to understand, and Dany was glad when he did, when she knew she'd crossed the point of no return. She'd decided to play with fire, and now she was smoldering, dancing, skating with Gabe. Touching him.

When the session ended at eleven, Jeremy, Carissa and Magda headed back to Gabe's to order pizza, and Gabe followed Dany into the rink apartment. Cigarette smoke fogged the air. At the kitchen table, neither Jake nor Jenny smiled.

At first Dany thought they were frowning at her.

Not so. Gabe.

She'd never seen Jenny look that way at Gabe. Bingo picked up on it. At Jenny's feet he growled.

"Bingo," warned Jenny.

Doris sniffed Gabe's shoes, and he petted her. Leaving her skates by the door, Dany asked him, "Want to go out on the deck?"

"Sure."

It was a quiet word, and his eyes avoided Jenny's.

Jake said, "So you're not coming with us, Dany."

Gabe, very still, never looked up.

"No."

Jake tipped his head back to smoke.

Beyond the kitchen Dany slid open the glass doors to the deck. The dogs stayed inside, and

Gabe locked himself and Dany out in the foul smells of the alley and the salt air of the sea.

The Gondolier had shut down for the night, like the rink, and the skeletal track curved black and still against the misty sky.

They lay in matching chaise longues.

"My mother suddenly doesn't like you."

"I noticed."

Touch me. Touch me, Gabe.

He did. He left his chair, knelt on the deck beside her and bent over her to kiss her, to slide his hand against her skin, to love her.

Gabe…

He loved her; he really loved her. In that dream of love, she opened her eyes to see his, and he released her.

Her stomach plunged. She knew the kind of news she was about to get. Decency wasn't Gabe's long suit, but he was loyal to her mother, and Jenny knew what he was about, and… *No, Dany, he doesn't love you.* Dany saw it all, and she was afraid she might cry then and there.

"Come on, fairy! We've been hunting you all night."

The voice came from behind the board-and-batten fence.

"All right, boys, calm down." Pooch.

Dany rolled her eyes. Were they really going to have to listen to this?

"No, you don't get it, *faggot*. We don't *want* you."

Dany and Gabe were still. There was no gate from Jenny's deck to the alley, just the private glass doors to the apartment.

Dany bit her lip, listening to the punks, smelling the scents in the air. Gasoline.

Gabe sprang up on the fence, scaling the chain-link like he had when they were kids. "Hey, beat it! Get out of here. Dany, call the cops."

Feet running, then a flare behind the fence, a flash of fire.

Pooch scrambled up the other side of the chain-link like a spider, escaping the flames, the punks or both. He swung over the top as Gabe jumped back down to the deck.

Dany was already half-inside. "Call 911, Mom!"

Gabe shoved past her to grab the fire extinguisher by the door.

He slammed the bottom of the cylinder, shook it as he headed for the other door, the door to the alley.

A fire alarm went off on the outside of the building.

"Don't open that door!" Dany screamed.

Pooch came in through the sliding glass doors and shut them.

Gabe felt the other door and turned to Jenny and Jake."Let's get out. Through the rink."

Pooch said, "I'm very sorry, folks. You're my hero, Gabe." He darted out to the rink door, running for it, and Gabe gestured with his head for Jenny and Jake to follow.

Jenny hadn't moved.

Jake lit another cigarette and stood. "Let's go, babe."

She smiled a little and shook her head. "Take the dogs." All three were whining anxiously and running back and forth in the room.

"Mom!" Flames glowed outside the glass doors. The fence was on fire.

"The fire department will come in time. It's The Gondolier. They'll come."

To save the historic roller coaster. It was up for landmark designation.

Dany knew how gases could expand in a burning building, how quickly a fire could become a flash fire. Smoke was raw in the air. No one moved.

Then Gabe's free hand pushed her toward the rink door.

"I'm not leaving without my mother!"

"Your mother's going, too." Jake jerked Jenny to her feet.

"Let go!" She yanked away. "Back off, you bastard. You don't touch me like that."

"Oh, fun." Dany's lips trembled. Her mother would rather let the rink burn over her head than leave. That was how she felt about leaving Rollerama and doors…all the doors.

Jake never got excited. He twisted Jenny's arm behind her back and held her other arm at an awkward angle. She kicked him and was suddenly silent and white, agonized by something he was doing to her wrist or arm. A cigarette dangling from one corner of his mouth, he said, "Get the door, Dany."

She did.

Jake paused only to sweep up Jenny's purse, lift the signed photo of Jim Morrison from the wall and drop it into the bag. He whistled for the dogs, and they all came, racing ahead, out into the rink, running for the main entrance. Jake marched Jenny out of the apartment while she called him names.

It occurred to Dany she should have her purse, but Gabe nudged her toward the rink. "Come on, Dany."

One word, her name from his lips, could buy a lot of cooperation.

She stepped out of the apartment, Gabe behind her, the fire extinguisher still in his hands.

Past the skate shop. Past the snack bar. The front doors were open a crack. Pooch had let himself out and not closed them. The dogs had gone.

Wise Man and the others would be out by the umbrellas.

It was then Dany remembered what she'd left behind.

You couldn't smell smoke in the rink. The fire must not have reached the apartment yet. Six feet of Gabe Lucero behind her, at her shoulder, touching her.

She turned, kissing his jaw. "I love you."

One of his arms was busy with the fire extinguisher. The other couldn't catch her fast enough. She ran in her socks; she'd never put on her shoes after skating.

When she entered the apartment, it was safe, no smoke, and she ran, ran to her room and grabbed her guitar case. No problem. She passed back through Jenny's soul kitchen, saluted the bead mural of Jim Morrison.

A roaring filled her ears, and she ran through for the rank, chased by a fireball that came from nowhere, tripping over one of her roller skates and grabbing up both but losing them as she was shoved through the air, shoved forward. A black shadow raced with her, and outside she hit the concrete, rolling like a log in violent hands, and her guitar in its case twanged an uncertain chord as her head banged the boardwalk.

She saw stars and through her streaming eyes she saw Gabe. His hands pressed hard on her shoulders, his body straddling her, his black eyes mean, the eyes of a man who could hit her. His breath came out that way, too, but he didn't raise his fist, just held her so hard and spit words at her, out-of-control words.

"You...stupid...*drunk.*"

Crying, she shook her head.

"You act like your life isn't worth *shit.* I hate people who do that. I hate you. I hate you because you drink, and you're *stupid.*"

"Shut up." She pushed his hands away and sat up and heard the ocean and sirens and saw the winos illuminated by an orange glow, the fire from the alley. One of her mother's dogs was befriending a stray, sniffing tails, wagging tails. Her head hurt. Everything hurt, burning. She crawled toward her guitar case. It was smoking, rank, and someone had thrown a piece of cloth over it, but the handle was cool. She picked it up and stood.

In a daze she stumbled past the Tilt-A-Whirl, over to the boardwalk wall. Someone held her. Gabe.

"Don't talk to me that way," she muttered. "If you hate me, let go." She shoved him.

There was Jenny by the ticket booth, gaping at the firelight on a Venice boardwalk she hadn't seen since 1971.

Jenny cast a glance of hatred at Jake, who just smiled, a long-haired devil. He still had his cigarette, and a second later Jenny went over to bum one.

Dany stooped to open her guitar case. The Gibson was fine.

Shadows in the fire's glow stood over her.

She lifted her eyes past her mother's bare feet and her skirt to her face.

"Whose guitar was that?" Jenny said. "Who did it belong to?"

Dany had never told anyone about this guitar. Had never told anyone it was special, a collector's item, a pawnshop treasure and a symbol. Important.

But her mother had known that her daughter wouldn't go back for a guitar unless someone else had played it first. Her mother knew *her,* as no one else did.

"Brian Jones." Dany shut the case.

Jake's laughter was the friendliest sound of the night.

As Gabe handed him the case, sirens sang, closer. The trucks were coming.

Gabe guided her over the wall, down to the sand and away from the flames.

"If The Gondolier burns down," she said, "I want to see it."

"If The Gondolier burns down, San Diego will see it."

She stanched her tears. No reason to cry. He'd called her a stupid drunk and said he hated her. Just words. Just words. Hate was love's jealous twin.

They found a place under the pier and fell back in wet sand and stared up at the pilings and the underside of the pier. Pivoting, she found Gabe's forearm thrown across his face. He said, "Who's Brian Jones?"

"Rolling Stones guitarist. He's dead."

A crab crawled nearby. Dany's socks were wet, and she drew up her legs, first one, then the other, to peel them off. She moved her hair in back of her head, and pieces of it came off, and she realized that she was burned, that she'd been on fire. She suddenly remembered Ginger and Celeste and wondered where they were sleeping and if the fire had wakened them.

"How did he die?"

Oh, Brian Jones. "Facedown in Jimmy Page's pool. I'm burned."

She let him examine the back of her head, the back of her body. "It's okay," he said. "Doesn't seem bad. Let's go see the paramedics."

Firemen shot hoses at The Gondolier. The apartment was gone, with Jenny's soul kitchen. Flames devoured the mural on the outside wall of Rollerama.

Jenny was crying, and Wise Man offered her a bottle in a paper bag. She just shook her head and clung to Jake.

With the paramedics working on her, Dany searched for Gabe.

Finally she spotted his brother and sisters in the crowd that had gathered on the boardwalk to watch the roller coaster burn. Jack hosed down the outside of the tattoo parlor, then gave up, as though deciding he'd just as soon have the insurance money. He brought a boom box out of his shop and put on the tape *The Doors* like a requiem for the place where Jim Morrison had slept.

Where was Gabe?

"You were an idiot, I hear," said the paramedic.

"Yes."

She got off with a few bandages on the backs of her arms and on the back of her neck. She wandered away from the paramedics still hunting among the faces along the wall for Gabe. Her mother stood in the crook of Jake's arms, and the Gibson in its case sat beside them. Someone had given them some clothesline—leashes for the three dogs.

Jim Morrison sang "The Crystal Ship" like a final kiss.

For thirty years, Jenny had loved him and now her monument to his memory was burning.

Someone plucked at Dany's sweater, and she turned, expecting to find Wise Man or one of the vagrants. It was Gabe. Behind him, the roof of the rink fell. She didn't hear what he said so much as saw it. "Let's go."

HIS BROTHER AND SISTERS walked ahead of them toward the apartment building. Jake had promised to look after Jenny, said he would take her to the marina, to the *Lien Hua.* Clinging to her guitar case, Dany barely saw the inside of Gabe's building, the staircase. She climbed in a daze, still seeing the fire, the timbers of The Gondolier. The rink falling.

"I would've liked to ride that roller coaster one more time." *With you.*

But he was taking her home.

She'd never been inside his place before. The light he flicked on sent cockroaches running for cover. An empty Venice Pizza box sat open on the counter, and some oils on big canvases leaned against one wall. Besides that, the walls were white, naked. The air smelled of paint and pizza.

Opening the glass door, Jeremy staked out the balcony for sleeping. The girls began unfolding sheets and blankets on the two sides of the big L-shaped couch.

Magda stared at Dany's guitar. "Are you going to play that?"

Dany shrugged, not really thinking it had been an invitation.

But Jeremy, from the balcony door, cocked an eyebrow.

"Sure."

From the remaining chair, with its falling-out stuffing, she opened the case, removed the instrument, tuned up. Woozy, she played "Soul Kitchen"... Jenny's kitchen... So many nights the clock had crept past midnight, past one, past two, yet Gabe had wanted to stay and Jenny had let him crash on the couch, the same way his sisters were now sleeping on *his* couch.

She stopped playing. "Sorry. Good night." Like the last song of the final set. The end of the night. She put away her guitar and followed Gabe into his bedroom.

A mattress and box spring on the floor. Nothing on the walls.

He went out for a minute, and Dany heard him talking to the girls in Spanish, and then he was back in the bedroom, shutting the door, locking it.

He turned out the light, and there were no windows.

As he pulled his shirt off over his head, Dany recalled the rink, all the times taken for granted with The Gondolier racing overhead. The world Jenny had given her, a childhood wonderland she'd never appreciated.

She removed her own clothes, too. She felt smoky and charred and exhausted. She didn't need a light to see Gabe. He was always behind her eyelids. She ignored his body sinking into the mattress beside hers till he reached for her and his mouth found hers.

"'I'm sorry' would go a long way," she said.

"I'm sorry."

It was unsatisfying.

Not like skin against skin. There should be this scent of smoke in his bed, on his body. *But you don't love me.*

She hated it that she cared. Unrequited love was not part of her personal makeup.

Regrettably, neither was *requited* love.

I wouldn't know what to do if someone really loved me.

Except perhaps send him away, as she'd sent Keale away.

"Dany. Relax."

His hand was tender, opening her. He had not done this under The Gondolier. When her breath escaped, she learned she'd been holding it. His mouth painted the skin of her thigh. Gabe... Gabe was doing these things, the way she'd always wanted. She stifled the cries she wanted to voice.

He brought himself to her, and the way he treated the condom was different this time, too. He kissed her and worked into her. "You're the one," he said, "who's good with words."

It was enough.

They were lovers.

His cheek caressed hers, and their kisses were beach humidity and the scent and taste of sex.

He said something she didn't catch.

"What?"

"Do you feel okay?"

"Yes."

She thought he was trying to be tender and that

it didn't come naturally to him. But it was more natural than his letting her be tender toward him. Even on top, she lacked that power. "What are you like," she asked, "when you let go?"

"I don't."

That was a smile.

She kissed him. She could never be as good at refusing love as he was. Once the rhythm of sex caught her, she couldn't stop, and he said, "There, baby," and she came with his hands holding her close to him, and he rolled her onto her back, beneath him, and she half-watched him and mostly felt his weight, felt him rocking in her until he shuddered, too.

A while later, he sat on the edge of the bed, as though deciding what to do next.

Dany shut her eyes, wanting him beside her, holding her again.

He went into the bathroom, came out a while later and slid between the sheets.

He turned to her, coming close, and she felt and saw him pushing her hair out of her face. He drew her hips against his. Kissed her. Kissed her. Kept kissing her.

Oh, don't stop.

She could hear the ocean somewhere…and taste him. *Gabe…*

He didn't make any promises. But with his body, he gently loved her again. Two times.

THREE TIMES.

Then it was light, and she couldn't recall having slept because she remembered touching him all night. They had never parted.

The rink was gone.

Neither of them left the bed. His eyes were a very dark brown, darker than her own. His hand rested between her legs. "The kids went to school."

She waited for him to move, to get up. He didn't. He stroked her.

"Don't you...have anything better to do?" It didn't come out as nasty as she'd intended.

It made him laugh. "No."

THEY WENT OUTSIDE at noon and walked down to the ocean and waded in. She wore some gym shorts of his and a T-shirt, and they didn't touch in the water or when they got out. While she bundled up in one of his towels in the sunshine, in intimate separation, she studied the charred Gondolier. One end, the end over the rink, had collapsed partway. The other end was untouched, unharmed.

"I wonder how my mother is." Jenny had finally left the rink.

"I'll drive you down to the marina if you want."

And get rid of me?

"On the other hand..."

They went to Common Grounds, and he bought her lunch and coffee, and they went back to his building, back upstairs, back to bed.

In bed she asked him, "Does this mean anything?"

"Yes."

The tangled sheets fell unnoticed to the floor. The sun went down. By then they knew each other's eyes, and knew what made it good was love. When she said, "I'm a little scared," he didn't tell her not to be.

He said, "Yeah. Well..." And that was all.

New subject. "Your family hasn't come back."

"It's probably okay at home."

"Why don't you try to get them to live with you? All the time."

"A bad mom is better than no mom."

"You say that like you know."

He shrugged. "I don't have much faith in the courts. I'm a Venice muralist. They'd end up farmed out all over the county." It was a big county.

He made dinner in the apartment's small kitchen, and after they ate, she played her guitar.

Beside the open balcony doors she finger-picked a Beatles tune, "I Will," and sang the words to him and never looked at him.

When she finished, she glanced behind her. He leaned shirtless against the bar, watching her.

It spilled out of her mouth, stirred by a lean brown body, a man's long uncombed hair. "What are you thinking?"

His mouth moved slightly before he actually spoke. "You're pretty."

It wasn't what she'd hoped to hear. She changed the tuning on her guitar to blues.

He crouched behind her, close to her, and finally took her guitar from her. "Let's go back to bed."

It was night sounds from the boardwalk that reminded Dany she hadn't seen her mother, hadn't gone back to the rink. She said something about it, and Gabe said, "She knows where to find you."

"She doesn't know where you live."

"I've told her. Jake will take care of her. And I'm taking care of you."

"It would be a novelty if you let me take care of you, instead, sometime."

Dead silence.

Time to change the topic again, pretend everything was fine. "Were you supposed to work today? For Jack? Painting?"

"That's the great thing about painting murals in Venice. No one's ever surprised when you don't show up." Another silence. "What did you mean, Dany?"

"Nothing." She hated herself. Her voice shook. "I thought I wanted to get out of Venice. I think I just wanted you. It's always tempting…to settle for less. But I think it's a sin to do that."

His eyes were interested but gave nothing.

No promises.

He rolled onto his back. "Remember when we were kids, little kids, and we used to get on the carousel, and we'd ride backward or forward but usually forward and pretend to be twenty-one?"

"Yes." The carousel had been a time machine.

Neither of them could say the other *remember*.

But Gabe said, "We never wanted to do that later, did we?"

Later meant after Terry Vashon fell over the railing. After Dany had come upon him trying to molest his son.

"You lied to me," she said. About Vashon. About its never happening before.

There was a long silence. Him breathing. Then, a single word. "Yeah."

She brought it up. "Is it…my drinking?"

His laugh held no humor. "Oh, yes."

The darkness embraced them, and she thought she heard cockroaches scuttling in the corners.

"I promise I won't. I promise I won't ever."

The way his eyes glittered, she knew he was foreseeing the first time she'd break her promise.

But all he said was, "I know that."

"Oh, it is only you, you dark ones, you nocturnal ones, who create warmth out of that which shines. It is only you who drink milk and refreshment out of the udders of light."

—Friedrich Nietzsche, *Thus Spake Zarathustra*

CHAPTER FIVE

Wild Child

THEY WENT TO THE MARINA that night in Gabe's car and found Jake and Jenny on the bow of the junk with the pit bulls. Keale was at the schooner, working into the night. "He has some new friends," Jake explained. "It's…interesting."

Gabe said nothing.

Jake offered Dany a daiquiri, and she shook her head. Yes, there was something to lose now. She was ready to give it up, to stop drinking. She wanted Gabe, and love made her strong.

Eyes dancing, Jake lit a cigarette. The blender whirred. He brought Jenny a fresh drink, virgin. They all lounged on the deck in the coolness, and Dany searched her mother for some change in

her. For twenty-five years she'd wished her
mother would leave Rollerama. Now Jenny had
done it, had left because of the fire.

Is she different? A little nervous, perhaps. But
flushed, too. There was an air of electricity about
her, a vividness. *You're beautiful, Mom.*

And Jake's eyes knew it.

She was still Jenny, with her long loose hair
and her gauzy skirt. She'd bought a new outfit
on Ocean Front Walk, but her style hadn't
changed.

It was too much to hope that—

"I met with the insurance guy today." Jenny
knocked ashes into the water while the junk
rocked at its berth. Bingo rested his head on her
lap, and Doris sniffed Dany. "I'm going to rebuild."

Dany's stomach tensed. She pulled her knees
up to her chest.

"It would be that," Jenny added, "or invest
in another business."

"There's an idea," said Dany.

Gabe had been sitting somewhere behind her,
on the upper deck of the junk. He slid down beside her, very close. Touching. The way he never
used to.

Her nostrils filled with the scent of sex. *I want
to be alone with you again.*

She wanted more. Gabe *knew* her. If he didn't love her... *He never will.* And if he did love her... Well, he was good at giving and not so hot at receiving. He'd said it was because of her drinking. He'd also said he never let down the walls, never let go. Never.

Around them in the marina, stays shivered gently in the wind.

Dany noticed her mother contemplating her in cold silence.

It provoked her to words. "Or we could build another memorial to the great Jim Morrison."

"Dany," murmured Gabe. As in, *Dany, don't.*

Her patience with fraud expired. The thirst grew within her, and she ignored it. She wanted Gabe, and she'd promised Gabe she wouldn't drink. But it was all so obscene, so phony.

"I bet you didn't even sleep with him."

Gabe put his hand against his forehead.

"You went back into the rink for Brian Jones's guitar," Jenny remarked, "when all along you had Jim Morrison's genes."

"I find the suggestion that I might be one of his spawn *revolting.* Why don't we talk about who my father *really* is?"

The tip of Jake's cigarette moved as he coiled a line on the deck.

Dany watched the cigarette.

He laughed and shook his head of long hair in the dark. Shook his head no. He wasn't her father. No such luck.

Gabe stirred, got up, and his long legs made their way to Jake, and both men eased along the space beside the cabin and went below.

Jenny asked, "What lie do you want me to tell you?"

The truth! "A lie I can live with!" The thirst sucked through her again. It seemed so harmless and it was what she wanted. Whiskey made her joyful whenever she faced that Gabe didn't love her. It made her happy when nothing else could, nothing but poetry and song. Nothing but annoying people, making them react. Testing them until they did react.

Her mother had leaned back against some life cushions and was smoking contentedly.

Dany said, "Why do I have to be his daughter? Why can't I be like Athena, sprung full-grown from Zeus's head? Why couldn't you have made up a story like that? It would make as much sense. I just want to be *me*."

"Oh, you are," Jenny murmured. "Don't worry."

"I have an idea for the new rink," Dany suggested. "*Disco*. Or maybe Elvis. We could call it Graceland Skateland."

"Why mess with success?"

"Success? The sixties *failed*. It's a good thing you didn't succeed or the whole world would be like Venice. Anything goes. The sixties began this country's fundamental deterioration of morals." She didn't believe this at all, but she said it with pleasure and took further pleasure in saying other things she didn't feel, hurtful things. "The place is full of gays and unwed mothers— freaks like you. It's disgusting. People without jobs, people on the dole. People who pee in doorways."

She thought she heard Jake laughing somewhere. "Old men with long hair."

Jenny had an odd smile on her face, like she was seeing a ghost.

"You shouldn't rebuild that skating rink. You should invest in the stock market."

Her mother laughed out loud. "You want to hear about morals?"

"Well, you'd know something about that. The world according to James Douglas Morrison?"

"Dandelion, the world is divided into people who tolerate and people who don't, and I know which I like better."

"Oh, yeah, you'd really tolerate a three-year-old waist-deep in..." She couldn't talk about that night in the alley.

"You must have been happy in Laguna Beach, Dandelion. No junkies. No winos. No freaks."

Jenny knew where to stab back. Dany couldn't miss the reference to her failed marriage, the hint that she hadn't been able to fit in with her husband's family. With normal people, as though the AmFib gang was normal. Jenny had implied that Venice was the only place Dany would ever really fit in because she had screwy genes, she was a wild child who couldn't settle down and have a real life. Whom no one wanted or had patience for.

No one except Jenny.

"How can anyone talk to you?" Dany demanded. "You're crazy. You've never given me any useful advice—just summer-of-love hogwash. No wonder my marriage failed. You act as though love for a dead man who probably couldn't remember your name, *if* you ever met, makes up for the fact that you've never tried to fit in with the world around you—even a world as weird as Venice."

"Dany." Jake was warning her. She'd gone too far.

She kept going. "If you really slept with Jim Morrison, tell me how it happened. Where was Grandpa? Where did it happen?"

Jenny stubbed out her cigarette. "On the roof."

Dany's heart pounded. "Where was Grandpa?" Dany's grandfather had died when she was eight, but until then he'd lived at the rink and run it. "Where was he?"

"Tripping."

Dany didn't remember her grandfather well. He'd always been interesting and colorful, owner of the oldest surfboard in Venice, or so he claimed.

I'll never know. I'll never know if she's lying.

It occurred to her then. The outrageous possibility. She didn't believe it, but she said it. "Grandpa."

"No." Jenny relaxed. "Good grief. You are desperate for a lie, aren't you?" She squinted at the dock light thoughtfully.

"Whiskey Bar" played on Jake's speakers, beating a rhythm of celebration, a carousel melody.

Dany stood, trembling. "Yes. Totally... DESPERATE!" She swayed on the rocking junk, slowly found her way down to the dock. Where was Gabe?

He emerged from below, tossed some words over his shoulder to Jake, nodded to Jenny and jumped down on the dock.

Dany stalked ahead of him. Whiskey bar...

A fog closed around them as they walked to Gabe's car, his Malibu. Dany closed her eyes, let the wind bathe her, on the way back to Venice.

At a light he said, "Don't be nasty to your mother."

"It's genetic."

Street people had gathered on the steps of his building, and some fraternity boys were harassing Miss Buffy near the umbrellas. Gabe yelled at them to go back to Greek Row or he was calling the cops.

They shouldered each other and finally left.

In Gabe's building, a young man huddled beneath the stairs, shivering. Gabe stopped, asked him something in Spanish.

He shook his head, answered with a nervous question, his eyes darting here and there.

Gabe asked him something else, and the shivering smooth-faced youth nodded, wide-eyed and skittish.

After he'd let Dany into his apartment, Gabe took a blanket downstairs. When he returned to Dany several minutes later, he said, "Sorry. I think he's schizophrenic." He locked the door of the apartment.

Dany didn't tell him she wanted a drink.

He opened the sliding glass doors and brought Dany her guitar.

She sat holding it. "He didn't play an instrument. He just sang. You look at live videos. Sometimes he just stands there. Other times he recites poetry. But it was all…so…sincere. Not sincere to people. Sincere to himself.

"And they were a tight band, like they could read each other's minds. Some of their songs are as complicated as orchestra music. Though rock-and-roll is better. Obviously."

Gabe turned off the lights in the apartment. The two of them melded close on the couch, her guitar resting on his thigh, too. "I sound like her. Talking about him. She does this for hours." Disgusted with herself, Dany changed the subject. "Do you ever want to live somewhere without cockroaches?"

"It would be a first, all right. What's it like?"

She remembered her house with Brett. "Lonely."

He laughed. After a while he said, "Maybe it's not true, what your mom says. But your mom…she gives what she can. I know she always did to me."

"What do you mean?"

"Suppose she doesn't know who your dad is. Suppose she doesn't remember. Suppose she was on drugs, just doesn't know what happened. So she's picked a story for you. She's given you a…history. Maybe that's what you get and you should take it for what it is.''

"A lie?''

Gabe considered letting it go. "Look. Your mom has…integrity.''

"Oh, right. Lots.''

"She does what she thinks is best for you. She makes up her mind and does it. You've got to admit, Dany, she gets along with you. She sticks by you.''

"Am I that undesirable?''

"You can be difficult. What I'm saying is, if Jim Morrison isn't your father, you're never going to know. Your mom picked a person she admired—''

"I don't admire him.''

Gabe lifted his eyebrows. "And she gave you a myth, your own creation story. She'll never take it away from you, Dany. She wouldn't do that to you.''

Trembling, on the verge of tears and not sure why, Dany said, "That sounds more interesting than useful.''

"So try using it.''

"Using it how?''

"When you're playing music. When you look

at the people listening. Maybe we're all children of the people who left something we admire.''

''That's metaphorical,'' she snapped, ''and it's not helpful.''

His smile was ancient. ''Then try this on for size. Your mother—and your father—helped make you who you are. Do you love yourself, Dany?''

''Passionately,'' she responded for the times it was true.

''Okay, well, somehow we get to where we are, and it's not bad, and it's what we know, and we have a bond with it, with the picture we have of ourselves and with all our memories, even the ones we hate. You called it yourself, Dany.''

''What?''

''Your mother's always told you that Jim Morrison is your father. Isn't there a small part of you that wants it to be true?''

She swallowed. He had named the reason she'd trembled, the reason she felt like crying. ''There's a really big part...that does.''

In the dark she crossed her legs on the couch and tuned her guitar, feeling her way, playing at blindness, trying chords. She knew certain chords perfectly because she'd heard them her whole life.

''Break on Through.'' Her own acoustic version. She started to sing and couldn't, couldn't play, either, so she stopped.

The goal was to talk without crying. "You'd think if you were a person who loved music and your mother was obsessed with rock-and-roll, you'd be able to talk to her. But I don't understand her. I don't understand a woman who wouldn't come to her own daughter's wedding because she won't leave a skating rink."

"She probably didn't like the guy. I didn't."

Dany's eyes shot at him. "Really?"

The look they shared reached back to Terry Vashon.

Gabe wanted out of the moment. "As for your mom, it probably wasn't really cool to be a single mother back then. Maybe it wasn't cool with her father. Did you ever think of that?"

"I wish she'd tell me."

"That's the nineties way. Explain your pain." He said it almost viciously. "You're thirty-one. She's fifty. You may as well start loving her like she is. And love her a lot, Dany. She's…"

He didn't finish.

Her mother had given him cookies and milk when he was twelve or thirteen. She had put out the blankets and pillow for him on the couch.

"Gabe. Did you ever…tell her…"

He shrugged. "Some. How he died."

And no more. "Boy, you two are something. Nobody ever thought to talk to *me* about it."

"Your mom knew what you could take."

"That's all you told her?"

He shrugged. "He hit me. She knew that."

And Jenny had probably guessed the rest. He was underestimating her mother. "You know, Gabe, if you needed someone—anytime—you could have come to me. Always."

"Dany, you were eleven."

"That year." He'd ignored her for two decades. She set her guitar aside. "You never let me help you."

"What kind of help?"

"Any kind. Like with Magda. You would have let my mother in."

"Your mother doesn't guzzle Jack Daniel's."

"That's a cop-out."

It was all he would say, and it wasn't enough.

He did not love her. He did not love her. But she loved him too much to push him away. So when he came toward her on the couch, she let him hold her, let him undress her and get closer and closer. He had condoms close by, and soon he was inside her, kissing her. Her back arched over an end cushion as he held her, made love to her.

He rubbed her cheek with his, then hunted out

her mouth. Yes. The door was this way. She was getting warmer. Hot.

Her orgasm was long and deep, and his answered, and afterward he kissed her more, kissed her whole body, thanking her.

She kissed him back. "When I told Keale I wasn't going on the ship, I thought it would be like this with you. I thought I'd be burned to nothing but that it'd be worth it."

He stilled and gazed at her very hard.

Shit. What did I say to make him look at me like that?

He eased off the couch, and she thought he would leave her. Instead, he lifted her in his arms and carried her to the bedroom, keeping the door open for night light, Venice boardwalk light.

On the bed he held her head and looked into her eyes, and everything swirled in the dark. The single look said, *Yes, this is the kind of love you'll never get over. It might not last but neither of us will get over this.*

"Gabe." She whispered, "I wish you'd say it sometime." *Even if you don't feel it.*

"It's less than what I feel." After a second he whispered, "Sometime you should try to see yourself as she sees you. You'd love yourself more."

"How do *you* see me?"

"You're a weed with bright sunshine flowers. You keep coming back."

He held her close, and the night was reflected in his eyes.

Minutes, hours, died in tenderness, and Dany knew things. That he might never try to protect her, might never be afraid for her at night when she walked alone on the boardwalk. That he might never ask her to marry him. That he might never say any of the things she wanted to hear. And that he would certainly never turn to her when *he* needed help.

But that he loved her. And in some way always would.

JAKE AND KEALE were leaving in two weeks.

Jenny reported the fact nonchalantly as she and Dany stood outside the chain-link fence the insurance company had erected to keep people from venturing under The Gondolier. Nearby, Gabe had resumed work on the mural outside Mr. Dark's Tattoo Parlor, which had been fire-damaged but not badly.

Jenny and the owner of the roller coaster had negotiated on the phone about what should be done. He'd offered her money for the rink business, and she had refused.

Dany recalled Jake matter-of-factly stuffing

Jenny's autographed photo of Jim Morrison in her purse before he'd marched her out the door. But she knew her mother must be thinking of lost memorabilia, of what hadn't been saved.

She adjusted her clothes, some cotton drawstring shorts and a flowing poet's blouse purchased at Love Me Two Times, the secondhand store on Market. She and Gabe has spent a morning clothes shopping for her and getting squared with the bank over her burned ATM card and identification and had bought Jenny a new dress, too, which he'd presented to her.

Dany found words that had eluded her then. "I said insensitive things the other night. I'm sorry I was rude." She *was* sorry, but she hated apologizing. She'd gotten out of the habit when she was married to Brett, since apologies made for boring conversation and he had wanted so many of them.

"I think I know the things you mean and the things you don't."

"I'm *very* sincere. I'm sincerely me."

"Yes, I know."

"I'll buy you a coffee, Mom. A latte."

"All right." Jenny gave her a sweet smile that said espresso was a good development of the nineties.

They found a back corner booth in Common

Grounds, and Dany went to the counter to place their order. Jenny liked caffe latte.

When she brought the coffees to the table, Dany said to her mother, "Did Jake ask you to go with him?"

"No." Again, a smile at her daughter's romantic ideas. "Can I smoke in here?"

"No. You shouldn't at all."

"Why not?"

"Cancer is an awful way to die."

"I'll take that under consideration. Tell me your plans, Dany. Jake said you and I can live on the *Lien Hua* if we pay for his slip at the marina."

"What a generous soul." Dany recalled the things Gabe had said, the way he'd explained Jenny. That her mother had given her a myth. She didn't quite believe it. "You told me you stayed at the rink for love. What did you mean?"

Jenny sipped her latte. "This may be hard for you to understand. But sometimes, when you're given the gift of feeling intense love, you don't want to let it go. You need to honor it."

Dany's heart thudded. *Like what I feel for Gabe. He loves me less, but I can't let it go.* It was what she'd always dreaded. She chanted softly, "We settle for lies. We settled for less, until there's nothing left to lose."

"That's true."

When had she taken Jenny's hand? When had it begun to feel right to hold on to her mother and look into her eyes and know that Jenny had always tried to point her toward the truth? Wasn't it Jenny who'd always encouraged her poetry and music, as though knowing it would give her some dignity, something to cling to?

I want more, Mom. I love Gabe.

Her mother seemed to know. Her mouth tensed a little before she said, "You and Gabe."

Dany withdrew her fingers to hold her coffee with two hands.

"It would be nice..." Jenny paused. The pause dragged. She didn't say more.

A radio played reggae, Steel Pulse.

Dany cleared her throat. She couldn't talk about Gabe. There was something else she wanted to tell her mother. Peace with Jenny was something she could give both of them. "I'm not going to complain anymore. About him. My father. I'm...proud of him."

A pair of blue eyes stared at her thoughtfully, as though trying to read what she really meant, what she really accepted.

Finally Jenny just sipped her coffee. "Good." Her eyes swept past Dany. "Here comes your boyfriend."

A second later Gabe slid into the booth, hugging Dany as he sat beside her. The conversation was casual. About her boss at the Whole Earth Café charging her for her uniform that had burned in the fire. About the workmen shoring up The Gondolier, to protect it while contractors gave bids on rebuilding the rink.

Jenny said casually, "Gabe, I was going to make you and Dany an offer. You could buy into the rink. Live there."

Dany froze. She knew what her mother was doing. Making it attractive to Gabe not to dump her.

Gabe's arm, across her shoulders, didn't move, but it lost some of its electricity, some of its intense connection to her.

He said, "That's a nice offer, Jenny."

"You're a nice guy."

Dany was embarrassed. *Am I such a bad deal that she has to bribe Gabe to keep me?*

The thirst came again. It was like a boiler inside her. She could hold it down for days, for weeks, for months. *Someday I'm going to blow it. Someday I'm going to blow it, and when that happens, it will be all over with Gabe.*

She loathed ultimatums and the people who gave them. She loathed being judged. The only kind of love was unconditional. The rest wasn't love.

The radio's reggae hour was over, and they began playing "golden oldies," starting with "You Were on My Mind."

Jenny sang along and sipped her coffee.

Gabe's fingers massaged Dany's scalp. Then he let go, and she knew it was because they both began to hunger too hard if they touched. "Buy me a coffee, Dany?"

"Okay."

He let her out of the booth and slid back in himself. He hadn't been alone with Jenny since before the night the rink had burned.

She said, "Just what are your intentions, Gabe?"

He checked an invisible watch. "This relationship is...rather new."

"Your acquaintance is...rather old."

He'd never seen Jenny's eyes so cold. Their expression said, *If you hurt my child, I will kill you.*

Her mouth said, "I know how strong Dany is. She was strong enough to save *your* ass when she was eleven years old."

It was the last time he'd let Dany save him, the last time he ever would. Gabe's eyes felt warm, too dry. He blinked to cool them, to wet them. "Let's not fight." He glanced toward the counter, to see if Dany was coming back with his coffee.

She was gone.

I'M GOING TO BE HAPPY. No one—no one—has the right to interfere with my happiness. It's a free country.

She kept the bottle in a paper bag beside her on the boardwalk wall and told Wise Man not to touch it. "I'm going to drink it all myself."

She tuned the Gibson and struck into "Passionate Kisses" and belted the words to the boardwalk. The tourists stopped walking and listened, and a well-dressed man in unscuffed loafers unfastened a money clip and dropped a ten in her guitar case. Playing a refrain, Dany said, "Thank you very much. I'm Jim Morrison's daughter."

The man regarded her piteously, drawing back—a look for the crazy ones, the freaks.

She sang her entire repertoire of songs by the Doors. "Soul Kitchen," "Break on Through" and "Whiskey Bar."

Jim Morrison had studied the psychology of crowds. When she was a teenager, Dany had tried to do the same thing, just to see what he'd read.

It was hard to find the right books. It was hard not to let her mother see what she was doing.

Her eyes reached for eyes in the crowd, shone at them. Robert Johnson songs. Country-and-western. Her own. The whiskey sloshed in her mouth, burned her throat, and she did not look for Jenny or Gabe on the boardwalk. Gabe would see this or hear about it, and it didn't matter.

It was time to fall, and Dany always preferred to dive. To explode in a celebration of Dandelion Morrison Wilde.

It became difficult to hit the right chords, but she kept playing. Someone took money from her case. She saw and couldn't object because she couldn't think of the right words. It made her laugh.

Until she looked out at the faces and saw Ginger staring at her.

If other people had given her that look, Dany would have flipped them off, dressed them down. From Ginger and her daughter, she just glanced away. And tried to play "Break on Through" again.

A body builder stopped in front of her and said, "Your music sucks. Why don't you shut up?"

She lost track of what she said back to him. She tried to punch him, but her guitar was around her neck. She put it away in the case, on top of all the money, and carried the case and the bottle back toward Gabe's building.

Ginger and Celeste gaped disillusionment when she went by.

Gabe was sitting on the steps.

She laughed when she saw him.

He opened the door for her and followed her upstairs.

The apartment spun. She set down her guitar and arranged herself on the couch to have another drink.

Gabe chose a chair, the one ratty chair.

"You're an asshole," she said. "I hate people like you."

He was rubbing his face, and he got up and went out on the balcony and shut the sliding glass door behind him.

It didn't make sense to her. *Oh, well.*

She stood and started for the door.

The sliding glass door opened, and he came back in. "Where are you going?" he asked.

"For a swim. To be alone."

"To make a scene?"

He thought he had her figured out. "You're an asshole," she repeated. "You just wanted sex. That's all you care about. My mother knew it. Jake knew it. Guess what? *I* knew it. Maybe it's all *I* want. I don't want some tacky suburban marriage. I've *had* that. You don't *get* tackier than SPF eighty and the AmFib Hetheringtons.'' The words slurred out of her mouth. She knew she was too drunk to speak clearly and didn't care.

He just stared at her.

''What are you thinking? You never say anything. You want other people to be weak, but *you're* never weak. Not with me. Well, screw you and everyone like you.'' She opened the door and slammed herself in the head with it.

He didn't laugh. ''You okay, Dany?''

''Yes.'' She wheeled around. ''I'm *fine*. Everything is *fine*.''

''You're going to have a black eye.'' He touched her face. His mouth looked some way she'd never seen it look.

She shoved him and walked out the door.

He loved her madly, and he didn't go after her, just leaned his head against the wall. She was testing him, consciously or unconsciously. He knew it had nothing to do with what their future would be. The future could be anything. She could try. She could succeed or fail. And the two of them would behave in certain ways. There would always be that thing they might or might not talk about—her potential for weakness. All the time he would wish she wouldn't take a drink ever, because anything could happen when she did.

If she did drink, he would lead his sisters and brother away from her. He might ask her to leave. The request might change her, and it might not, and the whiskey would hold all the cards until Dany decided she wasn't going to let it.

He would see her reach for a bottle and feel, *Oh, shit. Oh, shit, please don't.*

Should he follow her? She was vulnerable on Venice Beach, drunk like that. She could be raped. She could try to swim and drown. Someone could murder her for money she wasn't carrying.

He resented it and could not stop himself from going.

I don't want to take care of you this way.

He didn't want her to take care of him, either. In any way.

He felt in his pocket for his key, went out into the hall and locked the dead bolt.

"A Poet makes himself a visionary through a long, boundless, and systematized *disorganization* of *all the senses.* All forms of love, of suffering, of madness.... Unspeakable torment, where he will need the greatest faith, a superhuman strength, where he becomes among all men the great invalid, the great accursed—and the Supreme Scientist! For he attains the *unknown!*... So what if he is destroyed in his ecstatic flight....

—Arthur Rimbaud, letter to Paul Demeny

CHAPTER SIX

My Eyes Have Seen You

"GO HOME, DANY. You're drunk."

Lavinia, one of her co-workers at the Whole Earth Café, blocked the way to the back room.

"Tell Spud he can take this job and shove it. I am Jim Morrison's daughter. I'm the greatest living poet in Venice, and I'm not going to spend the rest of my life waiting tables." *I'm not going to settle for lies or settle for less.* She capped the well of sorrow inside her.

Is this all there is? Is there no true love?

Lavinia rolled her eyes. "Dany, please go home before Spud gets back."

"She's going home," said Jenny's husky voice, behind her.

Dany wheeled. What was her mother doing here? She never left the rink. Oh, but the rink had burned.

They found the sun and the sand. Dany drank as the sand burned her bare feet. She thought she stepped on a hot cigarette butt. "So, just tell me one thing. Just one thing. Gabe says you gave me Jim Morrison like a gift. That it's a gift. Is that true?"

The beach spun. She had to sit down.

Her mother sat, too, and poured out the Jack Daniel's. "I didn't give him to you. He gave you to me."

Dany tried to see in her mother's eyes, tried to ferret out the truth.

Gabe was right. Her mother would never give up her lie. If it was a lie. *I'm never going to know. If it's a lie, she'll never ever say. She's that smart. One lie. Never changes her story. For me. Because she loves me.*

"Dany, do you love Gabe?"

Dany had missed a moment, a transition. Gabe? "Sure."

"'Sure' isn't the right answer. I'm not talking about a take-it-or-leave-it love. Is Gabe the one you love?"

The waves reached for them and slunk away.

Jenny sighed. "I guess I was wrong."

"He's all I've ever wanted. For ages, I didn't realize it was him I wanted. But true love. I've always wanted true love, and you've always said there were all kinds of true love."

"Did I say that?" The words were reflective. "Perhaps I meant that true love can look many different ways. It doesn't always wear identical clothes."

"I don't want him if he doesn't love me the same way. I won't settle for lies. I won't settle for less."

"You need to give him a chance to love you. And as for loving you the same way, no two people love the same way. I've wondered if you're intentionally alienating him. If by being drunk you're giving him an excuse not to love you."

"An excuse would be better than his plain old not loving me."

"But if he doesn't, maybe someone else will."

Dany could only think of Gabe. He had

changed the night Terry Vashon died. And she was responsible for his father's death. In a drunken haze, she almost told her mother the truth. *But she knows—knows you were struggling with him when he fell.*

Gabe had never told Jenny what his father had done to him. Jenny might have guessed, yet—

I'm the only one who definitely knows.

Could it be the reason Gabe didn't or couldn't love her as she loved him?

"I don't believe it," she blurted out suddenly. "Sure, I'll change, but for *me*, not for him. I'll do it for poetry. With my gifts, I don't need love." Dany stood, making for the boardwalk wall. Spinning suddenly, she swept a bow to her mother. "Jim Morrison's daughter, at your service."

"Dany."

She felt sweat and salt, people staring. Her mother holding her face.

Her mother said, "You know whose daughter you are? *Mine.* I love you. If all you can believe is what you see with your own eyes, then hold on to that thought. You're my daughter, and I love you."

Dany felt her eyes streaming. She *wasn't* Jim Morrison's daughter. She was just a Venice Beach drunk.

And when she sobered up, Gabe still wouldn't love her.

SHE WASN'T UNDER the umbrellas, and Gabe didn't see her on the beach.

He asked Wise Man, "Seen the queen of the rink?"

"No, man. You know the queen of the rink?"

"No," said Gabe, and walked on, down toward the burned roller coaster.

That's where she'll be.

He passed his ladder leaning outside the Tattoo Parlor. He hadn't bothered to clean up when she'd disappeared from the coffeehouse. *Dany, where are you?* He wasn't searching because she was Dany or because of love. He was searching because of the disease that existed between people who drank and the people who loved them.

There they were, on a bench in front of the chain-link fence that had been erected to keep people out of the fire area. Dany's arms were folded across her chest, sullen comment on life. Beside her, Jenny blew cigarette smoke at the ocean. People walked past, skated past, never noticing the two women on the bench. Jenny seemed to see somewhere beyond them, to see the waves, the breakers, the boats at their moorings.

There was room on the bench beside her.

"What are you thinking, Jenny?"

She shook her head, blinking. "Nothing."

The ocean. *Jake.* Jenny Wilde wasn't too old to wish and dream.

"If you want to get away for a while," Gabe offered, "I can look after things here. You can trust me to do things the way you'd want them done."

"I know."

Dany's silence was snapping resentment. He knew why she'd started drinking. It wasn't about alcohol. Maybe it wasn't even about numbing herself. It was about unconditional love and life-time promises. It was her way of saying, *This is me. How much do you really love me?*

It was the only question. She didn't have to finish that bottle to make him see it. He knew how it was with alcoholics. He knew how it was, that there weren't any guarantees.

Are you even going to try, Dany? Are you going to try to do better than this?

If she didn't, if she wouldn't...

He stood and looked at her. "Let's go home."

DANY AWOKE in his bed, her stomach weak.

Gabe.

She listened and heard the wind and the Venice sounds, smelled the Venice smells. And paint.

Her memory was blinding and painful.

Well, you did just what you wanted, Dany. You showed him you aren't going to change for him. Good for you. Congratulations, you have a hangover.

Experimentally she sat up. It was dark out, but a light burned in the next room. She moved out of the bed. Queasy, she wandered toward the door. He was painting. Some abstract thing. No, there was a figure in it, on one of the big canvases. Gabe wore a pair of shorts and nothing else. He straightened up and glanced at her.

"I'm sorry."

"I'll bet." He started cleaning his brush, cleaning up. "Can I get you anything?"

"I'll take care of myself."

She found her way to the couch and collapsed again, lying on her side. "I wanted you to see. And I wanted to see what you'd do."

He gestured to the canvas. *This is what I'm doing.*

She tried all her lies. "I don't want babies. I don't want promises." *Say you love me. Please.* "I think I'm meant to be alone."

"Maybe."

"I'm not meant to be with you, anyhow."

"Why is that?"

Her heart stirred. She shrugged. "We love unequally."

His silence should have confirmed it and didn't. "I guess it's easier to say that."

"Than what?"

"Than to quit."

Drinking. "Look, I can quit. But you—you don't let me in. You turn to my mother. You've never turned to me. You don't love me the way I love you."

"I don't *want* to love you."

"Yeah, but that's not because I drink."

He crossed his arms on his chest.

"Maybe," said Dany, "it has to do with your father. Maybe that's why you don't want to treat me as an equal."

You are an equal, Dany. He squeezed his eyes shut. No. She was... He swallowed. *She knows. She knows, Gabe. She saw.* He hated it. He hated it even more that she'd tried to help and someone had died. The emotion was inarticulate. It had to do with being a man. Words spit out of him. "You're an alcoholic. So is my mother. You know how bad it gets? You kill someone with a car. Or you die yourself, aspirating your own vomit. Or you pass out in a gutter and someone backs over you in a car. Or you lose control and hit me, and I lose control and hit you back. It's not harmless.''

"Even if I promise never to drink, you won't believe me. It's too late.''

"You *did* promise.''

"Like I said. Would it satisfy you if I went to a clinic? No. Because you're lying to yourself. Maybe I will quit. But it won't be for a man who doesn't love me.''

He closed his eyes, like he couldn't stand it. "Fine. It's your problem.''

"Do you want me to leave?''

His head was in his hands, and when he looked up, his eyes were red. "Yes.''

"What if I stop drinking? Can we give it another try?''

"STOP IT!'' He didn't mean to yell. More words came out. "You do this for some reason. It doesn't have anything to do with me.'' He shut his eyes, because he knew there was a very real possibility that if he turned her out, she could become one of those women at the umbrellas.

And that if he didn't, it could end the same way.

"I love you. I'll love you if you're down there.'' He pointed and made sure she knew just where he meant. "I'll love you if you're here. But I won't want to be the person picking you up all the time. Pick yourself up. This isn't my problem. I don't want my life to revolve around it. I'll find some woman who has problems, but she won't have this problem. Maybe she'll nag or spend a lot of money or bug me about things that don't matter. But she won't do this.''

Dany nodded. ''When I feel a little better, I'll get out of your hair.''

We settle for lies. We settle for less, until there's nothing left to lose.

He didn't answer but went out onto the balcony and shut the glass doors behind him.

She went to the bathroom and found one of her lipsticks. She wrote on the mirror, ''I want babies. I want promises. I want you.'' Then, embarrassed, she tried to wash it off, and it wouldn't all come off. A film remained, like a secret exposed.

SHE HALF DOZED on his couch, and he didn't come near her. He left the apartment as though he hoped she'd be gone when he got back.

Sobering up was awful. She remembered things.

Ginger looking at her that way, like, *Oh, God. You, too.*

Her mother practically admitting that Jim Morrison wasn't her father, that she *had* provided Dany with her own creation myth.

And Jenny's analysis of her daughter's drinking. Daring Dany to see if sobriety could allow Gabe to love her. Or if it might open the door to someone else loving her.

Dare to love and be loved, Dany. Dare to settle for nothing less.

Her Escape Account would never provide escape. There was no escape, even if she went somewhere else. That money could never help her.

Through the black windows, she saw only night. The bank wouldn't be open now.

You're just drunk, Dany. She cried, glad Gabe wasn't there to see it.

She didn't want him taking care of her anymore.

HE LET HER OFF at the marina the next morning, with her clothes in a grocery sack and her guitar in its case. He didn't get out of the car, and they didn't kiss, but he said, "What you told me...about my not letting you close...it's true. Everything."

She touched the dashboard absently. "I'm not sure it matters. It's taken you, what, twenty years to make a pass at me? Let's not kid ourselves.

I'm not going to settle for less than I want, Gabe.''

"It's taken you just as long. I've never liked seeing you with other guys.''

"I won't settle for less than what I want.''

"Maybe you should settle for what you have. Some of us don't believe in less. Or more.''

"You'll believe when you find it.''

"You're wrong.''

Jenny and Jake were on the aft deck of the junk, and when Dany saw the way they were talking, she stopped on the dock and tried to leave.

But they saw her first, and Jake waved.

As she boarded the junk, she heard Jenny saying, "Let me talk to Dandelion.''

"You got it.'' Jake kissed her and left, jumping down to the dock. Slipping past Dany, he said, "Come down later and check out the schooner with your mom.''

Dany joined her mother in the sunshine on the junk.

Her mother noted the guitar case and bag of clothing.

She checked Dany's face.

"I'm okay,'' Dany said. "Really.''

Jenny considered her carefully. "Do you think

you could handle a million-dollar property without screwing up?"

"Excuse me?"

"You'll have to dicker with that bastard who owns The Gondolier. You know, in the whole history of that roller coaster, I've never liked the people who owned it or the people who ran it."

"What are you saying?"

"Jake wants me to come with him. On the schooner. I'm asking you to be my business partner."

"What?"

"That rink has to be rebuilt. You could oversee that, don't you think?"

I'd screw up.

But for the first time ever, her mother was showing interest in something beyond Venice Rollerama, beyond a long-dead one-night stand. *Jake.* Her mother didn't necessarily want to sail around the world. She wanted Jake Donahue. Love. Maybe her mother had been waiting at the rink, waiting all this time for the real thing.

Dany hoped Jenny wouldn't settle for less. "Okay. I'll do what you want till you get back."

Her mother held out her hand. They shook on it, then kissed.

Hugging her daughter, Jenny whispered,

"Help him have faith in you, honey. He loves you."

"Thanks, Mom."

She had spent most of her life complaining about her mother.

All along Jenny was the one who'd believed in her. And for all the words she spoke, her example had been to wait—to wait for the love that was real and right, a love returned. To have faith that it would come—and never to settle for less.

DANY SPENT THE NEXT DAY hunting the boardwalk for Ginger and Celeste. She felt vulnerable with the day pack on her back, and she really didn't know what she would say to Ginger when she found her.

Finally she gave up looking, got a coffee at Common Grounds, and went over to the boardwalk wall to drink it.

They were standing by the Tilt-A-Whirl, and Dany began to move toward them when she recognized Ginger's denim vest and olive drab pants, army surplus, when she saw the familiar figure of the toddler beside her.

Something stopped her.

A bearded man, talking earnestly to Ginger.

She was shaking her head, and as Celeste

started to wander off, Ginger reached for her hand.

Keale Johnson moved first, picking up the child, holding her against his side, resuming conversation with her mother.

Oh, God. Go! Go! Dany leaned forward, sending Ginger telepathic messages. *He's pretty nice. Look how he's holding your kid. He's cute. Take him. Take him. You could do worse.*

She thought, *But only take him if you really love him.*

Don't settle for less.

Ginger shook her head again, reached for the baby and turned away. She headed up the boardwalk, merging with the crowd, while Keale stared after her.

A second later he was talking to the Tilt-A-Whirl operator, grabbing a pen and piece of paper. Running after her.

A family of tourists got in the way.

Dany stood. Trying not to spill her coffee, she hurried through the crowd, trying to see them. The cash in her day pack made her feel naked—no, more vulnerable than that.

She couldn't find them.

Where were they?

Ducking down the alley behind Common Grounds, she spotted Ginger and Celeste round-ing a corner. Ginger was reading a piece of paper. He must have found her.

Dany ran. "Ginger! Wait."

The woman swept up her daughter suspiciously, then seemed to relax as Dany drew closer.

With a glance behind her down the sunny alley to make sure they were more or less alone, Dany took off the day pack.

"Go to a bank. Right away. This is all yours."

Ginger backed away, shaking her head.

"Please. I don't want it. I don't want anything." Her eyes felt watery. *Take it, dammit.* "Please. Go take care of your baby. Shit." She dropped it on the ground and turned away, hurrying up the alley.

A second later feet pounded behind her. A woman carrying a toddler and a day pack and running, too. Toward her.

"Dandelion," said Ginger.

She looked back.

Ginger held out her hand. "Thanks. Thanks very much."

"If the doors of perception were cleansed, everything would appear to man as it truly is, infinite."

—William Blake,
The Marriage of Heaven and Hell

CHAPTER SEVEN

Waiting for the Sun

DANY SAW GABE the day the schooner sailed. He and Magda came to see the ship off. Dany kept her distance and so did he. She didn't see much of him, living at the marina, sleeping on the *Lien Hua* with her mother's dogs.

She half hoped to see Ginger and Celeste on the dock, half hoped Keale would take them away, but they didn't appear.

As he said goodbye to her, Jake Donahue leaned near Dany, and his hair brushed her face. "I'll tell you something about that junk, Dany. Women who spend enough time around it end up getting married."

"I've been married. And my mom has spent a lot of time around it, Jake."

"Bet it still works."

"My mom has spent a lot of time around it."

He winked at her.

Keale Johnson waved to her from the deck and shook his head as though to say, *Too bad it didn't work out.*

Holding her mother, Dany said, "I'm going to miss you."

"Not half as much as I'll miss you."

Time grew slow and important as the ship cast off with Jake at the helm, and they turned out into the bay.

Dany found a bench to sit on, knowing that when the ship disappeared from sight, Gabe and Magda would be gone, too, would have left the dock to return to Venice.

It was harder to watch a schooner sail out of sight than she would have guessed. *I'm alone, now. I've got to make it on my own.*

In some way, this solitude was the future she'd always feared.

She stood at last and turned to go up the dock.

Her heart pounded. Gabe was still there, waiting for her to come near.

Their eyes met. She stopped walking.

He looked at her for a time. "Need a ride anywhere?"

"I'm staying on the junk. I've got a bicycle."

"Hey, Mag, let me talk to Dany a minute."

His sister wandered yards away, down the dock.

Gabe hesitated. He'd decided to tell her something. "So, those things you want."

"I don't deserve them."

He shook his head. His hand touched her hair. "Yes, you do."

Her eyes filled with tears. She deserved them—but wouldn't get them from him. There would be someone else.

He kissed her mouth, startling her. "I miss you. I miss who we were when we were kids."

His mouth again. His hands held the warm skin of her neck, and dreams became vision, and vision was enough for that moment.

She kissed him back, then edged away.

Impatient, Magda joined them, and Dany seized the distraction. "Cool shoes." Converse All Stars. "I have some."

"Thanks," said Magda.

"Can I call you?" Gabe asked.

"After...a while." *After you're sure.*

Hugging herself, Dany started ahead of them

and hurried along the dock, hurried back to the marina where the *Lien Hua* was berthed.

You Make Me Real

HE DID NOT CALL, and Dany accepted it. She did not drink, and she filled the empty spaces. The rocking of the junk by night. The boardwalk with its street performers by day. The rink. These things filled the spaces.

Her mother wanted Gabe to redo the murals, and Dany promised she'd call him and didn't. She finally asked her mother, *Do you mind if I look for another artist?*

Another artist would never be the same.

Jenny said, *That's fine, honey. I trust your judgment.*

On August second, she slept in the partially renovated rink for the first time. For a bed she used the single piece of furniture she'd moved in, which was a couch she'd bought at Love Me Two Times. Her mother's dogs kept her company, growling at sounds on the boardwalk, wagging tails and wandering out into the unfinished rink, where the new floor had not yet been put down.

She went to bed at ten, and sometime in the night the dogs began barking. She sat up. These dogs never barked. Was someone trying to get in?

She dressed quickly and hurried through the apartment and out into the rink. Doris stood at the double doors that led outside, barking happily and wagging her tail.

"Cool it, Doris." It was probably just some drunks using the doorway as a men's room.

Dany was wide awake now.

Maybe she'd go out and play her guitar. It was two in the morning, but she wasn't afraid. It was her world, and she refused to lock herself inside, the way her mother had.

She pulled on her denim jacket over her cut-offs and T-shirt and took the Gibson from its case. All three dogs raced around her in circles. Oh, hell, she'd take them with her. Three leashes. She'd tie them to a bench.

Bingo was going to tear up whoever was on the other side of that door—at least lick him to death. "Bingo—enough."

She unlocked the new entrance and pushed open the door to the beach night, and someone under the alcove said, "'There are things known and things unknown, and in between are the doors.'"

The dogs sniffed the frayed hems of his jeans. He smelled like paint.

The neon light of The Gondolier glowed as though the roller coaster would run this summer, which it would not. September, she'd been told.

She was careful not to scrape the Gibson on the doors and to lock up behind her.

"You keep strange hours," she told Gabe.

Winos lurked nearby, drinking and rowdy.

He set down his paintbrush. "I didn't like your new decor. Boring."

Cocking an eyebrow, Dany let the dogs drag her away from the building and turned to inspect the wall.

The old legend was back, in its old spot, same writing: "JIM MORRISON SLEPT HERE."

The rest of it was bigger, as obnoxious as a teenager with three rolls of toilet paper and nothing to do but cruise a pretty girl's house. Sexy, personalized lyrics. "COME ON, DANY, LIGHT MY FIRE." It deteriorated from there into the dirty and the very personal. He'd found his calling with cans of spray paint; what could she expect?

"I'm so flattered…"

Her eyes caught the words trailing off to the right.

"I LOVE YOU, DANDELION. WILL YOU MARRY ME?"

He watched her uncertainly in the dark.

"Depends on how fast you can repaint that wall."

He laughed and came closer. His arms swallowed her, and all her cravings for escape quieted and stilled.

When she saw his eyes, there was a light of innocence in them, as though the carousel had turned back time, cleaned up the past, then set the clock forward again.

"I love you," he said.

A match struck, the heat of lips. A long, forgetting kiss.

"Are you settling for less?" she asked.

"I told you—I don't see things that way. I love you."

He lowered his mouth to hers again.

Wise Man stumbled past them in the night and stared at the wall. "When's Jim coming back?"

Gabe eased his mouth away from hers. "Soon. Real soon." He smiled into Dany's eyes. "I'm a very fast painter."

Dear Reader,

There is a Garrison Keillor story I love that involves a couple opening their home to their son's friends for a party. At one point, the father comes downstairs to find his son and the other kids flipping through old photograph albums and openly ridiculing the father's hairstyle, et cetera. I love this story for the truth in it, for what it says about the way children perceive—and treat—their parents. Part of adulthood seems to be coming to terms with our feelings for our parents—not only recognizing their flaws and coming to appreciate the gifts they gave us, but acknowledging the ways that their flaws, as well as their virtues, have shaped us and made each of us unique.

Although Jenny Wilde is a product of the sixties and my mother is not, I identify with some of the tensions between mother and daughter in this story. Dany struggles with the fact that she is a different person from Jenny, that in some ways she wishes Jenny was different. But in the end she comes to feel the gifts of her mother's faith in her and of Jenny's unconditional love for her. And she realizes that she wouldn't change her mother for the world.

My mother's faith in me has always been remarkable. At fourteen I enjoyed writing stories—*long* stories—for my own amusement. I seldom shared them with my parents, and they never invaded my privacy by attempting to read what I didn't want to share. But one morning at breakfast, my mother told me she had been reading about John Steinbeck and learned that the author had known from a very young age that he would be a great writer. I knew she was telling me this for a reason—that she believed in me and was inviting me to believe in myself. What a gift of faith this was! In my mind and heart I felt that I could be a great writer. I continue to hold on to that belief, because my mother, with her faith and love, made me feel it twenty years ago. She makes me feel it now.

If I had a wish for all of you reading this, it would be that you have faith in your own dreams—the kind of faith my parents have given to me—and that you inspire the children you know with faith in themselves. Believe! And may your dearest dreams come true.

Sincerely,
Margot Early

Harlequin Romance®

Delightful

Affectionate

Romantic

Emotional

Tender

Original

Daring

Riveting

Enchanting

Adventurous

Moving

Harlequin Romance—the
series that has it all!

Harlequin® Historical

From rugged lawmen and
valiant knights to defiant heiresses
and spirited frontierswomen,
Harlequin Historicals will
capture your imagination with
their dramatic scope, passion
and adventure.

Harlequin Historicals…
they're too good to miss!

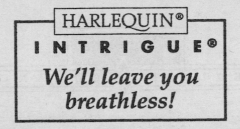

LOOK FOR OUR FOUR FABULOUS MEN!

Each month some of today's bestselling authors bring
four new fabulous men to Harlequin American Romance.
Whether they're rebel ranchers, millionaire power brokers
or sexy single dads, they're all gallant princes—and
they're all ready to sweep you into lighthearted fantasies
and contemporary fairy tales where anything is possible
and where all your dreams come true!

You don't even have to make a wish...
Harlequin American Romance will grant your every desire!

Look for Harlequin American Romance
wherever Harlequin books are sold!

HARLEQUIN SUPERROMANCE®

...there's more to the story!

Superromance. A *big* satisfying read about unforgettable characters. Each month we offer *four* very different stories that range from family drama to adventure and mystery, from highly emotional stories to romantic comedies—and much more! Stories about people you'll believe in and care about. Stories too compelling to put down....

Our authors are among today's *best* romance writers. You'll find familiar names and talented newcomers. Many of them are award winners—and you'll see why!

If you want the biggest and best in romance fiction, you'll get it from Superromance!

Available wherever Harlequin books are sold.